T0274094

Acclaim for

THE LOCKET'S REVENGE

"Gripping and intense, sometimes tragic but always hopeful, *The Locket's Revenge* delivered everything I was hoping for in this duology–and more! Richmond's immersive writing style draws readers right back into her undersea world of beauty, intrigue, and danger. Locklyn, Darin, and their crew must face impossible choices and their greatest fears in a race against time and looming disaster, leading to powerful growth and a conclusion as poignant as it is satisfying. Fans of *The Mermaid's Tale* won't want to miss this epic finale!"

– LAURIE LUCKING, award-winning author of *Common*

"*The Locket's Revenge* delivers more of everything I loved about its predecessor–more mystery, higher stakes, and more romance. Locklyn and Darin's love is sweet and real and had me deeply invested. Richmond brings us even deeper into the stunning underwater world she has created, and I never wanted to come back up! Fans of *The Mermaid's Tale* will definitely want to dive back in for this heartfelt conclusion."

– ASHLEY BUSTAMANTE, author of the COLOR THEORY trilogy

"*The Locket's Revenge* is a high-adrenaline fantasy with a dystopian edge, sure to pull readers through its pages with pressing questions and satisfying answers. If you're ready for an undersea adventure filled with sweet romance, this enchanted duology is for you."

– RACHELLE NELSON, author of *Sky of Seven Colors*

"*The Locket's Revenge* will take *The Mermaid's Tale* readers on an extraordinary undersea adventure where the stakes are higher than ever. Legendary monsters come to life, and the entire aquatic world shudders with the ramifications of Locklyn's choices. In her scorn, the menacing enchantress Circe, armed with a weapon of unfathomable power, is coming for vengeance. And . . . she's not coming alone. Richmond's *The Locket's Revenge* is a seafaring fantasy epic you won't want to miss."

– WAYNE THOMAS BATSON, bestselling author of THE DOOR WITHIN and THE MYRIDIAN CONSTELLATION

"Readers will take a deep dive into immersive world-building in the underwater fantasy realm of *The Locket's Revenge*. L.E. Richmond's sequel to *The Mermaid's Tale* is even better than the first, brimming with sweet romance, inspiring themes, and plot twists that would shock even the most powerful Sea Enchantress. Locklyn and Darin's story will keep readers wanting to swim back to its pages up until the satisfying conclusion!"

– SARA ELLA, award-winning author of THE CURIOUS REALITIES duology, *Coral*, and the UNBLEMISHED trilogy

"A fabulous sequel with all the trademark Richmond poignancy. A story that left me breathless with anticipation and with a sweet, longing ache of what might have been, and hope for the things yet to come."

– AJ SKELLY, bestselling author of THE WOLVES OF ROCK FALLS and MAGIK PREP ACADEMY series

THE LOCKET'S REVENGE

THE LOCKET'S REVENGE

L.E. RICHMOND

Published by Enclave Publishing, an imprint of Oasis Family Media, LLC

Carol Stream, Illinois, USA.
www.enclavepublishing.com

ISBN: 979-8-88605-158-2 (printed hardcover)
ISBN: 979-8-88605-159-9 (printed softcover)
ISBN: 979-8-88605-161-2 (ebook)

Cover design by Kirk DouPonce, www.DogEaredDesign.com
Typesetting by Jamie Foley, www.JamieFoley.com
Map design by Matthew Harned

Printed in the United States of America.

This one is for Helena.
You are the one I run to when I feel
beauty's poignancy deep in my soul,
because I know you will feel it too.
Love you always, Sis.

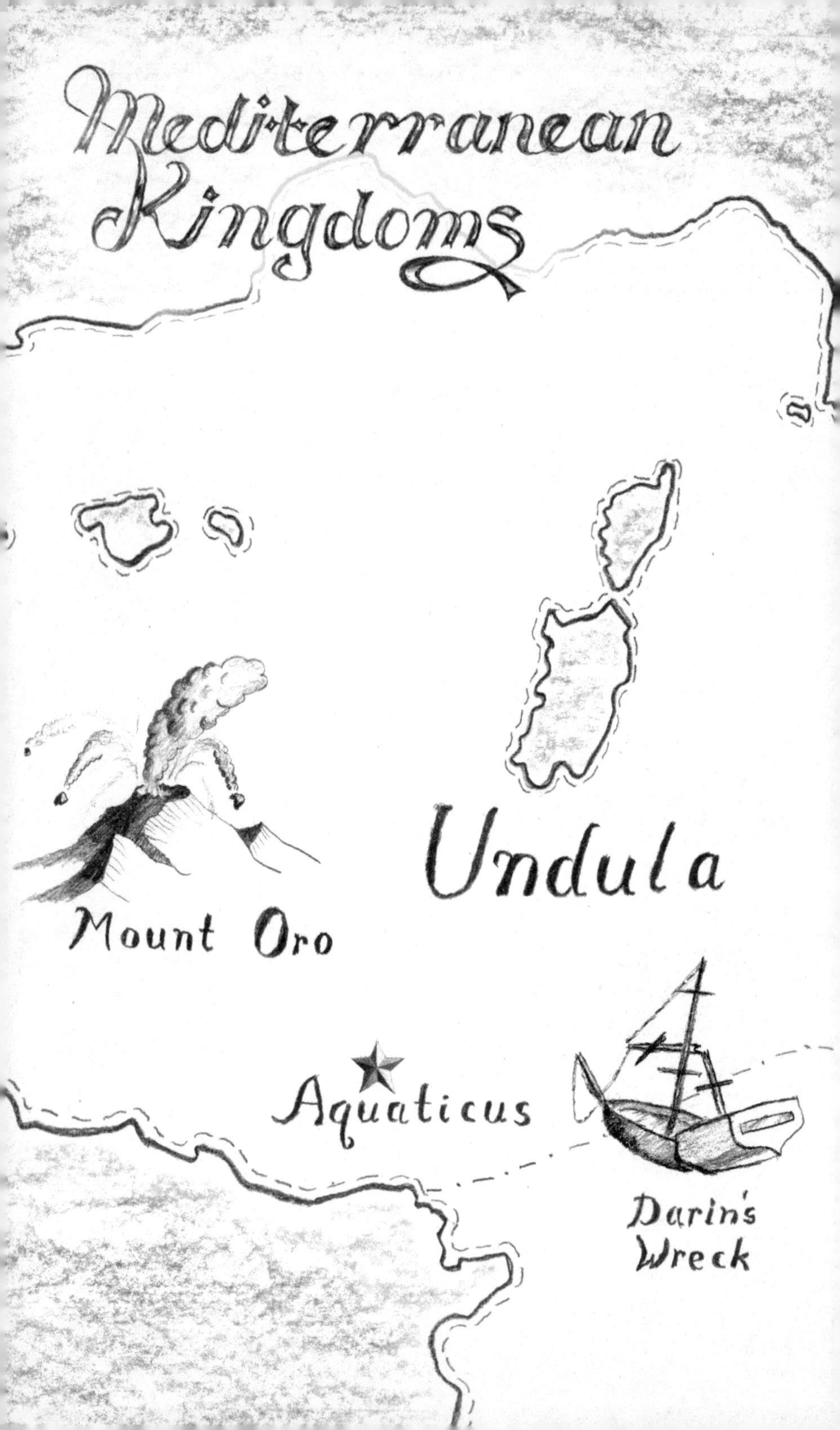

Mediterranean Kingdoms

Undula

Mount Oro

Aquaticus

Darin's Wreck

Llyra's Lost Treasure
Circe's Cave
Rayan Mountains
Oublier Faire Kelp Forest
Orwell's Hideout
Douglas Pass
Imber
Nebula

He answered and said, “But I see four men unbound, walking in the midst of the fire, and they are not hurt; and the appearance of the fourth is like a son of the gods.”

DANIEL 3:25

PROLOGUE

THE SILVER CHAIN GLIDES THROUGH her fingers, link by link, metal brushing the raised scars, which are invisible to most eyes, sending exquisite jolts of pain slithering up her nerves. But she does not flinch. Life is pain now.

She had thought the pain would kill her once.

As she lay on the rocky bottom of that lake, pain singing through every nerve. Unable to cry out, as the skin of her face dripped from her cranial bones like molten metal. Watching the dark shape of her worst nightmare soaring above her through the water, bellowing for escape . . . she had been certain death was moments away. She had prayed it would come–begged the Wave Master to send her relief.

But, like the man she had loved, death did not come for her.

And after that first endless night of torment, she had never prayed again.

She had saved herself.

The tunnel through which every small creature from Loch Ness escaped led to Loch an Ordain. There had been moments when she was sure she would die there, rocks digging into every inch of her mutilated body, claustrophobia clawing welts of terror into her psyche.

But, at last, she had reached Loch an Ordain.

And there she had found her.

Morrigan.

The closest thing to a mother she would ever have. The woman who had given her rebirth. Who had nursed her back to health. Who had trained her in the ancient arts of dark magic. Who had promised her that she would one day be the greatest enchantress under the sea if she could do two things.

Regain her voice.

And kill the man who had betrayed her.

Her thumb caresses the catch of the locket. It releases and the two halves separate, falling open in her palm. There is a split second of silence.

Then the voice fills her cave. The voice of another betrayer.

Images swirl in the water.

The Surface.

Trees.

Golden light.

Vibrant flowers like nothing seen under the sea.

A hairy, four-legged creature racing across sand, barking like a sea lion.

And a man crouched at the edge of the surf.

"If you come out of the water, we can be together. Forever, Llyra. I promise you."

The locket's hinge bites into her palm as her fingers clench convulsively. A line of scarlet appears and spreads, drifting over the silver, as she whispers a dark incantation.

And the voice changes.

New images fill the water around her.

A man's face, mouth gaping wide in a scream of terror.

The monster's dark form and glowing eyes, more colossal and correspondingly more ghastly than her nightmares.

Fiery waves of desolation, exploding through the water.

And even as the man shrieks in pain, begging for help, for her to save him, his face begins to melt, skin sliding from bone to expose red muscle and purple nerve, stripping away every defense.

With a movement so small it is almost lazy, her index finger and thumb shift, sliding the two halves back together, closing the bauble in her hand. Silence fills the cave, pulsing with restrained power.

A smile tugs at the corners of her mouth.

Morrigan was right.

His agony would be her healing.

Only when she had siphoned every drop of her pain into him, watching it tear him apart from the inside out, could she claim the promise her foster mother had given her.

The promise of true greatness.

And an immortal name under the sea.

1

LOCKLYN

I LAUGH. NOT MY NORMAL LAUGH–ALL bubbles and mirth–but a high, strained cackle that erupts from my lips like a geyser from a whale's spout. I grip Darin's forearms, warmth whispering up my fingers from the feel of him, using him to hold myself up in the water as unaccountable weakness sweeps through me.

"That's funny," I say as the horrible sound of my laughter dies away in the still water. "That's really funny, Darin."

For some reason, I can't look at any of the others, but stare into the golden eyes above me, willing his face to break into a smile, his shoulders to shake with mirth, before he pulls me into his arms. I allow his nearness to wash away the pain of losing him, my fear that I would never see him again, my guilt for leaving him.

After a moment, he does smile, but it is all wrong. It is the polite, strained smile you would offer to a stranger you accidentally bumped into in the square. His eyes slide away from mine. "Have we met? Orwell tells me I recently suffered some memory loss."

The water solidifies around me–I can't get enough into my lungs. My fingernails bite into Darin's forearms and he flinches, pulling away from me, but I hang on.

"No," I say, and my voice echoes around the valley. "No," I say again, shaking him. "You know me, Darin. You know me."

He is still trying to pull away, and the look in his eyes, like a lost seal pup confronted with an aggressive shark, is a stonefish spine directly through my heart.

"Darin, please." I'm gasping now, fighting to drag water into my lungs. "Please. It's Locklyn, Darin. You held me the day I was born. You taught me to fight. You gave me this!" I release him, reaching down automatically. As my hands meet smooth, hard scales and a fleshy fin, my heart plummets. "Where's my anklet?" I spin in the water, eyes roving the seafloor.

"Locklyn." A voice tries to pierce my consciousness, but my fevered brain is impervious, repelling every thought except the one reality that is tearing my world to shreds.

"You brought it back from that wreck! The one that started everything. I can't believe I lost it! You told me to make all the other Mermaids jealous!"

I can see how crazy I sound in his wide, golden eyes. "I-I'm sorry . . ." he starts, and for some reason, the words cause something inside me to snap, sending rage flooding through me.

My hands clamp onto his arms again, and I shake him so hard his teeth click together with a sharp snap. "You're not sorry!" I yell. "You can't be sorry, because you don't even know what you're sorry for! I'm your best friend! How can you look me in the face and say you don't know me? How *can* you?"

He opens his mouth, eyes wide and frightened, and the sight shatters the sliver of my heart that remains intact into a million shards. Darin wasn't afraid of anything. Least of all a little, blue-haired Mermaid. He's gone. He's not dead. But he might as well be.

A hand closes around my arm, dragging me away from Darin. "Locklyn, stop." It's Conway's voice that finally pushes through the haze of anger and pain. "It's not his fault, Locklyn." The words are soft, tinged with something I can't identify, and I break. Sobs wrack my body and I crumple into Conway's arms, heaving silently into his shoulder as hot, green, acidic tears pour down my cheeks.

From a long way off, I hear Ginevra's voice, higher and colder than I've ever heard it before. "How did this happen?"

Orwell's voice comes next, but he doesn't answer Ginevra's question. "There, there, son." His tone is gentle and soothing, like someone speaking to a merchild. "The rest of the herd is back now. I could use your help getting them settled in the stable."

The sobs shaking my body redouble, and Conway's arms tighten around me, his hands rhythmically stroking my hair. Movement flurries around us, punctuated by sporadic chittering from the dolphins. After a long moment of silence, Ginevra speaks again, lower this time.

"I don't understand, how . . ." Her words trail away into a gasp. "Conway. He must have followed us. To the lair. And he didn't know about . . ."

Circe.

I push out of Conway's arms so hard that he staggers in the water. Then, I am flying back the way we came, up the rocky mountain path. Voices ring out behind me.

"Locklyn, what are you doing?"

"Come back!"

"Are you crazy?"

"Locklyn!"

I think I hear someone start to follow me, but emotion is coursing through my veins like liquid strength, and with my new tail, I don't think even Darin could have caught me.

I will find her. I will make her give Darin back his memories.

And, if she won't, I will, for the first time in my life, kill another Merperson.

Gladly.

2

DARIN

THE SHAKING IN HIS HANDS IS FINALLY beginning to subside. He strokes the smooth, silvery nose of the dolphin butting against him, still feeling the sharp prick of the little blue-haired Mermaid's nails biting into his biceps. The memory of her eyes, light blue and alight with joyful recognition, fading into black, laced with a pain he does not understand, makes his heart flutter against his ribs like a trapped manta ray.

Guilt attacks as he remembers her frenzy, her desperation.

You know me, Darin. You. Know. Me.

Bubbles whoosh out of his mouth in a sigh as he drops his head into his hands. The dolphin's nose pokes at the side of his face, but Darin ignores her.

I don't know anything.

One day ago I didn't know my own name.

And Darin might not even be my real name. Everyone around me could be lying to me and I wouldn't know.

I would never know.

His first memory is of a beautiful, golden-haired Mermaid offering him a drink. It must have put him to sleep, because his next memory is waking up on the edge of a shining, iridescent kelp forest. For several long moments, he lay there, his mind grasping for something, anything, to latch onto. But there was nothing, and the more his mental struggles proved fruitless, the more powerless he became to check the swimming emotions building inside.

Darin's fingers clawed a rock from the path beneath him, and he clenched it so hard that beads of blood welled up along his palm, staining the rock's edge red. At least the blood was real. The stinging pain was real. But the blankness in his mind remained, and no matter how Darin pushed at the walls trapping him inside the tiny, empty box that was his consciousness now, he could not break out. Claustrophobia gripped him, coating his tongue with the taste of despair.

Who am I?

Who am I?

Who am I?

With a shout of frustration, Darin flung himself off the path, hurling the blood-stained rock with all his might at the passage wall. Then he began to swim, churning the water into billows of foam with every sweep of his muscular tail, using every thrashing movement to lash out at the helplessness encroaching on his mind.

After a day and a half of swimming, he found the valley. Hearing someone moving about in the stable, he slipped quietly up to the doorway and peered in. A giant Merman with white hair and a beard reaching nearly to his scarlet tail hovered inside with his back to Darin, scooping posidonia into dolphin pens with a trident. As Darin watched him, his frame suddenly stilled, the trident in his hands flicking into the upright position of a weapon.

"Who's there?" His deep, gravelly voice was not loud, but was menacing nonetheless.

Darin's inability to answer this very simple question, the one that had been pulsing at the edges of his consciousness for nearly two days, made him reckless.

"What right have you to ask?"

"The right of every owner to know the identity of those who trespass on his property." The Merman still had not moved.

"That right is only as good as the ability of the owner to enforce it," Darin said derisively, turning to continue swimming.

He felt, rather than saw, the trident leave the other's hand. Hurling himself forward, Darin barely managed to keep the teeth of the trident from skimming along the flesh of his back. Rolling over in the water, he dove for the sand below, his fingers latching onto the handle of the weapon.

Something slammed into his back with impressive force and he spun forward, barely managing to keep his hold on the trident. Righting himself, Darin whirled around just in time to see the scarlet tail whipping toward him again. His body flipped horizontally in the water so that the tail sailed beneath him, and Darin jabbed downward with the trident, hearing a satisfying grunt of pain as the prongs connected with the giant's shoulder. Seconds later, the weapon jerked in his hands, and Darin barely managed to hang on as the Merman darted forward, dragging him through the water in an attempt to wrest the trident from Darin's hands. Something in his brain clicked into place, and he began to work his way, hand over hand, along the trident's shaft until he was close enough to bring his tail crashing into the other's midsection.

The Merman gave another grunt, but then yanked with astonishing strength, causing Darin to shoot through the water as the Merman released his hold on the weapon to close his hands around Darin's throat instead. As blackness swirled at the edges of his vision, Darin fought blindly, lashing out with both the trident and his tail, but the giant's hold on his throat did not ease, and the haze clouding his vision morphed into utter darkness.

When Darin awoke, he found himself sitting at the foot of a long, mahogany table, bound to a chair with kelp rope. As the haze over his vision cleared, he saw the giant sitting across the table, tucking into an enormous plate of food. The Merman's gaze flickered up to meet Darin's, then back down to the plate in front of him.

"Hungry?" he asked lightly.

"Do you plan to feed me?" Darin retorted. "Because, in my current state, getting food from my plate to my mouth is going to be difficult."

"My plan is for you to tell me who you are and what your purpose in coming here is, at which point I will determine whether to untie you or slit your throat."

Darin opened his mouth, the helplessness rising inside again as his mind thrashed for something to form an identity out of. But there was only blankness. There was nothing for him to tell this giant. Because, at this point, he had no identity. He was no one.

"Why don't you tell me who you are?" he countered. "It seems only fair after you tried to kill me."

The other threw back his head and roared, causing the entire table to jiggle as his torso shook with mirth. "Believe me, son, I don't *try* to kill people. If I had wanted you dead, you would be on your way to the Wave Master's kingdom, not here speaking to me." Still chuckling, he settled back in his throne-like chair, folding his hands across his chiseled abdomen. "But as your host, it does seem only fair that I introduce myself first. I am Lief Orwell."

Darin stared, waiting for him to continue. The giant's eyebrows rose. "I must admit, that is not the reaction I normally receive when I introduce myself. You have never heard of me?"

Jellyfish began to squirm in Darin's gut. Apparently, he should know who this was. But he had no idea. Not even an inkling.

"Not a whisper," he replied.

Orwell's forehead creased for a moment before he smiled. "Clearly, I have an aggrandized view of my own renown under the sea." Something about the humility of his self-deprecation eased the desperation choking Darin's mind. "Once, I was a Schatzi who roamed the sea seeking wealth and adventure. Now I am but a gatekeeper, who has pledged the remainder of his days to the Wave Master's service."

"A gatekeeper?"

"I guard what you seek," Orwell said quietly.

"I am seeking nothing," Darin rejoined, his defenses rising.

"Merpeople do not enter the Rayan Mountains seeking nothing. I have acceded to your demand to know my identity. Now it is your turn. And be warned, lies will not advance your quest. Not here."

Is it possible to lie if you have no idea what the truth is?

Orwell's eyes narrowed as he studied Darin for a long moment. Then, with a suddenness that caused Darin to leap against his bonds, Orwell slapped the tabletop.

"Of course."

"Of course what?" he responded guardedly.

Orwell's eyes were filled with a pain Darin did not understand. "You don't know."

Darin looked at the giant Merman, confused.

Orwell leaned forward. "Tell me," he said softly. "Did you wake up next to an iridescent blue kelp forest about a day's journey from here?"

Darin stared at him. *How does he know?*

"Did a beautiful, golden-haired Merwoman offer you a drink at any time in the past few days?"

Darin's heart picked up speed. "How do you know?"

Orwell's eyelids flickered shut for a moment, then opened. "The beautiful Merwoman you met is called Circe. She is the most renowned enchantress under the sea. And the drink she gave you has erased every memory of your life up until this point." His eyes looked directly into Darin's. "That is why you do not know who you are."

"But why would she give me a potion to make me forget my life? Am I her enemy?" Darin's breaths were shallow, salt water brushing in and out over his tongue.

Bubbles whooshed from between Orwell's lips in a long sigh. "It seems that every being under the sea is Circe's enemy. She needs no cause for cruelty."

"Is there no way to reverse the enchantment? Can this Circe undo the spell? Cause my memories to return?"

"I have no doubt that she could," Orwell replied. "But I have never known her to do so."

Anger was beginning to simmer again. "You expect me to sit back and accept this condition as my new identity? To build a life from nothing at, what"–he glanced down at his bound body–"twenty-five? Thirty years old? What if I have a family? A wife? Children?" His voice faltered. "I have to remember." It was almost a plea. "I have to."

Orwell nodded. "And I will do all that is in my power to help you, only on one condition."

Darin eyed the Merman warily. "And what is that?"

The giant leaned toward him, the aged lines of his face more pronounced than ever. "Live," Orwell said, and the bubbles from that single, exhaled word flew down the table, dissolving seconds before tickling Darin's face. Confusion must have been evident in his expression, because the other leaned back in his chair with a laugh. "It will be better for you to build a new life for yourself now than to spend the rest of the years the Wave Master has granted you in pursuit of a past you can never reclaim."

Darin comes back to himself in the barn, his hands absently stroking the head of the dolphin nestled into his side, humming contentedly with her eyes closed. With what feels like enormous effort, he drags a mouthful of water into his lungs.

Whoever I was, this is not who I want to be.

On the verge of senseless anger that explodes like a geyser over anyone unfortunate enough to be in my vicinity.

He blows out a stream of bubbles, and the dolphin squirms as they brush her sleek head. "Ticklish, eh?" he asks, before blowing on her scalp again so that she wriggles and lets out a series of guttural chirps uncannily similar to chuckling. The corners of his mouth lift as a tendril of warmth uncurls tentatively inside his chest.

I'm alive. Even though I know nothing about myself, at least I'm alive.

"Darin?" He turns around at the sound of the voice and sees the dark-skinned mermaid with the pearl-white tail leaning languidly against the door jamb. Nerves swell inside his chest and he tenses unconsciously, meeting her cool, black eyes. "Locklyn's gone," the Mermaid says. Her eyes narrow ever so slightly, and Darin knows that this would mean something to the Merman he used to be.

"The little blue-haired Mermaid? The one who–"

"Who attacked you? Yes, that's Locklyn."

A thousand questions pulse in his throat. He forces them back. "I'm sorry," he says, watching her obsidian eyes shift at the words. "I'm sure that I should know you. But I don't. Will you tell me who you are? And . . . how I know you?"

She gives her head an irritable little shake, causing the shells at the ends of her many braids to click together. "Why are you apologizing? It's not your fault."

He looks at her, the corners of his mouth lifting a little. "Well, in that case, I most certainly rescind my apology."

Her mouth quirks. "And don't let me catch you at it again. I'm Ginevra, queen of Nebula. I forced you and your sister-in-law to lead an expedition to find the most famed treasure under the sea. Because, without said treasure, I would be forced to hand over fourteen youths from my kingdom to the government of Atlantis to be fed to a sea monster in the north."

Darin stares at her. "You do realize it would be unkind to make up stories for a man who doesn't know any better than to believe them?"

She smiles a little wickedly. “No, I hadn’t thought of that.”

On a whim, he darts forward, seizing her hand theatrically. “Oh, mighty queen, have pity on me!”

Her laughter fills the stable, high and clear as sea glass chimes. “I never thought I’d see the day Darin Aalto would grovel before me.”

“What would Darin Aalto do?” he says quietly, and the laughter dies from her lips, leaving her eyes blank and weary.

She opens her mouth, but before she can respond, the stable door bangs open behind them. Ginevra jumps, snatching her hand from his, and they both turn to see the black-haired boy who pulled Locklyn off Darin earlier hovering in the doorway.

His eyes flicker between them for a moment before he says, “Orwell needs us all. Now.”

WHY?

The guttural, inarticulate soul-cry that only a Merperson would utter.

Every creature under the sea suffers pain.

But only Merpeople demand a reason for the hurt, their insistence on answers beating against the barrier separating the Wave Master from His creatures.

As I hurtle along the passage toward Circe's kelp forest, I feel oddly removed from the broken heart inside my chest, as though I am on the outside staring in, unable to bear the full extent of my own anguish. So I focus on the black stone walls spinning past, craning my neck to stare up, up, up, pretending that if I strain hard enough, my eyes will pick up strands of moonlight, filtering down from The Surface.

A flash of white catches my eye, and I jerk my head to the side just in time to see a soft, ribbon-like tentacle sweep past my face. Slowly, I look back up to see the glowing bulb of a phantom jellyfish drifting directly above me. Something brushes my right arm and I turn my eyes downward to see the tentacle that swept past my face wrapping itself languidly around my wrist.

My hand fumbles at my back for a weapon before realization

hits me—with the force of the first time—that my pants are gone. By now, my entire forearm is encased in soft, white tentacle, and I am starting to feel pressure on my elbow as the jellyfish begins to inexorably drag the tentacle upward, toward its pulsing mouth.

But, as I am dragged toward the glowing bell, the fear that I expect doesn't come. Instead, irritation prickles.

We didn't meet one antagonistic creature on the way up here three days ago, and now phantom jellyfish are appearing out of nowhere? Could your timing be any worse, you great, ghostly cephalopod?

Next time, show a little more consideration and attack the entire party, rather than waiting to target the Mermaid all on her own.

As the ridiculous thoughts ricochet through my brain and my body drifts ever nearer to the jellyfish's mouth, a deeper realization pushes through the jumble.

Losing the knife storage was actually a worthwhile trade.

I am so close to the jellyfish that I can see its stomach pouch peeking through with each pulse of the bell. I crunch in on myself, flipping upside down in the water and walloping the phantom with my new tail. Body fluids explode outward, clouding the water, and I let out a gasp before clamping my mouth shut to keep from inhaling the remains discoloring my surroundings.

Holding my breath, I untangle the limp tentacle still wrapped around my wrist, before shooting back up the path, dismay tingling through me.

I meant to stun it.

My eyes skim down my new appendage, taking in the blue and purple highlights shimmering faintly against the silver. The remembered image of the exploding jellyfish causes my throat to close as I fight back tears.

I thought a tail would change me, and in a way, it has. But I don't feel like myself anymore.

I thought the difference would be that I'd feel stronger, but right now, I feel weaker than ever.

Something else brushes against my face, and my eyes fly open. It is a kelp stalk. A blue kelp stalk that hangs limply in the water, the faintest hint of residual glow flickering around it. I shoot backward, out of the edge of the forest, and stare at it.

The kelp forest appears to be dying. The stalks of kelp that were thick and robust a day ago are shriveled and limp, flopping from side to side with every current. The pulsing blue light has evaporated, the only trace of its existence this faint residual shimmer in the water.

I continue to stare at the pitiful sight before me, until realization sends me forward, pushing the useless kelp stalks out of my way effortlessly, dragging lungfuls of water through my nose to test for the glorious smell of my remembrance, brain poised for the slightest sign of encroaching sleep. My eyes rake the rock wall on my right for an opening and when, after about ten minutes, I finally spot it, my heart falls.

The entrance to the cave is dark. There are no shadows or golden flames cavorting on the walls. No scent of potions brewing within. No sound of a voice glorious enough to stop the tides issuing from a centuries-old locket.

I dart inside. The cave is completely empty. Not a fleck of ash in the fireplace. Not one forgotten bottle on the shelves.

The sight does not surprise me.

Not after seeing that the magic which once animated the kelp forest has disappeared.

The Sea Enchantress is gone.

4

DARIN

HIS EYES NARROW AS THEY ROAM FROM face to face around the dark wooden table, trying to be unobtrusive as he scans every feature, searching for one that he recognizes, to awaken his dormant mind.

Across from him sits a hulking, stone-faced man, shorter than Orwell, but broader.

To the Merman's right sits Ginevra, long eyelashes brushing her cheekbones as she languidly runs one finger along the design worked into the edge of the table.

Behind Ginevra's chair hover two Merwomen with skin as dark as hers, but with black hair and olive green tails. Both are holding nets and spears.

To his right sits the black-haired boy who summoned him and Ginevra from the stables. The youth seems jumpy, eyes constantly darting toward the curtained entrance of the tent.

Darin's eyes continue their journey and meet those of the figure to his left, a small, mossy-haired Merman with pale, almost transparent eyes.

The Merman introduces himself. "I'm Arledge. I'm sure you don't remember me."

"I don't remember anything, so no," Darin answers flatly. "How did we know each other?"

"We didn't know each other well." Arledge's eyes drop to where his fingers are knotted together. "Your group rescued me and my sister"–his voice cracks–"a-after we were captured by scavengers."

Darin skims the table. The only Mermaids present are Ginevra and her two guards, none of whom could possibly be Arledge's sister. His mind goes back to the creamy skin of Locklyn's face, accented by her waves of navy blue hair.

"Is Locklyn your sister?" he asks cautiously. Arledge's head jerks up, and Darin sees with horror that his pale eyes are swimming with steamy green tears. "I'm sorry." He feels like a sea dancer who doesn't know the choreography, constantly blundering into those around him, causing hurt and consternation unintentionally, but with no idea how to stop.

Arledge swallows convulsively. "My sister died almost a week ago. She was attacked by a giant crab as we were entering the Rayan Mountains."

"I'm sorry," Darin says again, the phrase sounding hollow in his own ears. He knows he should say more, but no words come, and just as the silence between himself and Arledge is stretching uncomfortably thin, Orwell clears his throat.

All eyes swivel to the head of the table, where Orwell is sitting in his carved throne, fingers loosely interlaced on the table before him. "Our current situation is–not to mince words–dire. Circe, the most feared sorceress in the Seven Seas, now has in her possession a locket containing the voice of the Mermaid Llyra, which she undoubtedly has the capability to wield as a powerful weapon. To add to this, it appears she knows the location of the monster caged in Loch Ness. Putting these two facts together, it seems highly likely that she intends to go north and release the monster, using her own powerful magic, combined with the voice of Llyra, to control the creature for her own sinister ends."

There is silence around the table for a moment before the black-haired youth bursts out, "What about Locklyn? If Circe has gone, she'll fall asleep in the kelp forest and there will be no one to wake her up!"

"She shouldn't have gone swimming off like a crazed fringehead," Ginevra says loftily.

The young Merman rounds on her. "Last time I checked, having a heart that isn't made out of ice doesn't constitute lunacy."

"Conway." Orwell's voice causes the youth to flop back in his chair, hands raised in surrender, but from the look in Ginevra's eyes, some sort of damage has been done.

"If Locklyn is going to Circe's lair, she will not return for another day and a half. We must use that time to plan and make preparations, so that as soon as she returns, we will be able to set out without any more delay." Conway starts to speak, but Orwell raises a hand. "Locklyn is a clever girl, princeling. I believe she will return. But, to ensure she has not fallen into difficulties, one of us will go after her as soon as this meeting is concluded." Conway gives a quick nod, and Orwell continues. "As I said, we must leave this place within two days. We will make our way to the city of Atlantis and present our intelligence to the Council of the Guardians, appraising them of the fact that a dangerous sorceress now has the means to release and control the monster caged in Loch Ness. If we can gain their support, we may be able to put together a group that stands a chance of thwarting Circe. If they refuse to listen to us, we must secure travel accommodations and travel north ourselves."

"But how will we ever be able to stop the sorceress?" Arledge asks.

Orwell studies the young Merman a moment before replying. "I will be honest with you, Arledge. Our chances of stopping her without the Council's aid are very slim. But we must try. I saw the devastation of which that monster was capable in its infancy, and I can only imagine its capabilities now. The North Sea will become a ravaged wasteland before Circe and the monster turn their sights toward the Mediterranean and then the rest of the Undersea Realm."

"I think securing the Council's aid is the least of our worries." All eyes turn toward Ginevra. "At this point, we have no way of reaching Atlantis aside from swimming, and from the Rayan Mountains, the journey will take a minimum of forty days. Besides, I, for one, cannot go directly to Atlantis. If I do not return to Nebula within thirteen days and call off the army massed on the border to Undula, the prince"–her voice bites as she waves a hand in Conway's direction–"will not have a kingdom to return to after his adventuring is through."

Conway sits upright. "You left your army with orders to attack Undula if you failed to return in thirty days?"

Ginevra's dark eyes are like chips of flint. "As I told your father, I tell no lies. And my first priority is my kingdom. I wanted to ensure that we would receive our due. One way or another."

Conway's lips compress and he looks away. But for an instant, admiration flickers along with the anger in his eyes.

"How did you get back here?" Arledge asks Darin. "You were captured by the Atlanteans and they were taking you away in their submarine, but now you're here . . . " His voice trails away as he takes in Darin's blank expression.

"No, Arledge. You're right." Ginevra seems to have abandoned her disdainful calm. Darin turns to stare at her in bewilderment. "Darin, you were captured by the Atlanteans, but you must have escaped. It's possible you hijacked their submarine. And if so, it's probably waiting–"

"–outside the entrance to the tunnel!" Conway finishes, a huge smile on his face.

But Ginevra turns from him to Orwell. "If the submarine is truly there, then we have a chance," she says.

Orwell pushes up from his throne, hands braced on the table before him. "Then what are we waiting for? Even traveling by submarine, we will have days to finalize our plans regarding Atlantis and the North Sea. For now"–he points at Ginevra and Conway–"you two must return to the entrance of the tunnel to ensure the submarine does indeed wait outside. If it is there, one of you ought to stay and guard it while the other returns with the news. In the meantime"–he motions to Arledge and Ginevra's two guards–"these three will help me to pack provisions and supplies for the journey, while I release my dolphin herd into an enclosed valley nearby where they will be able to live and graze until my return."

Darin's eyes meet Orwell's, questioning.

Orwell nods. "And you, Darin, will head back up the path toward the kelp forest to find our missing Mermaid."

5

LOCKLYN

WHEN I SEE HIM SWIMMING QUICKLY UP the path toward me, my heart begins to bounce up and down. He came to find me. He must have remembered the way to the kelp forest.

His memory is coming back!

But as he speaks, the hope burgeoning in my chest plummets down to the rocky seafloor below. "Orwell sent me to see if you were alright."

I swallow hard on the lump swelling in my throat. Everything inside me wants to swim away from this shell of Darin as fast as I can without a glance back. Pain will be an inevitable part of every interaction between us, as the sight of him probes at the memories of what we once had.

I look up into his familiar face, a face that two days ago, I feared I would never see again. The lost expression in the golden eyes I love breaks my heart.

Slowly, hesitantly, I reach out and take his hand. His fingers are slack against mine. "Do you remember anything?" I say.

He looks down at me. "No," he says. "Nothing that would identify me as a Merperson. I know what words mean–obviously– and I know what objects are. But everything before drinking the potion Circe gave me is blank. When I first met Orwell, he attacked me. My body knew how to fight back, but I have no idea why."

My eyes widen. "Orwell attacked you the first time you met?"

"He is one Merman I would recommend *not* sneaking up on," Darin says wryly.

"Well, you survived to tell the tale."

"Yes," he replies. Then pauses. "But why?"

I release his hand and turn to head back down the path. "We should probably swim while we talk. Believe it or not, you're the greatest Schatzi in Aquaticus, the city we both come from."

He cocks his head. Surprised? Intrigued? "I was a Treasure Hunter?"

"You still are. And it looks like we're all going to be spending a lot of time in the near future looking for an enchanted locket, and I fully expect you to pull your weight."

His teeth flash in a roguish smile, and I look away, my heart throbbing.

"If I'm going to pull my weight, we'll need to spend a lot more time together, Keeper of my Memories. So I'm a treasure hunter. And I have a best friend." His smile is more hesitant this time. "Tell me more."

Right now, I need to help Darin. I do not need to spiral down the emotional twister I was riding before he was captured. He's still Darin, even with none of his memories. His humor is still there, and his ability to read people. And clearly his fighting skills.

"You and I have always talked about taking a trip to the North Sea. We planned to go to The Surface to see the lights the Land Dwellers call Aurora Borealis. Merfolk call them The Wave Master's Brushstrokes."

"The Wave Master's Brushstrokes. I like that."

"You have a brother too," I say. "He married my sister. They have four children, three boys and a girl."

"If my brother married your sister, then I'm your . . . brother-in-law?"

"Not exactly. You're the brother of my brother-in-law."

"Same difference."

"Not if we're being technical about it."

"Do we need to be technical about it?"

Well, on the very off chance that I ever marry you, it actually would be very important to be technical about it.

I just give my head a shake and continue. "Anyway, you always helped Amaya and Beck, my sister and your brother, every chance you got, because the treasure hunting business is far more lucrative than net making. You tried to help me too, but I wouldn't let you because I'm too sensitive about being viewed as a useless Crura."

His brow furrows. But his eyes dart to my tail. "You don't have legs."

I give him a half smile. "Until two days ago, that would have been an inaccurate statement. The tail is a recent acquisition."

He surveys me with confusion. "I don't even know where to start. Firstly, why did you have legs? Secondly, I'm assuming that didn't make you popular, but obviously I don't know because I can't remember anything. Thirdly, how under the sea did you suddenly get a tail?"

"The short version is that my great-great-grandmother double-crossed Circe," I say. "The very enchantress you met."

"Met is a loose way of putting it," Darin mutters.

"Llyra didn't hold up her end of their bargain to give Circe the locket with her voice magically sealed inside, so Circe cursed Llyra's descendants as punishment. One Merperson in every generation of her family would be at home neither on land nor in the water. And I drew the short straw, I guess." I exhale bubbles. "But you know what's strange? Now that I finally have a tail, I miss my legs. In some ways, they made my life miserable, and yet I don't feel like myself without them."

"That's not strange." Darin has been scanning the unchanging black walls on either side of us, but now he turns to me, golden eyes serious. "Experiences define us. You're looking at a prime negative example of that. Since I can't remember any of the experiences that shaped who I am, do I even have an identity anymore? You say I'm a Schatzi, but I can't remember discovering a single wreck. You say I'm a devoted brother and uncle, but I wouldn't be able to pick my family out of a crowd. You say that we're best friends. But I don't remember a single shared experience with you." He looks apologetic. "I don't feel anything toward you other than vague friendliness. You seem like a nice girl, and I'd like to get to know you better. But there's nothing else."

His words rip through me. But it's what he adds under his breath that keeps me from swimming away, unable to hear anymore. "I can't remember. Wave Master, I just can't remember."

The lump in my throat swelling again, I face him. "But I do remember, Darin," I say quietly.

His eyes are tinged with despair, and I take hold of his arm to pull him to a stop next to me in the water, forcing him to listen.

"We'll make new memories," I say. "Memories for both of us."

6

DARIN

THE VALLEY IS DESERTED.

He and Locklyn spin in the water, startled questions erupting to break the silence that has hovered between them for the last hour.

"Where is everyone?"

"Did Circe come back and do something to them?"

"Did they leave without us?"

"They wouldn't just leave . . ."

Locklyn darts to the stable and peers through the driftwood lattice. Her eyes are dove-gray and wide with alarm as she turns back to him.

Strange. I thought her eyes were blue.

"The dolphins are gone."

"All of them?"

He darts up beside her, and, hovering next to her, the reality of how petite she really is hits him for the first time. The strength of her personality makes her seem bigger somehow.

She turns to look at him, the delicate lines of her face scrunched with confusion, and he has a sudden, insane impulse to lean down and kiss her.

Locklyn's voice jerks him back to reality. "Why would they take all the dolphins? We only need enough to carry the treasure and the supplies."

Memory stirs, and he lets out a groan. "I just remembered something. We're not taking any of the dolphins. Orwell said he was going to release them into a valley not far from here. We're traveling back by submarine."

"By–what?"

Before he can answer, a voice rings across the valley. "There you are!"

Locklyn and Darin swivel to see Conway emerging from the passage leading to the open ocean. "We need to leave."

"What's the rush?" Locklyn asks.

"Darin didn't tell you?"

Embarrassment floods through him, and he's unsure what to say that won't make him sound like a self-obsessed amnesiac.

Before he can speak, Locklyn says lightly, "We had other things to talk about. So what's the plan?"

"Turns out Darin here hijacked the Atlanteans' submarine. We're using it to return to Atlantis, with a quick stop at home along the way so Ginny can call her warrior maidens off Undula's borders. Apparently, she left them with strict orders to raze Aquaticus if she wasn't back by the time the last sand grain fell through the hourglass on the last day of the month." Conway gives his head an exaggerated shake.

"That's what I would have done," Locklyn says with a nod.

Conway tosses up his hands. "Remind me not to cross either of you."

Locklyn's lips twitch. "There's your main pastime gone."

Darin follows the pair as they banter cheerfully back and forth. Loneliness tinged with jealousy wraps around his soul.

The tunnel they follow widens, the floor becoming sandier as the plains draw nearer. His eyes scan their surroundings, skimming over the sea urchins, corals, and whelks encrusting the rocky walls. As they round a corner, something white snags Darin's attention, and terror grips him. Conway and Locklyn are still chatting, swimming onward as though nothing is wrong.

"Stop!" His shout explodes through the water, and he darts forward to shove them against the tunnel's rocky wall, ignoring their gasps of surprise as he yanks the coral knife Orwell gave him from the sheath at his waist. He faces the gargantuan white silhouette of an Anakite crab, crouched against the wall not ten lengths away.

"Darin," Locklyn's voice is soft. "It's dead."

He grips his coral knife, still peering through the water, unwilling to take his eyes off the beast. "How do you know?"

"Because we killed it, genius." Conway rolls his eyes. The right shoulder of his shirt is torn, and Darin can see blood oozing from a cut underneath. The prince must have landed on a coral.

"Conway!" Locklyn's voice cracks through the water.

Conway tries to staunch the bleeding in his shoulder with his fingers. "Sorry," he says stiffly, after a pause.

Darin shrugs an acceptance of the apology, unable to look at either of them as he pushes his dagger back into its sheath.

"Darin?" Locklyn's fingers brush his arm, but he doesn't look at her. "Darin, I'm sorry. We should have warned you about the crab." When he still doesn't speak, she says again, "I'm sorry."

"Stop apologizing!" He doesn't know where the outburst came from, but the anger is an old friend, rearing out of his helplessness and lashing out at anyone within reach. Locklyn pulls back, her hand dropping.

"Don't speak to her like that." Conway's tone is icy, and, for the first time, Darin hears a hint of royalty in his voice.

"Conway," Locklyn starts.

But Darin cuts in. "I may have lost my memories, but I would bet every sea urchin in these mountains that never in my previous existence did I need advice from you. Take your scratched arm and bruised pride to Orwell. He'll fix you up."

The blood drains from Conway's face, leaving only two scarlet patches beneath his black eyes, which glitter with fury. "Now there's the Darin I know," he says. "Hard, arrogant, and bull-headed. Some things haven't changed."

Locklyn places a hand on his arm. "Please go," she says, and there is no room for argument in her voice.

With one last deadly look, Conway turns, swimming away from them, past the still white form of the Anakite, up the tunnel and out of sight. Silence swells between the rock walls. When Locklyn finally does speak, he sees that her eyes have gone green–a vivid, poisonous shade.

"I don't care what you've gone through." Her crisp words seem to vibrate through the tunnel, echoing inside his head. "But nothing gives you the right to treat the people around you like sea slime. You are the strongest person I know, Darin. But using your own circumstances as an excuse to punish those around you? That's weak. Pathetically weak."

Without another word, she turns and swims up the tunnel. It is a long time before he can force himself to follow her.

7
LOCKLYN

I JUST WANT TO CURL UP ALONE IN THE corner of the submarine and sleep all the way back to Aquaticus.

But when the submarine comes into view, I know at a glance that sleep will be a long time in coming. Our group, Darin included, hovers in a semicircle around the door to the submarine, muttering together furiously. As I approach, Ginevra's voice rises above the rest.

"We have to leave him behind, Orwell."

Coming up to the back of the huddle near Conway, I flutter my tail, bouncing up and down in the water to peer between the shoulders of Kai and the taller of the two Nebulae guards. But all my bobbing avails me nothing. I'm too short to get a good look at what is inside the door.

"To do so would be to pass a certain death sentence on him," Orwell warns.

"To take him with us would be to hone a lethal weapon for our enemies!"

"What's going on?"

Everyone turns to look at me, except Conway, whose profile is enough to tell me he is still seething over the altercation with Darin. Ginevra is the one who answers.

"It seems that stealing isn't Aalto's only criminal pastime." She gestures to the door of the submarine, and I jostle my way to the front of the group. "Add kidnapping to the list."

Looking into the interior of the ship, my eyes encounter the scarlet pair belonging to the colorless Merman who sits cross-legged on the floor, seaweed ropes binding him to hooks protruding from the submarine wall. He smiles at me and chills skitter along my spinal column like icy fingers.

"Ah, my little cousin returns." The timbre of his voice is smooth and sonorous. "But, oh dear." He clicks his tongue disapprovingly. "What persuaded you to give up your greatest asset, my sweet?" His eyes skim my body, coming to rest on the shining periwinkle and silver scales of my tail.

The sight of his crossed legs sends a stab of regret and longing through me.

I will never be able to sit that comfortably on the floor again.

I cross my arms. "I fear we do not see eye to eye on what my greatest asset is. I have spent the last two decades becoming more and more convinced that neither legs nor a tail make any difference. It is the life we live, rather than the body in which we live it, that is of true value."

His laughter is as beautiful as his voice, but with the same deadly aftertaste. "Did you hear that sweet cliché from a fortune teller at the local market, love?"

Orwell's voice pushes between us, rougher than I am accustomed to hearing. "What is your name?"

The achromos smiles, and the triangular welt on his colorless right cheekbone scrunches in on itself, as the jewels embedded into his incisors sparkle in the submarine's white light. "You may call me Igor."

"Oh, may I?" Orwell says brusquely. "Well, Igor, if you'll excuse us, we need to decide whether or not to leave you stranded in the middle of the ocean." He drags the door shut with a click before glancing down at me. A whoosh of bubbles spurts from his lips in a sigh. "I've never been able to tolerate sea snakes, Locklyn. They bring out the worst in me."

"We have to leave him," Ginevra says again from behind us. "That submarine is barely the length of a humpback. We wouldn't be able to discuss plans without him listening in on every word we say. If we release him in Atlantis, he will most likely turn us into the authorities for theft and kidnapping. If we release him in Aquaticus or Imber, he'll be hunted down for being a foreign mutant. We might as well leave him here to find his own way."

"We cannot leave him directly outside the gateway to Llyra's Treasure," Orwell states decisively. "Not when the way there is mostly clear."

"There's still the siren and Circe's forest," Ginevra says.

I intervene. "The forest is dying. Circe must have used spells to sustain it that lost their power when she left."

Ginevra huffs. "Then let's take him halfway to Aquaticus and leave him on the plains. That will give us enough time to complete our business in Nebula and reach Atlantis without him following us and causing trouble."

"His chances of surviving alone on the Vasitas Plains are slight," Orwell says. "I, for one, do not desire any more deaths on my conscience."

Ginevra's eyebrows rise.

"Orwell is right," I say, and her eyes harden into a glare. Her lips part, but I forestall her. "I've spent my entire life being harassed by those who thought they knew whether or not I had the right to exist. Many of them believed ending my life would be a service to the Wave Master, since they claimed He had created Merfolk with tails and I was an affront to His design." We stare at each other, azure eyes into umber. "The right to take life belongs to the Wave Master," I say firmly. "To take that right onto ourselves ought to be a matter of utmost weight, but we do it almost thoughtlessly. We're so confident of our own justice, we forget that someday we might be on the other end of the knife, wondering if the person executing the death blow is as confident of their own right as we used to be."

Lips puckering, Ginevra's gaze doesn't waver from mine. A voice breaks the stillness around us.

"She offers good advice, this one." My heart gives a dull thump as I meet the golden eyes staring down at me. The silence with which he was able to advance, right up to my shoulder, unnerves me slightly.

"The quickest way to reach a decision would be to put it to a vote," Conway says, and I give him a small smile, whispering, "King in the making."

The corners of his mouth lift before he turns to the rest of the group. "All in favor of leaving Igor on the Vasitas Plains?"

Not a single person raises their hand. Ginevra fiddles with the shaft of her spear, staring at the sand beneath her, and the memory of her eyes as she hesitated during our death match fills my mind.

The queen of the Nebulae isn't a killer.

Conway gives me a theatrical little bow. "Thanks to our orator here, the decision is unanimous."

I try to return his smile, but the expression feels forced. "Do you know how to steer a submarine, Orwell?" I say.

He barks a laugh. "I've been living as a hermit in the Rayan Mountains for the past hundred years, my girl. I know how to steer a seahorse-drawn chariot, but that is the extent of my skill. Perhaps sparing Igor will have a dual purpose, since he must know how to navigate the craft."

"We cannot allow our enemy to–"

Ginevra's argument is cut off by Conway and Darin. Their "I can do it" collides in the water.

Everyone turns to them. "How under the sea would you know how to steer a submarine?" Ginevra snaps, glaring at Conway.

"I guess I was just born brilliant."

Her scoff is drowned out by Darin's observation. "Perhaps Conway ought to do it. I obviously don't remember navigating the submarine here, but I was hoping the sight of the controls would spark a flash of memory in me."

I glance covertly between the two of them just in time to see a look of gratified surprise cross Conway's face.

"No sense waiting around, is there?" he remarks. "The submarine is packed, and since it will take us three days to reach Imber and another to reach Aquaticus, the sooner we start, the better."

Orwell opens the door wide, and as the members of our group file past him into the submarine's interior, I hang back, focusing on the light brush of ocean currents against my skin, and savoring the last moments before confinement. Close confinement.

This should be an interesting trip.

8

LOCKLYN

"WE SHOULD REACH IMBER IN THE NEXT couple of hours," Conway says.

I don't turn, keeping my face pressed to the cool glass of the porthole, gazing out at the chasm of magma gliding beneath us, its crimson glow illuminating patches of an unknown golden plant growing along its banks.

"Why did I wait to travel until a dire quest prohibited any sightseeing?" I say, keeping my voice low so as not to wake the rest of the group.

"Hate to break it to you, but much as I loved your legs, they weren't the ideal propelling mechanism. You would have spent most of your time swimming around in the open ocean, where there aren't exactly abundant sights."

His voice is almost normal, and I long to make a witty retort. The banter between us is light and effortless. And right now, with the Undersea Realm in danger of being ravaged by a fire-breathing monster, and the Merman I've loved all my adult life suddenly a stranger, I want effortless. I want it so badly.

A tiny, dark creature suddenly shoots from the fiery river below, the red glow silhouetting its small humanoid torso and eel's tail. It sails past the submarine's porthole, pausing for a moment at the top of its arc to peer at me with glowing orange eyes.

"Conway, look!"

But the mulciber is already splashing back into the magma below as Conway cranes to see out the porthole without letting go of the steering rod. My whispered shout has only served to wake the people nearest us.

"What is it?" The sharp edge of Ginevra's voice is softened by sleep.

"Only a mulciber," I whisper back. "I'm sorry, I just got excited because I've never seen one before. Go back to sleep."

"A what?" Conway asks curiously, his eyes trained on the water rushing past the front window of the submarine.

"A mulciber. They're magma-dwelling sprites and most of them are excellent metal workers. Darin told me that if you search along the banks of a fire river, you sometimes find exquisite tiny metal trinkets on the sand, items they deemed flawed and tossed out."

"Did I ever bring back any of these trinkets?" Darin's voice is closer than I expect.

"You brought me a pail once." I glance at him while trying to ignore the subtle increase in my heart's rhythm.

"A pail?"

"I'm a dugong shepherdess," I say. "The pail was for the milk."

"Did your singing make them produce more?"

My heart stills, and my eyes widen. "Do you remember me singing to them?"

He gives a slight shrug. "It was a guess."

I close my eyes for a brief moment, as if that will shut away the pain. "You told me you found it on the banks of a fire stream," I say. "On the handle, there was a tiny ding in the metal that looked like a miniature L. You said it was a sign the mulcibers had made it especially for me."

An odd expression flits across his face, but he says nothing.

I gaze out the porthole again, scanning the dark water for more mulcibers. I hear Darin's voice again, this time from the other side, but he's not speaking to me.

"I owe you an apology."

I turn my head a fraction to see Darin hovering next to Conway at the front of the vessel. Conway is still staring straight ahead, and the only sign that he has heard anything is a tightening of his posture.

Darin goes on. "Although I can't remember who I was, I know that if I was–what was it you said?–hard, arrogant, and bullheaded, that's not the person I want to be again. My behavior to you back in the tunnel was all of those things, and I apologize."

There is a pause before Conway says stiffly, "Apology accepted." Darin gives a nod before beginning to turn away. "And, Aalto?" Darin turns back. "For what it's worth, while your hardness and arrogance could definitely use some work, you weren't bull-headed *all* the time."

Darin laughs, and the familiar bubbling sound sends warmth coursing through me.

The rest of the group has rustled into wakefulness.

"How close are we to Imber?" Orwell inquires.

I expect Conway to answer, but Ginevra does first. Her face is pressed against one of the middle portholes. "The gates of the city are beyond the next ridge. The Ustrina River becomes a waterfall that flows into the moat."

"We must decide what our next move is to be." At Orwell's words, every eye flickers toward Igor, who is still slumped against the submarine's wall, his breathing deep and even. Unease twists inside me as I study his milky face. Most Merpeople I've seen look younger and more innocent in sleep, but his expression seems sharpened in slumber, more conniving. Almost wicked. My eyes seek Orwell's, wide with an unspoken question.

"Nothing we discuss in the next five minutes will be lethal in the wrong hands," Orwell states, then says, "I believe not all of us ought to disembark at Imber."

Ginevra's head turns swiftly. "What?"

"Speed is our greatest asset," Orwell says. "You, lady, have business which you must attend to in your own country, but for the rest of us, any time spent in Imber is merely a delay in accomplishing our dealings in Aquaticus. Prince Conway must confer with his father regarding the success of his mission and the implications for Undula. Darin and Locklyn ought to alert their family of their safe arrival and ascertain all is well with them. The rest of us need to purchase supplies obtained much more easily and cheaply in Undula's markets–and prepare to set out for Atlantis as soon as possible."

Ginevra's lips have gone thin and tight. "And what of him?"

All eyes swivel again to Igor, who has not moved. "If you are willing, that task will be yours," Orwell replies. "For the sake of our mission, a delay of his trial until we return is desirable. Could you find a place for him in Nebula's dungeons?"

Ginevra gives a brief nod, just as Conway announces, "We're here."

I dart for one of the portholes.

"Wind and tides," Darin breathes next to me.

Imber is no more like Aquaticus than Malik is like Ginevra.

The walls of the warrior queen's city are built of black obsidian, studded at regular intervals with small, pointed white objects that I at first think are stones. As we drift closer, I realize they are shark teeth so massive, they must have been taken from the heads of dozens of great whites. Instead of the fine mesh netting that serves as a dome above Aquaticus, Imber is encased in a bubble of rippled sea glass, a half dome resting on top of the city walls. And unlike Aquaticus, where the gates are open from dawn to dusk, the gates of Imber are firmly closed.

"Is it still night?" I ask, wondering if the days in the submarine have somehow messed up my timekeeping skills.

Ginevra tosses her head. "In Nebula, we are never rash enough to leave our gates open to all who might choose to enter."

"Hence the dearth in trading partners," Conway mutters.

I choke back a laugh.

A muscle twitches in Ginevra's cheek, but she restrains a retort. "The gatekeepers will allow me to enter. It should not take me more than three days to set Nebula's affairs in order. By seahorse chariot, the journey to Aquaticus is less than a day. Let us plan to meet outside the gates on the morning of the fifth day."

At Orwell's nod, she drives the butt of her spear into Igor's shoulder. The Merman's eyes flicker open slowly, their red irises skimming around the group before coming to rest on Ginevra's face. "You desire an audience with me, princess? Please, please, I am quite at leisure."

The white flash of her tail is so sudden, I barely see the movement before hearing the thwack of it connecting with Igor's side. The achromos makes no sound beyond the whoosh of water leaving his lungs, but his eyes harden. "Save your mockery, nudibranch," Ginevra says coolly before turning toward the door with a crisp gesture to her guards.

Kallan and Baia dart forward, quickly detaching Igor's ropes from the submarine wall. A swift slash from Kallan's spear severs the rope binding his ankles, leaving his wrists tightly knotted together. The submarine door clangs metallically as a quick shove from Ginevra sends it sliding to the side.

"In five days then," she says, before gliding out of the submarine. Kallan and Baia follow slowly, with Igor sandwiched between them.

"Could I go out for a moment before we head for Aquaticus?" I ask Orwell. "It feels like a long time since I've tasted ocean salt."

Orwell nods, and I move toward the door, turning with my hand on its frame, when I hear my name. Our leader's eyes sparkle with mischief. "Just don't bring back a mulciber."

A smile splits my face. "But if I ever get back to my dugongs, I'll really want some more metal pa–"

"Locklyn." Darin's voice is a strangled shout. "Locklyn!"

The whining screech of metal on metal reaches my ears a split second before the door of the submarine slams into my hand, bones cracking in an explosion of pain.

9

DARIN

DARIN COLLIDES WITH CONWAY AS they lunge toward Locklyn. Darin's hands grip the handle, dragging the door open. Conway's arms loop under Locklyn as she slides down, spirals of blood oozing into the water from the jagged slash visible through the mauve bruises blossoming on her palm.

On the other side of the door, Ginevra is supporting a hunched-over Baia, whose gasps are clearly failing to bring water into her lungs. Kallan and Igor are both gone.

"I didn't see what happened," Ginevra says wildly. "I was signaling the sentries when I heard Kallan scream. When I turned around, Baia had had all the water knocked out of her and Kallan was darting under the submarine. I was about to follow when I heard Locklyn yell and–"

She stops at the sight of Locklyn's mottled purple hand, a white flash of bone visible through the red rip in her skin. Darin glances at Locklyn's face, and relief courses through him seeing her closed eyes and slack jaw. By the Wave Master's mercy, she's passed out from the pain.

A gagging sound to his right causes him to glance at Conway, whose face has gone even paler than usual.

"Give her to me." Darin reaches out to take Locklyn from

Conway. For a fraction of an instant, the other's grip tightens, but then Darin feels her weight sliding into his arms, and Conway backs away, face averted. Darin shifts Locklyn to a more comfortable position, her head resting against his shoulder. Her hand jiggles limply, hitting his tail, and, even in unconsciousness, her face spasms. "She needs a doctor, Ginevra."

As if in response, the gates behind them begin to slide open, unseen chains clinking musically. At the sound, Ginevra starts to turn, but a second noise forestalls her.

Kallan slides between the propellers and comes to a stop against the submarine's wall. Her face is contorted with pain, and the water around her is slowly turning scarlet from the blood seeping between the fingers of her right hand, which are pressed to her torso. With a little gasp, Baia darts towards her friend.

"What happened?" Ginevra stares into the eyes of her bodyguard, who fights to straighten in the water, before giving up, gasping in pain.

"My lady, I caught up to him quickly." Kallan's words come out in wisps of bubbles. "With those absurd props he has in place of a tail, it was laughably easy. But I had not expected his hands to be unbound." Her voice falters at the look on her queen's face.

"And?"

"He caught hold of my spear and wrenched it out of my grasp." The response is almost inaudible. "When he attacked me, I fled."

There is a long moment of silence. Then Ginevra's voice is glacial. "You fled?"

"Ginevra," Orwell intervenes. "Locklyn and Kallan both require immediate medical attention. The rest of us ought to leave at once to search the surrounding waters for Igor. If we are unable to recapture him, our mission will become more urgent than I can express. There is no time to waste."

Darin glances to the open gates behind Ginevra and sees, with a jolt of surprise, that each side of the entryway is now lined with a row of silently watchful Nebulae maidens. Not one face bares a smile, but somehow, the expressions on the stony countenances convey the last emotion he would have expected.

Joy.

Ginevra's eyes remain on Kallan for an instant longer before she turns, gesturing to the four Nebulae nearest her. "Take them," she commands curtly, pointing to Locklyn and Kallan. "That one"–her hand flickers dismissively toward Kallan–"to the barracks. That one"–she gestures to Locklyn–"to my quarters."

Without a backward glance, she swims through the gates, the other guards falling into formation behind her. As the two Nebulae approach Darin, he glances around. The rest of the party are piling into the submarine as Baia trails behind the two Nebulae supporting Kallan toward the gates.

"We can take her, my lord," the Nebulae bodyguard in front of him says stiffly.

My lord?

His eyes skim over Locklyn's pale face, and, on an impulse, he leans down and whispers,

"Get well quickly. We have a lot of memories to make."

He watches as she is carried slowly away from him.

10

LOCKLYN

AS THE ROOM AROUND ME SWIMS INTO focus, I pray I am still dreaming. It is a beautiful room, in a stark, geometric style, but the décor is strange. Unsettling.

Smooth silver walls.

Obsidian sculptures depicting bold warriors.

A vanity wrought out of some kind of metal covered in a variety of hair supplies.

A silver wall mount hung with knives, morning stars, and a trident that looks as though it is made out of sea glass.

I turn my head slowly on my pillow, eyes resting on the object sitting on a bedside table. And, unwillingly, a smile tugs at the corners of my mouth.

It is a large glass tank half full of magma, with a smooth rock rising like an island in the center. On the rock sits a tiny humanoid creature, its eel's tail curled neatly around itself. In one hand, the mulciber holds a miniature pair of pincers, in the other, a ring, its silver circumference barely large enough to encircle a Merperson's pinkie finger.

I lean forward, trying to see how the tank remains supplied with fresh magma, when a voice behind me makes me jolt upright in the bed.

"They make the worst pets, you know."

Ginevra swims languidly over to the vanity table. She sits and pulls the shell off the end of one of her braids, her fingers dexterous as they unwind the silvery strands of hair. Glancing down at my right hand, which I have unconsciously cradled against my chest, I see that the palm is heavily bandaged, though my fingers have been left free.

"The most entitled little pests you'll ever meet," Ginevra continues. "If you don't drop in new stones and scraps of metal every other day, they go into sulky fits, which mostly involves lying in a corner of their cage pretending to be dead. And if you ignore that, they construct bellows and blow such large air bubbles into the bottom of the tank, all the magma eventually explodes out the top. It was a terrific mess. So now I let the little eel have his own way."

I glance over at the tank and see that the "eel" has perched the ring atop his skull like a crown and is hovering next to the glass, holding his pincers like a trident, with a distinctly sour expression on his tiny face.

The resemblance to Ginevra is so uncanny that I burst out laughing. A slight smile twists Ginevra's lips. "Like I told you, they're pests," she says, running her fingers through newly free strands of hair before starting on the next braid. "But that ring isn't horrendous, Hugo."

Hugo takes the circlet off his head and examines it critically. "I didn't know you could keep mulcibers as pets," I say, watching as he takes a miniscule hammer from his belt and taps at an invisible dent in the metal.

Ginevra gives a short laugh. "You shouldn't. My sister found Hugo on the banks of the Ustrina River with an urchin spike through his tail. She brought him to the palace and we took care of him until his tail healed. Then we returned him to the Ustrina and released him into the magma. But when we reached the palace, we found he had followed us. We took him to the River again, and when we saw him following us back to Imber, we shut the city gates on him. But the next day we found him outside the palace doors, clutching a set of silver bracelets. One for Michal. One for me." She shakes her head. "Bribery doesn't work on me. I'd have sent the little beggar back. But Michal's soft. So he stayed."

"In your room?"

"Like I said. He's entitled."

The questions in my mind are solidifying. "Is this the palace? The palace in Imber?" Ginevra's expression is indecipherable as she gives an affirmative nod. "Why am I here?" I say slowly.

"You couldn't really travel with bone shards sticking out of your hand."

I scramble through my memories. "The door," I say. "It slammed into my hand."

"You mean that sea slug, Igor, used shattering your hand as a diversion before escaping."

"What!" She's moved to the vanity, and I stare at the back of her head. "He escaped?" When she doesn't respond, I push myself further up on my pillows, trying to meet her eyes in the mirror. "Ginevra."

She just gazes at the shells taken from the ends of her braids, which she runs through her fingers. Clink. Clink. Clinkety. Clink, clink.

"Ginevra," I say again.

Her eyes finally meet mine in the mirror, hostile and shuttered. "What do you want me to say? He knocked the air out of Baia with a kick to the gut. Kallan and I turned around in time to see him slam the submarine door into your hand. No one knows how his hands got untied. Kallan pursued him and caught up, but when he threatened her with her own spear, she turned tail and swam." Her voice is scornful. "What a day for the Nebulae, warrior women of the sea. Bested by a single Crura."

"You do remember that up until a week ago, I had legs," I say conversationally.

"Your legs, or lack thereof, aren't the point, Locklyn," she snaps. "The point is that Igor shouldn't have escaped. And he did. On my watch."

I try to subdue my desire to panic. "The worst he can do is return to Atlantis and petition the Council for a sea-wide warrant for our arrest," I think out loud. "If he gets there before we do, that would make it almost impossible for us to enter the city."

"Why do we have to go to Atlantis anyway?" Ginevra demands suddenly. "When we first discussed our plans at Orwell's, we thought we'd need to go there to secure a submarine to travel to the North Sea. But we have one now."

"We have to alert the Council about Circe and ask for reinforcements," I remind her.

She only swivels back to the mirror. "We have a submarine and he doesn't," she says. "There's no way he will get to Atlantis before we do."

At that moment, the door bangs open, admitting a slight Mermaid who looks to be in her mid-teens. Her silvery hair matches Ginevra's, but her tail is olive green and glints with adhered sea glass shards.

"Rihanna," Ginevra's voice is edged with irritation. "One word. Knock."

"Sorry, sorry, sorry," the teenager intones brightly, darting toward the vanity and beginning to shuffle through the basket of jewelry sitting in the corner. "You've been gone so long, it hasn't been necessary."

Ginevra's scowl deepens. "What were you doing in my room while I was gone?"

"Secretly meeting with the scullery boy, obviously." Rihanna's dark eyes crinkle mischievously as she meets her sister's irate stare. "We can't all have as impeccable taste as you. Has Conway fallen head over tail for you yet?"

She's gone too far. I can see it in the tensing of Ginevra's face and her flashing eyes. She flies off her stool and, for an instant, I am certain she is going to strike her younger sister. Instead, she moves to the door, and I have to marvel at the grace and dignity of her movements.

"Out."

The single word sends Rihanna scuttling, her hands full of jelly hair ties and Ginevra's discarded shells. With a deadly softness, Ginevra slides the door closed behind her and moves back to the vanity, her back rigid as she lowers herself onto the stool. Silence envelops the room, sticky as oyster innards.

"So," I remark, "why–"

"Don't."

Silence oozes through the room again, broken only by the sporadic clinking of shells dancing across the vanity's smooth surface. "What did you think I was going to ask?" I say when the quiet becomes too much.

Ginevra's fingers still for a moment, and then she swivels to face me. "You were going to ask why he doesn't care about me," she says abruptly. "Weren't you?"

"You might not believe this, but I was actually going to ask why Rihanna had to use your room to meet with the scullery boy."

The bell-like notes of Ginevra's laughter fill the room. "The little flirt shares a room with Michal."

"Your middle sister?"

The laughter dies from Ginevra's lips. "Yes." Her voice drops. "My best friend."

"Did . . ." I hesitate. "Did something happen?"

Ginevra surveys me for a moment, and when she speaks, her voice is brittle. "When the Atlantean delegation came to demand fourteen Nebulae youth, I laughed in their faces. But they had the last laugh. Igor threw a fragor in the throne room, and the resulting blast disfigured the left side of Michal's face. She can't see out of that eye anymore, which means her value as a warrior is gone." A thin trail of bubbles slips past her lips. "Which means the assembly tonight is almost certainly going to vote to make Rihanna regent."

I choke, coughing out salty spume. "Rihanna?"

Ginevra meets my eyes, and I think I see camaraderie sparkling in hers, but it disappears so quickly and I tell myself I must have imagined it. "They're all fools. Even with both eyes gone, you couldn't find a better regent than Michal. She's–" her voice falters.

She lifts her graceful head, the beautiful clouds of her silvery hair wild and crinkly from the braids. "She's not like me."

We gaze at each other a moment. "Why would that make her a good regent?" I finally say.

Ginevra's lips twist. "You don't have to pretend, Locklyn. You, of all people, should know I don't have a diplomatic bone in my body."

"But you're a good leader," I protest.

"Am I, though?" she asks. "Or am I just a spoiled little girl who's good at getting her own way?"

Her abruptness surprises me. "Why would you say that?" I ask. "Ginevra, you took the throne at ten years old. Ten! And not only have you managed to hold your kingdom together for ten years after, you've strengthened Nebula. You're feared under the sea."

I expect her to give a reluctant smile, but instead she stuns me by bursting into tears. I throw off my blankets and am at the vanity in an instant, wrapping my good arm around Ginevra's shaking shoulders. She takes a shuddering breath. "I'm tired of being feared."

I swallow as I gently stroke my bandaged hand over her silvery hair. Gradually, the heaving of her shoulders stills, but since she doesn't pull away, I stay beside her. Music bubbles up, and I begin to hum, a wordless melody I've never sung before, but that flows naturally from somewhere deep inside. It's a tune that embodies the pain of unfulfilled desires tinged with the hope of future peace.

She eventually straightens, and I draw away, perching myself on the end of the bed as she turns back to the mirror and begins to run an urchin brush through her hair. I stay silent as she rises and sifts through the jewelry basket, eventually pulling out a circlet of dark metal studded with emeralds, which she settles atop her bright head.

"Come here," she snaps suddenly, as though she had already asked me several times without being heeded. Resisting the urge to not respond, I slowly join her at the vanity. "Sit!" she raps out, as though I am a recalcitrant dolphin. Obediently, I sink onto the stool she just vacated and watch apprehensively as she begins digging through the basket again. I catch a glint of gold as she pulls something out. She turns me toward the mirror. Her fingers are sure as they twist my blue curls into a pile on top of my head, and I watch, mesmerized, as she uses a set of golden combs, linked by a finely wrought chain, to secure the hair in place.

"All right, you're ready," she declares, turning toward the door. She stops. "Almost ready." She glides swiftly across to Hugo's tank and fishes around inside. The next moment, a band of warmth encircles my pinkie finger, and I look down to see the glitter of Hugo's ring, a circle of perfect, miniature dugongs. "*Now* you're ready."

I open my mouth, but at the sight of her fiercely narrowed eyes that dare me not to even think about thanking her, I change my words. "Ready for what?"

"You're coming to the Assembly with me. Let's go."

I stare at her.

With a huff, she yanks the door open and jerks her head toward the hall outside. "Are you suddenly an immobile coral?"

My lips twitch, and I push up off the stool, skimming past her as I head into the hall. "You know," I say, as she follows me, "I think I could give you a few tips on being less scary."

The queen of the Nebulae's laughter fills Imber's silent halls.

11

TWO HUNDRED YEARS EARLIER

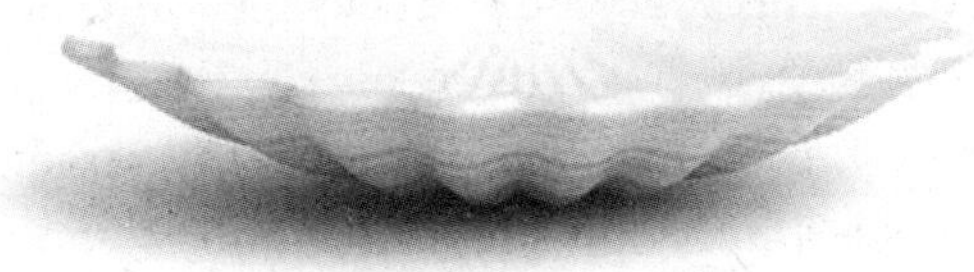

ON AN ISLAND IN THE MIDDLE OF A FIRE stream, a mulciber sets down his tongs. He picks up the silver locket he has created and studies it closely.

"It is missing something."

Going to his tray of cut gems, he sifts through the stones.

"Moonstones and sapphires would complement the dolphins and waves."

After some time, he steps back. "It is my best design yet."

The shore of the stream across from his forge is littered with rejected products, but this locket will not be joining them. It will be for his wife.

He turns the locket over to study the back. The unmarked silver is beautiful.

He hesitates before picking up his finest engraver. With steady hands, he etches three words onto the locket.

"Perfect."

He straightens up the forge before going home. The locket will stay here until his wife's birthday tomorrow. As he opens the door, he catches a whiff of something. There is a barracuda nearby.

He slams the door and dives into the stream, heading for home.

He does not realize the door did not latch. A few minutes after his departure, a juvenile pygmy shark swims up to the forge. Using its nose to nudge open the door, it swims inside. Its reckless tail knocks into the locket. The chain tangles around its tail fin. The shark leaves again, swimming toward its usual hunting spot.

It has barely reached the shore of the fire stream when another pygmy attacks. The two fight, slamming playfully into each other until the locket becomes dislodged and falls to the sand.

The sharks leave, and the next day, when the mulciber returns to his forge, the locket is gone. He searches the forge, but eventually concludes it must have been stolen by his rival smith.

Days later, a young Schatzi arrives at the stream. He sifts through the rejected items on the shore, and is about to decide there is nothing worth salvaging, when a chain half-buried in the sand catches his eye.

He picks up the locket and studies it. Turning it over, he reads the inscription on the back. "Forever and always." He places it in the pouch at his waist and swims away. He must return to Aquaticus. Talia will be singing tonight. He wonders why the mulciber threw that away. It is perfect.

12

LOCKLYN

SHE WAS MEANT TO BE A QUEEN.

The thought fills my mind with a glow of admiration as I linger in a corner of Imber's great hall, watching Ginevra. She hovers in a small balcony which juts from the front of the room, looking down at the sea of upturned faces below. On either side and slightly behind her, Rihanna and a young woman with an eye patch, whom I assume to be Michal, are stationed. Neither of them carry Ginevra's aura of authority, intangible as a mist hovering around her solitary, shining form.

The silence stretches and strains against the confines of the room, and I struggle not to fidget, forcing my body to remain still while trying to occupy my mind with studying the Nebulae nearest me. The maiden directly in front of me has so many piercings in her ear, I am sure there must be more metal than flesh there. The silver lines of a tattoo curl up her neck from the collar of an urchin spine-studded jerkin encasing her muscular torso. My eyes shift to the girl in front of her, whose jerkin is silver chainmail embedded with onyx chips. A rich girl. Her soft black hair is braided into a thick plait that flows down her back, and I am just determining that she has a sweet demeanor when she faces me.

Her eyes are a shade of green so neon it is almost yellow, and as she narrows them at me, her lips curl back from her teeth, revealing sharpened incisors affixed with onyx to match her chainmail. I shrink back against the wall behind me, and her snarl morphs into a smile, just as the pounding starts.

The hilt of the trident Ginevra holds strikes the ground again and again, and every spear shaft in the great hall follows her, the beat becoming faster and faster. Then Michal's trident begins a different cadence–three quick taps to complement Ginevra's pulsing beat–and about a third of the room follows her. The drumming is beginning to reverberate in my chest, and I feel an inexorable pull to sway to its rhythm.

A shrill shriek startles me, and my heartbeat slows as I see Rihanna on the balcony. She scrapes the edge of a coral knife deftly along the haft of her sea glass trident, creating a high-pitched wail. Mixed with the pounding spears, it forms an unearthly, heart-rending kind of music.

The beat moves faster and faster, twisting and changing as the Nebulae follow their queen, until finally, with one last knife scrape from Rihanna, silence envelopes the room once more. Ginevra glides forward until one of her hands rests lightly on the balcony railing. The high clarity of her voice makes any increase in volume unnecessary.

"Warriors."

"Lady." The word is so unanimous, so beautifully simple and elegant, my throat closes. I watch the entire hall place the tips of their spears on the shoulders of the warriors in front of them and bow in one fluid, graceful motion.

"One month ago, I left my kingdom," Ginevra declares. Her tail sways almost imperceptibly. "I left it in order to ensure the continued prosperity of Nebula–to ensure that no dishonor perpetuated against our kingdom would go unchallenged." The hall is so still, I can hear the bubbles breathing from the lips of the warriors nearest me. "And I return triumphant," Ginevra's voice rises. With a theatrical flair, she gestures behind her.

A towering glass cylinder, filled with the treasure I recognize from Llyra's wreck, glides toward her on bronze wheels, propelled from behind by unseen hands. The pots of magma illuminating the hall cause the treasure to glow, and a collective gasp ripples up from the assembly.

"Our nation's interests are secured," Ginevra continues. "And, in my absence, our kingdom has remained secure under the guidance of my sister and your appointed regent, Michal Kaveri."

The silence in the room shifts. It is no longer unified in adoration of the queen. Now it is strained. Taut. Discontent. Michal's face twitches for an instant before falling into lines of impassivity once more.

Ginevra's voice sharpens. "In continued pursuit of our nation's interests, it is necessary for me to leave again in three days' time."

A snort shatters the stillness of the hall. Every head swivels to the source of the disruption. The rich girl. The one with adder's eyes.

Ginevra turns slowly to stare at the girl. The silence stretches taut once more, and I wait, knowing with absolute certainty that in this battle of wills, the adder girl doesn't stand a chance. The seconds slip by, until finally, the neon eyes drop away from the dark ones.

"The nature of my mission requires the utmost secrecy." Ginevra's tone reveals no hint of the interruption. "And I do not know how long I will be away." Her tail pauses in its slight swaying. "In the interests of continued peace and prosperity for Nebula, Michal will continue in her post as regent. Unless"–she pierces the adder girl with her eyes–"anyone wishes to propose another candidate."

I don't even know Michal, but I know what it's like to experience rejection because of something you can't control. Hope for her begins to swell in my chest.

A voice cuts through the water directly in front of me. "I wish to propose another candidate."

Ginevra's eyes flash. "On what grounds?"

"On the grounds that Michal Kaveri is unfit to lead a kingdom of warriors," says the tattooed girl coolly.

I look beyond Ginevra's elegant form, now rigid with tension, to Michal, whose posture has sagged. Her tail, an even darker green than Rihanna's and without any sea glass embellishments, and her hair, slate-gray rather than the silvery white of her sisters, make her whole form seem dark, shadowy, almost unreal compared to the glowing forms of Ginevra and Rihanna.

"Under Michal's leadership, Nebula has remained secure for the past month," Ginevra's voice is as cold as an icicle. "Two spies from Aquaticus were apprehended and are currently awaiting sentence in our dungeons. The mulcibers produced three times their usual quota of weapons. In no way has Michal proven herself unfit for leadership."

"She's blind in one eye," the girl retorts. "She can no longer use a bow. And her skill in other areas of combat is far exceeded by that of your sister Rihanna."

"My sister Rihanna," Ginevra says with deadly calm, "is a child. Her skill with a trident may exceed Michal's, but, I assure you, her skills in diplomacy and negotiation are"–her eyes flick toward her youngest sister–"negligible."

"You took the throne at ten years of age." The tattooed girl is not cowed by the iciness of Ginevra's manner. She only seems to become more insolent. "Rihanna is a warrior. The same can no longer be said of Michal."

"I don't want to be regent!" Rihanna's voice is high-pitched and childlike. "Not because I lack diplomacy or negotiation skills"–she shoots a scathing look at Ginevra–"but because I'd rather live out my days in Oro than stay cooped up in a palace settling petty disputes all day! Michal can keep the post of regent, and she's welcome to it. Because I'm not going to do it."

"If the vote of the warriors is to confer the title of regent upon you, you have no choice in the matter." The formality of Ginevra's tone is an impressive contrast to that of her younger sister. "As your queen, my support is behind Michal Kaveri to stand as regent in my absence. But as another candidate has been proposed, I will put it to the vote of the warriors."

"No." Anger drops the pitch of Rihanna's voice to a growl. She darts to the balcony railing and pauses beside Ginevra, the glass on her tail reflecting the reddish light of the magma pots and surrounding her in an iridescent, angry glow. With a flick of her wrist, her coral knife leaves her hand, hurtling end over end toward the tattooed girl, who has no time to move. The tip of Rihanna's knife buries itself in the wooden shaft of the girl's spear, inches above her fingers. Rihanna rounds on her older sisters. "I'd like to see anyone"–her voice quivers with fury–"try to force me to do *anything*."

There is a ringing silence, broken by the scrape of coral on wood, as the tattooed girl extracts the knife from her spear. Then, the hall erupts in cheers.

"There's a leader!"

"Rihanna!"

"That's what we need in a regent!"

"Action over diplomacy!"

In the red light of the magma pots, I watch Rihanna's eyes widen in shock. She opens her mouth, but Ginevra's fingers close on her wrist, clamping tight. "Let it be put to a vote." Her voice cuts effortlessly through the tumult, which dies as all eyes go to their queen. "All in favor of Michal Kaveri retaining her current post of regent in my absence?" My eyes skim the hall, counting raised spear tips. "Thank you. And all in favor of Rihanna Kaveri assuming the post of regent?"

Above the mass of raised spear tips, Ginevra's gaze is bleak and the edge in her voice is like coral against glass. I can't look at Michal. "By the vote of the warrior assembly, Rihanna Kaveri will assume the post of regent of Nebula in my absence." She raises her hands, quelling the cheers rising toward the balcony. "Tomorrow I will inspect the city's security perimeter. On the day following, I will hear grievances. But tonight"–she manages to manufacture warmth in her voice–"tonight, I want my people to rejoice at their queen's safe return. In the city square, a feast fit for a Land Dweller emperor's table awaits you. Go in gladness."

The throne room doors swing into motion, and the warriors' spear shafts begin to pound again. Ginevra inclines her head, then raises her hands before turning and gliding out of the balcony, followed by Michal and Rihanna.

The bedlam that follows her departure sends me back against the wall to avoid the Mermaids all fighting to be first out of the throne room to the food. The tattooed girl thrashes through the other warriors, tail slapping aside anyone in her path.

Then I remember that Conway once told me Nebula produces next to none of its own food.

On second thought, perhaps punching one's way to the door seems warranted.

The room empties in seconds, but a thread of sound beckons, drawing me toward a doorway in the back corner of the room. Words emerge as I swim closer, though the lovely voice is one I don't recognize.

"It's fine, Evrie. Truly."

"It's fine for you!" Tears choke Rihanna's voice. "You're free, aren't you? Now you can swim off with Ginevra through the Seven Seas, having adventures, while I'm stuck here, settling flintstone thefts and regulating mulciber capture!"

"Maybe this will teach you not to indulge in fits of temper like a spoiled child," Ginevra says frigidly.

"A spoiled child?" Rihanna's voice rises. "The people chose me to replace Michal as regent! Clearly they don't see me as a child."

"Everyone knows you're not a child, Rihanna." I realize with surprise that the rich, soothing voice must be Michal's. "And you're strong. The people will follow you. Which is what will make you a good regent."

Ginevra was right. She must have been an excellent regent.

For an instant, there is quiet. Then Ginevra says gently, "Come with me, Michal."

Michal's words are edged with hesitation. "Should I perhaps stay to help?"

"I don't need your help!" Rihanna spouts. "The people chose me, Michal! Me! I don't need you! Just go with Ginevra!"

"Rihanna," Michal says softly, but Ginevra's voice is louder. Harder.

"That's enough."

"You can't–" Rihanna starts.

"I said, that's enough. The people have chosen you, as you say. They have chosen you to lead them and that is what you must do. From this night until the night I return, our kingdom is in your hands. And everything you do–or do not do–affects not only you, but every one of your subjects." Ginevra's tone alters. "There is a council of advisors and nobles who will help you. And the army, as you know, is the best in the Mediterranean. I foresee no likelihood of an attack."

Rihanna's voice quavers. "So, that's it?"

"Rihanna, if you want me to stay–" Michal begins, but Rihanna explodes again.

"I don't want you to stay! I don't need you! Either of you!"

The whoosh of a tail through water is my only warning to fling myself sideways. Rihanna streams through the curtain covering the doorway, green tears streaking her face.

The doors to the great hall close with a bang, but conversation continues. "I think I should stay with her, Evrie. She's fifteen."

"She doesn't need us. Let her try leading on her own."

"But what about Nebula? I know you're angry at her, Evrie, but think. The mistakes she will make won't just affect her anymore."

"She's completely self-absorbed, Michal. Everything's always about her. She doesn't even pause to consider how you might feel about losing the regent position because of something that isn't your fault. No, the only thing that matters is she won't be able to swim around practicing trident throws and spending time with the scullery boy."

"She really does like him, you know." There is a hint of a smile in Michal's voice. "Most of us are pretty self-absorbed at fifteen, Evrie."

"But not you, Michal. You've always seen other people and care enough to take time to find the best in them."

"It's because of the Wave Master." The beauty of Michal's voice accentuates the power of her words. "I know He loves them." There is a pause. "That's the only thing that's gotten me through, Ginevra. You remember the night after the Atlanteans came, I was in so much pain, and in a nation of warriors, I knew I would have no place. But when I finally slept, I dreamed of Him."

I press into the curtain, not wanting to miss a word.

"The warrior council was dragging me through the gates of Imber, shouting that a one-eyed Mermaid had no place among the Nebulae. They threw me into the Ustrina River. As I began to sink, the magma searing my skin, I begged Him to save me. For a moment, there was nothing. But then I felt His hand on my arm. I thought He would pull me from the River, but instead, He appeared beside me in the magma. He put His arms around me and we swam up the River, away from the crowd. The magma still burned, but everywhere my skin had contact with His, there was coolness. Healing. When I woke, I still couldn't see, but the pain in my eye was gone. I knew then, Evrie, the rejection I would experience from the warriors–that would be my fire river. I wasn't supposed to try to escape it, but I knew He would be with me."

The silence that follows is so long, I lift the edge of the curtain ever so slightly to look in. Ginevra's pure white tail shines like a beacon, her arms wrapped tightly around her sister as they embrace. At the sight, my throat swells. I let the curtain fall.

Ginevra's voice is unrecognizable in its warmth. "Come with me, Michal. Rihanna will be fine. She might think she doesn't need you, but I know I do. You make me better, sister. You don't even want to know how horrible I've been this last month."

There is a light laugh, then Michal says, "When should I be ready to leave?"

13

DARIN

HIS BODY IS TENSE AS HE LEANS AGAINST one of the submarine's walls, picturing the bloody slash in Locklyn's palm, a shard of bone visible through the ripped skin. In the frozen shock following Igor's attack, he had allowed the Nebulae women to take her from his arms and through Imber's city gates. Now he wishes he had insisted on going with her.

The dark emptiness of his mind presses in heavily. Her presence had soothed him. Her stories were beginning, slowly, to rebuild a shadowy sense of himself. Her belief that he was not defined by the memory theft wrought by Circe's cursed potion was encouraging him that he could become a worthy Merman in the future, with or without his memory.

His eyes find Conway at the controls, and he wanders over. "So, you're the crown prince of my–our–kingdom."

Conway's jaw tightens. "Yes," he says, not taking his eyes from the water streaming past the submarine's front window.

"Being responsible for an entire nation would terrify me," Darin remarks. "Even if I had all my memories."

"Well, you're lucky, aren't you? That happy responsibility is going to fall to yours truly."

Irritation flickers, and Darin almost turns away. But Locklyn's voice seems to whisper in his mind, checking him.

I don't care what happened to you. Nothing gives you the right to treat the people around you like sea slime.

"What did I do to you? I can't remedy an offense I have no memory of committing."

Conway fiddles with the controls. "You didn't do anything. I'm just . . . tired of steering."

"That is the most pathetic lie I have ever heard."

"So, I can't even lie up to your standards?" Conway snaps.

"What in Oro's depths are you talking about?" As Conway hesitates, Darin becomes aware of the others nearby. "What is he talking about?"

Orwell and Arledge's faces are blank, but Kai's low voice rumbles out, "You were both in love with the dolphin tamer."

"Dolphin tamer?"

"Come on, Aalto. Who is the only one of us who could possibly tame a dolphin?"

Darin's hand flies out, jerking the silver lever and bringing the submarine to a shuddering halt. "Circe's potion did many things. But increasing my patience was not one of them. Stop talking in riddles."

Conway's cheeks turn crimson. "It isn't your memory loss that makes you a fringehead. It's the fact that the most amazing Mermaid I've ever met somehow wasn't good enough for you until she had a tail. Did you think having a Crura wife would damage the prestige of Aquaticus's most acclaimed Schatzi?"

Crura wife? What is he talking about? "Locklyn? Why would you think I would give two periwinkles about her having a tail?"

"We swam together for a month!" Conway's voice is rigid. "I would see her looking at you like your smile caused the ebb and flow of the tides! But you treated her like a patronizing older brother. Until now."

Is he right? Was I so arrogant that Locklyn's legs would bother me? Darin's head jerks to the others. "Is he right?"

"I never saw the two of you together, son." Orwell's voice is kind. "But she spoke of you . . . most highly."

"I barely knew either of you," is Arledge's response as he gazes dully out the porthole.

Darin's eyes seek Kai. For an instant, there is conflict on the Merman's face. Then Kai says guardedly, "My impressions are nothing more than what I spoke. But I never thought it was contempt that kept you from expressing what was in your heart."

The words only add frenzy to the turmoil in Darin's mind. The subject is too personal, and though he seems outside it, he finds it embarrassing to be discussed so openly. *But I asked for it.* Orwell and Locklyn both told him to focus on rebuilding his life. But then a new identity would be only for him. Everyone else's view will be colored by the Merman he was before.

He throws an angry glance at Conway, and regret flashes across the other's face. "Aalto, I–"

"You've said enough."

He wants nothing more than to rip the submarine door open and swim out and away.

If I am to start a new life, I wish it could truly be new.

"Aalto." Darin reluctantly turns to Orwell. He sees in the other's expression the Merman who spent most of his days roving the Seven Seas. "Go," Orwell says. Darin looks at him in confusion, and Orwell reaches for the submarine's door and slides it open. "Go," he says again. His hand reaches into the pouch at his waist, and he holds out a chain, from which is dangling a tiny hourglass. "Return by the time the sand runs through twice. And take a weapon."

For a moment, Darin is completely still. Then his fingers snag the chain, and he drapes it around his neck. Grabbing his dagger from his sleeping place next to the wall, he darts through the door and is gone.

14

LOCKLYN

"OUR CODES CLEARLY STATE THAT during the first year of life, a merchild has a higher claim on its mother than her military duties. Demoting Officer Rilian is not in keeping with the spirit of these laws."

From where I float in the balcony behind Ginevra, my eyes wander wistfully toward the doors of the great hall. It is our final day in Imber. Ginevra, Michal, and I will set out at the first stroke of the time gong. While I admire Ginevra's wisdom and her dedication to resolving the disputes of her subjects, the glimpses I have had of Nebula's capital make me yearn to explore this city that is so different from my own.

"Listening to this is shriveling my mind into a flake of plankton." The mutter causes me to glance at Rihanna, who is whisking her tail irritably beside me, her fingers fiddling with the strands of the peridot necklace looped twice around her neck. She dips her chin toward the curtain in the corner of the great hall, then leans close and says in a hushed voice, "The exit in the side chamber is a secret. It's technically supposed to be known only to the royal family. But since you seem able to tolerate my oldest sister, it's more likely that I'll strangle her someday than that you'll sneak in and assassinate her."

The corners of my mouth twitch. "Aren't you supposed to be learning how to govern the kingdom?"

Rihanna rolls her eyes. "Ginevra has forced Michal and me to attend these 'grievance sessions' ever since I could throw a trident. I can't believe Michal got out of this one because she has to pack." A dimple appears in Rihanna's cheek. "If we go now, I'll show you the mulciber foundries and the training grounds. And the seahorse stables."

I glance down at the dozens of Merpeople still waiting for an audience with Ginevra. "All right," I whisper, and Rihanna's teeth flash white. Drifting backward, she quietly slides the cover over a chute leading to the curtained room where I overheard her arguing with Ginevra the night she was made regent. Guilt pinches my stomach as I cast a glance at the queen of the Nebulae, but her attention is riveted on the Merman now hovering below her, and I slip into the chute after Rihanna's retreating form.

Rihanna holds the outside door open for me silently, but as soon as we are out in the street, she trills, "Free at last!" and takes off. I follow.

Imber's palace is in the center of the city, just as it is in Aquaticus, but the street layout is different. In Aquaticus, the streets intersect at right angles, forming a grid pattern. In Imber, there is only one street. It spirals out from the palace in the pattern of a nautilus shell, ending at the city gates.

As we speed away from the palace, I gaze at the dwellings passing by. They are made out of stone, metal, and the leftover shards of wrecks, as they are in Aquaticus, but whereas my city's houses are triangular, with turrets and embellishments on the dwellings of the wealthy, Imber's houses are square and utilitarian. Aside from the palace, none of the houses have any embellishments whatsoever, except for strings of white objects draped over the doors of some of the dwellings.

I move a little closer, and convulsively swallow a gulp of water. "Rihanna, are those bones?"

Rihanna turns. "Yes."

"But . . . they look like . . . Mermish bones."

"Of course." Rihanna sounds bored. "All the old-timers have strings of the bones of their enemies. Ginevra put a stop to the practice when she took the throne. She said the tradition was barbaric and stripped our enemies of the little dignity they had left. So the young warriors hunt tiger sharks, and string their teeth to make chimes. But Ginevra knew she'd have mutiny on her hands if she tried to force the existing bone strands to be taken down." She swivels back, clearly tired of the topic. "Let's go. We'll have to hurry if we want to make it to the training hall in time." Her tail picks up speed.

As we pass a stone house with a pile of tiny tridents on the stoop, the door flies open and a harassed-looking Merman emerges. "Have either of you seen two merchildren?" he asks. "A lad and a lass?" Rihanna and I shake our heads. "Those two little wobegongs!" complains the Merman. "They need the Academy. They have too much energy to be cooped up at home. Always going out searching for stray mulcibers and trying to slip into the training hall to practice with the targets."

I'm about to linger there to ask what his merchildren look like, but Rihanna grabs me and drags me away. "We haven't seen them—sorry!" she calls over her shoulder.

"Since the Nebulae Merwomen are warriors, do the Mermen raise the children?" I ask her after we've gone a ways.

"Not all the Merwomen become warriors," Rihanna says scornfully. "You should see some of the girls in my class—they can barely hold their tridents. All Nebulae merchildren attend the Academy from five to ten years old. Then, the most talented Merwomen are trained to be warriors, and the most talented Mermen are trained in administration of the nation's essential industries—mulciber husbandry, teaching at the Academy, and strengthening Imber's defenses."

"And those who aren't the most talented?"

Rihanna waves a dismissive hand. "Someone has to do the grunt work."

I watch her as we continue to skim through the streets, wondering if she ever thinks of those around her who do the grunt work as real Merpeople with feelings and dreams and ambitions of their own.

In my mind, I see my hut in the reef, with dugong pens around back. The small lean-to off to one side where I store the milk and conduct my cheese-making process. I am one of the grunt workers Rihanna scoffs at. A dugong shepherdess working night and day to barely scrape by.

My eyes flicker down to the bubble-encrusted scales propelling me through the water.

For the first time in my life, I might have another option outside of struggling for survival. What is my dream?

With a stab of pain, a familiar face fills my mind.

For the last four years, Darin's been my dream.

I've been pursuing the hope, even when I refused to acknowledge it, that one day our inside jokes, our hours of talking and silence, our secrets and confidences would morph into the love of a lifetime.

Instead, his mind was wiped of all those things, and our relationship is as tenuous as a severed octopus tentacle. The wounded stump might regenerate into something stronger. But at the moment, all I can feel is the consuming loss of what once was there.

"Locklyn." Rihanna's voice cuts through my musings. "We're here."

Lost in my thoughts, I have barely taken in anything about my surroundings for the last few minutes. But now, I stare.

The sprawling complex in front of me is more than three times the size of the palace. To one side, there are stables, with the biggest sea horses I have ever seen visible through the half doors of their stalls. On the other side is a netted enclosure, similar to the octopus-wrestling ring at the Shark's Fin, only much larger. Inside, pairs of Mermaids spar, using knives, tridents, and spears. An instructor, with muscled arms crossed over her dugong-hide jerkin, swims among them, observing. With a shock, I watch one of the Mermaids nearest me dart forward and slash her opponent viciously across the face with her knife. Gossamer strands of blood curl from between the other Mermaid's fingers as she staggers back, clutching her cheek.

My gasp causes the attacking Mermaid to spin, and I see the girl who snorted during Ginevra's speech. She bares her teeth at me before turning to press her advantage on her wounded opponent.

"Locklyn!" Rihanna's voice is impatient, and I turn to see her holding open the door to the main entrance.

"Did you see that?" I exclaim as I join her. "That Mermaid with the yellow eyes actually cut her sparring partner!"

"Of course she did." Rihanna's tone suggests I am rapidly approaching the ocean floor in her estimation. "Fighting isn't a game. There have to be real consequences. Why do you think Nebula has the best army under the sea?"

Still a little stunned, I have no reply. Rihanna is through a side door so quickly that I barely make it in after her without catching my tail as it closes.

I stop just inside, trying to get my bearings, when something whooshes past my face. My body automatically hurtles against the wall, terrified to find a trident protruding from the center of a Mermaid-shaped target at the other end of the room.

"Nice throw, Brosnan." The shout is high and bubbly, and I turn my rounded eyes onto Rihanna, who is gazing at the boy who threw the trident like he is the most wonderful thing she has ever seen.

15

LOCKLYN

"LET'S SEE YOU HIT THE FIN, RI," THE boy calls back, and Rihanna zips over to an impressive array of spears and tridents racked on the back wall. I follow her, wondering what kind of Merperson situates the entrance to a throwing range where the next individual who enters could be impaled by a stray trident.

"Rihanna . . ."

She ignores me as she selects a spear with a gleaming obsidian point and joins the boy. Quickly drawing her arm back, she hurls the weapon, which imbeds itself in the target, exactly where the fin would connect to the tail on a real Merperson.

The boy smiles at her, and she glances away.

I smile in spite of myself.

"I thought you weren't coming," I hear him say as they swim toward the target to retrieve their weapons, unconcerned about the projectiles being thrown by the other Merpeople practicing nearby.

Rihanna huffs. "We were stuck listening to Ginevra resolve petty grievances. Until we snuck away."

"We?" The boy turns toward me. "Who's your friend?"

"Oh, this is Locklyn. She's from Aquaticus. And despite being Ginevra's friend, she isn't a complete crustacean."

I grin at the boy, who looks slightly horrified at Rihanna's lack of tact. "High praise. Brosnan, right?"

Brosnan returns my smile. "Saying exactly what she thinks is one of Ri's worst–and best–qualities."

Rihanna shoves his shoulder. "Do you want to hear exactly what I think of you?"

"Please." He folds his arms and waits.

"You'd better watch how you talk to Imber's regent," she retorts.

"What?"

"Michal got deposed last night at the assembly. They wanted me." The words are haughty, but her eyebrows pinch together in distress.

Brosnan seems taken aback. "How's Michal?"

"Michal! That's all anyone cares about!" Rihanna's voice is so loud, the other Merpeople in the range turn to stare at us curiously. Brosnan reaches to pull the trident and the spear from the target.

"I have to get back to the palace," he says quietly. "We can talk on the way."

Rihanna is still fuming as we exit the throwing range and make our way out the double doors. As soon as we are in the street, she spins on Brosnan. "Don't you care how I feel about this?"

My eyebrows rise involuntarily, and it is all I can do not to interject a crisp comment about exactly how much anyone cares about her feelings in this situation. Brosnan just looks at her and says calmly, "How do you feel?"

"I hate it! Everyone keeps acting like I'm so lucky, and Michal's the one to be pitied, but she's good at this, and I'm not. Listening to grievances makes me want to scream and pull my hair out. I'm fifteen. I just want to spend time with you, and become a better warrior, and not worry about any of this! And everyone acts like I'm a terrible Merperson for feeling that way."

"No one thinks you're a terrible Merperson," Brosnan says.

"She does!" Rihanna points an accusing finger toward me, her eyes beginning to swim in steaming green tears. "It's written all over her face."

Brosnan glances at me. I choose my words carefully. "I don't think it's terrible to feel that way. It's natural. But have you considered how Michal is feeling, Rihanna? She lost her eye in a brutal attack. And because of it, she was publicly humiliated by nearly everyone who demanded her position be stripped from her and given to her younger sister."

Rihanna's lips tighten as she continues to fight the tears threatening to brim over. Brosnan's fingers wrap around hers, though he says nothing.

Rihanna speaks haltingly. "Michal always takes care of everyone else. It never crossed my mind that she could be upset. She never is." Rihanna swallows. "But she never tells me anything, either. She tells Ginevra, never me. And Ginevra's the same way. They've always been best friends. And now they're gallivanting off to the North Sea for who knows how long, and I'm going to be left behind. Like always."

Brosnan pats her shoulder a little helplessly as she begins to cry. I glance past them, straight into a pair of yellow eyes. The Mermaid is sparring with a new partner next to the net, but her gaze is riveted on us. When she catches my look, her jeweled incisors flash at me, and she darts under her opponent's guard, slashing her across the face. Just as she did to her previous partner.

Bile rises in my throat, and I instantly turn away, just as Brosnan says, "Come on, Ri. If Cook wakes up from his afternoon nap and finds me gone, I might end up in this evening's soup." At her watery chuckle, he adds, "And if the grievances end and Ginevra notices you and your friend are gone, I might be helping Cook put *you* in the soup."

16

DARIN

THE HOURGLASS AROUND HIS NECK HAS just drained for the first time when he sees it.

A hulking, dark shape sends a thrill coursing through him.

His eyes can't fully discern what it is, but he knows deep inside.

Even without my memories, I am a treasure hunter.

His tail propels him forward, and the contours of the battered vessel grow clearer with every stroke.

When he is close enough, his fingers glide over the crusty wood. "Hello, beautiful."

He darts up and over the ship's railing, searching for a way down into the bowels. There is a trapdoor in the center of the deck and he pries it open, peering into the darkness below.

Gills of a blobfish, I forgot a light.

As if in answer to the thought, a glow appears in his peripheral vision. Darin swivels his head to see a ctenophora drifting lazily past. Pouncing on it, he ties its legs around his wrist, leaving the body bobbing over his arm like a luminescent balloon. Then he descends into the ship's cavernous depths.

The space is bare. Too bare. Impaired as his memory is, he knows there is no point in sailing a ship without cargo.

A Schatzi must have found this.

Slowly, he swims the perimeter of the hold, half hoping he will find some forgotten trinket which will provide a clue as to the ship's purpose. In a dark corner, there is a flash of movement. Darin is just drawing near to investigate when a male esox flies at him out of the shadows, razor teeth snapping. Reeling backward, he catches a glimpse of the female, circling protectively over a clutch of eggs.

Darin darts upward, yet he feels scales brush his bicep before tiny fangs sink into his arm. Waving wildly, he manages to dislodge the esox just as he re-emerges onto the deck. Preoccupied with examining the droplets of blood welling from a dozen puncture wounds, he fails to notice he is no longer alone until a voice says, "Aalto?"

Darin's coral knife is in his hand before the second syllable of his name has died. Two Mermen, who were clearly examining the boat, move backward, empty hands raised. "Aalto, it's me," one with curly, emerald hair says.

The knife in his hand does not lower. "Who?"

The green-haired man glances in bemusement toward his companion, whose brown hair matches his muddy tail. "What are you playing at, Aalto? It's me, Carlow Eaton. What are you doing here?"

"Yeah, I heard you'd been charged with theft from the crown," the other Merman says, eyes narrowing.

His gut tells him these two are the last Merpeople he should confide in that his memory has been erased. "You should be more careful what rumors you listen to," Darin says coolly. "Why are the two of you here?"

The two Mermen exchange a glance. "Times have been tough since you disappeared, Aalto. It's been nearly a month since a wreck was discovered. Nen and I thought we'd go to the last place we'd heard of a successful treasure hunt."

He has no idea how to respond, since he still does not know who either of them are. Absently, he reaches to twine his fingers in the chain around his neck and his memory jolts. "I have to get back," he says abruptly and turns away.

At the railing, he pauses to unwind the legs of the ctenophora still twined around his wrist. As he is about to dive over the railing, pain explodes across his left temple. Strands like squid ink pulse at the edges of his vision as he whirls, just in time to see Nen inserting another rock into the pouch of a slingshot.

"We were checking to see if your crew missed any treasure on this wreck," the brown-haired Merman says. "But I'll wager that Malik will be happy enough to get an update on the treasure you stole from him, that we might get a little reward for bringing you in."

The second rock catches Darin directly above the right ear, causing the world to go black.

17

DARIN

SO THIS IS CONWAY'S FATHER.

Apparently, he brought this Merman treasure time and again. He should remember the king's face. But the black-bearded visage glowering down from the coral throne is foreign and, try as he might, Darin can see no resemblance to his son.

"So," Malik demands, "where is the treasure you promised me?"

"The majority of the treasure we collected was to repay your debt to Nebula," he responds coolly. "Queen Ginevra took it back to Imber, in order to call off the forces stationed along your border. Prince Conway is traveling behind me, bringing a small amount of treasure to replenish Undula's coffers."

Malik leans back on the coral throne. "My scouts informed me yesterday that the Nebulae were retreating. Clearly, your claims about Llyra's Treasure were not idle boasts. Tell me, how much gold remained?"

The others had told him the treasure they took from the wreck barely scratched the surface of the wealth concealed there. But Malik's entitlement sits wrong. "Shouldn't you be asking how your son fares?"

Malik's lip curls. "You should know as well as I, Aalto, that Conway's absence has made certain financial considerations easier on me. As far as I am concerned, if he weren't bringing Undula's share of the treasure, he could stay away until his ascension to the throne."

Anger flares inside, and Darin feels sudden compassion for the black-haired youth with the hard eyes. He keeps his expression impassive. "You're in luck. Conway should be here by tomorrow, then he will depart with a group of us, myself included, on a quest to the North Sea. It is clear why he seems so delighted to forgo *your* company."

Malik eyes him coolly. "Conway can go to the North Sea if he pleases. But I'm afraid I will require your services here. Undula's coffers could use what remains of Llyra's Treasure. And you will be leading the mission to retrieve it."

"Highness, I would be more than happy to join such a quest," Carlow puts forth from his place to Darin's left.

"As would I," Nen agrees from the other side.

He glances at each of them with dislike. "The rock to my skull and posidonia ropes on my wrists suggest you two might have a problem with my leadership," he says wryly. "I'm afraid I will have to decline your offers to join my crew."

Carlow and Nen tense, but Malik throws back his head and laughs. "Finding a treasure that has been lost for over a hundred years does entitle the Merman to choose his own crew. You are dismissed, gentlemen."

"But, Highness," Carlow protests, "we had hoped–that is, we had thought–perhaps some token of gratitude for bringing . . ." His voice trails off as Malik rises from the throne and towers above him. Malik glares down at the shrinking Merman before his lips curve into a gracious smile.

"You have my royal gratitude," he says smoothly. "And there is no better reward than the knowledge that you have served your country." His fingers flutter, and the guards on either side of the silver doors leap to push them open. Carlow and Nen linger a moment longer before reluctantly bowing and exiting the room.

After Malik re-seats himself, Darin addresses him. "Highness,

I desire nothing more than Undula's good. However, the matter which calls our group to the North Sea is of the gravest importance. If you will allow me to depart with my crew, I give you my word that upon my return, I will lead a quest to retrieve what remains of Llyra's Treasure."

Malik's eyes narrow. "What is this gravely important matter which calls you north?"

Darin draws in a lungful of seawater. "There is reason to believe a powerful Sea Enchantress is journeying that direction to release a captive monster. Unless she is stopped, it is likely she will use this menace to terrorize the entire Undersea Realm."

Malik regards him for a long moment. "Who will be joining you on this mission?" Malik asks finally. "Besides my son, of course," he adds.

"Locklyn, Kai, Arledge, Lief Orwell, and Ginevra." He is concerned his lack of knowledge of full names except Orwell's will seem informal to the king, but to Darin's surprise, Malik's expression is suddenly filled with satisfaction.

"The queen of Nebula will be joining you? On a trip to the North Sea?"

Darin scans the king's face, trying to understand his sudden shift in mood. "Yes."

Malik leans back and claps his hands. "Your aim is noble, Aalto. Go to the North Sea to stop this Sea Enchantress. You may complete the mission for me upon your return." He gestures again to the guards. "Show Mr. Aalto out. I am sure he is anxious to see his family."

18

LOCKLYN

I DON'T HEAR A SINGLE WORD OF Rihanna and Brosnan's conversation on the swim back to the palace, my mind is so focused on concocting excuses for our absence.

But I don't have to use any of them.

Michal is waiting in the side chamber as Rihanna and I appear. Her face is unusually grave. "Ginevra needs to talk to us," she says. "In her room."

As Michal pushes open the door to the apartment where I first woke up in Imber, I think I see Ginevra bent over Hugo's tank, talking to the mulciber. But, by the time we are all inside, she is sitting on the edge of her bed.

As soon as the door swings shut behind us, she speaks. "Someone has been relaying Nebula's secrets to Malik."

"How do you know?" Rihanna's voice sounds querulous. Michal says nothing, her serious eyes locked on her sister.

"The General came to see me." Ginevra's tone is clipped. "She has suspected it for some time, but yesterday her scouts finally found proof." She looks at me. "You know the wreck Darin found? The one on the Undula-Nebula border? The General's scouts found a bottle on board, and inside was a message detailing the location of the raid planned for next month."

Rihanna's mouth opens and closes like a guppy, and Michal's brows constrict.

"Is now the right moment for you to leave your kingdom?" I ask Ginevra.

"That's why I called you three here," she replies. "I'm torn. Nebula needs strong leadership now more than ever. But if that monster is released, even the strongest leadership will not prevent our kingdom from being turned into a desolate wasteland. And I am an asset which that mission desperately needs."

She's not wrong.

"I'll stay, Evrie." Michal's voice retains its usual calm despite the tension in the room. "Stopping Circe is vital. You should go. I'll stay and help Rihanna."

"Why should either of you stay?" For a moment, I am confused, thinking the voice is Ginevra's. Rihanna seems to have grown taller. "Having intercepted this message, we know to change our raid plans. And now that she knows where the drop-off location for messages is, the General will be able to set a trap to catch the traitor the next time he or she attempts to communicate with Undula."

Something close to respect flickers in Ginevra's eyes as she surveys her younger sister. "Malik is growing bold," she responds. "I am afraid he will view my prolonged absence as an invitation to strike against Nebula."

"But you can't stay." Rihanna's words are matter-of-fact. "Michal is right. You need to go with this crew to stop Circe. The warrior council will have greater respect for Michal when she returns successfully from a dangerous quest. Perhaps they will see that the loss of her eye has not changed her warrior's heart."

A lump comes to my throat at the expression on Michal's face. Young Brosnan's word has taken effect.

Ginevra is still looking at Rihanna, indecision etched on her features. "It sits wrong with me to leave you alone."

"I won't be alone," Rihanna declares, her shoulders and chest thrown back. "The judges will be able to assist me in making decisions. The General has held her position for over four decades. She will be able to guide me, just as she guided you."

"What do you think, Locklyn?" Ginevra's question surprises me, and I fumble inwardly for an answer.

"Malik didn't attack while you were gone before," I say at length. "Rihanna is right that the odds of the General catching the traitor soon are high. She will not be without support and resources. And we could use you." My eyes go to Michal and I smile. "Both of you."

"Let me try, Ginevra." Rihanna's voice sounds childlike again for an instant. "Having to lead made you who you are."

The queen's tail gleams a brighter white as she rises from the bed. She gently places both hands on her youngest sister's shoulders. "I don't want you to be me, Ri."

Rihanna's face splits into a mischievous smile. "I don't want to be you either." She grows serious again as she reaches up to cover her older sister's hands with her own. "But I do want to be the best version of myself."

There is a ping as Hugo throws the trinket he was working on against the side of the tank in one of his fits of temper. Then, to my surprise, Ginevra says, "The weight of a kingdom is not a light one. But I believe your shoulders can bear it." She lightly kisses Rihanna's cheek. "Now," she declares, "we ought to go and enjoy whatever supper the cooks have prepared. After tomorrow's first gong, it will be some time before we eat anything palatable again."

19

DARIN

I'M SUCH A FOOL.

His eyes skim the unfamiliar buildings, and he scrapes at the surface of his mind, trying to generate any spark of recognition. As the guards ushered him through the palace's jewel-studded doors, the smart part of his brain had urged him to ask for directions to the Aalto residence. But his lips remained closed. Something stubborn and defiant rose inside, choking the words that would have exposed, yet again, his complete helplessness.

Surely, he could find his family on his own. Wasn't it possible that swimming through the streets of the city in which he had grown up would jog his memories?

Now, after an hour of aimless swimming, panic is beginning to stir. Not only do none of the streets seem familiar, but he is beginning to realize he has no idea how to get back to the palace. The thought occurs to question some of the passersby. Perhaps one of them knows his brother? But, almost instantly, realization washes over him that he cannot remember his brother and sister-in-law's first names.

Why couldn't something else have happened to me? If I had lost a limb, I would be able to forge a new life for myself, building on the old one.

But how can I make a new life with no identity?

A swelling, frustrated anger makes him want to rail at the Wave Master whom Orwell told him is the director of life beneath the sea.

Why did you let this happen to me?

Do you take delight in my suffering? Does it amuse you to see me helpless?

Helplessness pushes you toward the Helper.

The words are crystal clear, originating from somewhere outside his broken mind. He stares unseeingly at the stream of Merpeople slipping past, his heart's dull rhythm quickening.

Help me, then. Whoever you are.

"Darin?"

His head quickly turns to the door in the wall next to him, which has opened. A middle-aged Mermaid with an amethyst-colored tail, eggplant hair pulled into a knot at the base of her neck, and starfish feet crinkling the edges of her bright eyes, gazes down at him.

"Darin! It is you!"

Two hands, scratchy with calluses, close around his limp fingers, dragging him upward. Then the Mermaid's arms are around him, squeezing with strength surprising in someone whose head is barely level with his chest. "You're alive. You're safe," she murmurs, and he feels the heat of tears sliding down her cheeks.

It's only when she finally pulls away, looking up into his face, that he is able to form words. "Yes, I am alive," he says, forcing a laugh that comes out more like a croak. "Whether I'm safe is a little more debatable."

The Mermaid's face furrows, the starfish feet around her eyes becoming more pronounced. She opens her mouth, but he suddenly can't bear to hear her ask the question.

"I lost all my memories," he says, awkwardly. "I'm sorry. I don't know who you are."

The color drains from her face.

"I'm sorry," he says again.

"Don't say that," she admonishes gently. "You have nothing to apologize for. Come inside."

As he ducks through the doorway behind her, a strange smell, sharp, but not unpleasant, assails his nose, and he glances around, eyes catching on the pot bubbling over the magma crack in the corner.

"What are you making?" he asks, unsure what else to say.

"A fresh batch of ignis," she says, then kindly explains, "it's a salve for treating burns. Squid ink and dugong milk are the key ingredients."

"Are you a physician?" Darin asks as she motions for him to take the stool next to the table.

She settles across from him. "Not exactly. I'm a midwife and herbalist. Aquaticus boasts several physicians, trained in Atlantis, who serve the wealthy, but I never attended school there. I apprenticed under the previous herbalist and eventually took over his practice serving the poor of the city."

"How–" He doesn't know how to phrase the question tactfully.

"How do I know you?" she completes it for him. "Do you remember or know who Locklyn is?"

"Yes," he says, a little surprised by the name. "Only because I know her currently. I don't remember her from before."

Something deepens in her eyes. "I'm Locklyn's aunt, Chantara."

"Locklyn's safe." The words come without conscious thought. "She's in Nebula, healing from an injury. But she is going to meet us here in three days."

"Thank the Wave Master," Chantara whispers.

"How long"–he clears his throat–"how long have Locklyn and I known each other?"

"Let's see," Chantara muses. "You and Beck started coming to visit me with Amaya around the time Locklyn was born." Her face clouds. "Wave Master knows, after what my brother and his wife did to Locklyn, Amaya didn't have much desire to spend time at home."

"What did Locklyn's parents do?" he asks.

"They left the poor little one in the reef to die when she was born with legs."

He is aghast. "How under the sea did she survive?"

"Sheer stubbornness, mostly," Chantara says with a short laugh. "You and Beck and Amaya helped. When she was five, Amaya gave her a dugong and Locklyn used it to start a herd. Since then, she's pretty much looked out for herself."

Something sharp jabs into the scales on Darin's hip. Looking down, he finds himself staring into the gummy smile of the smallest narwhal he has ever seen, its horn gleaming pristinely from its upper lip.

"Ecgbert!" Chantara says sternly, and the narwhal turns its broad face toward her, tail wiggling with delight. "I'm sorry, I've never been able to break him of the poking-to-get-attention habit."

"He's still a baby, isn't he?" Darin says, reaching his hand cautiously toward Ecgbert, who darts forward, butting his rubbery forehead against the proffered palm.

Chantara sighs. "No, no, he'll be thirteen next month. He's just miniature, and I have no idea why."

"Where did you get him?" Ecgbert closes his eyes in ecstasy under the forehead massage.

"Prince Conway and Princess Ginevra gave him to me."

Darin looks at her. "That's–uh–interesting. They don't get along too well as far as I've observed. They almost seemed to despise each other."

"Well, I haven't seen either of them for years," Chantara says. "But, contrary to what most of us believe, hatred is not love's antithesis. Indifference is. Hatred, on the other hand, is sometimes simply love that has been thwarted."

Darin smiles slightly. "I see where Locklyn gets her wisdom."

Chantara smiles back. She stands and goes over to move the bubbling pot of ignis away from the direct heat of the magma crack. "We should go," she says.

He attempts to force buoyancy into his tone. "To see my brother?"

From the sympathetic look she gives, it is obvious his forced heartiness was about as convincing as an ancient frogfish's camouflage. "What are his children's names again?" he asks quickly, before she can say anything.

"Beck and Amaya have three boys, Zale, Ren, and Fisk. They're eight, six, and four. Avonlea, their daughter, is about a month old. She's just starting to swim on her own." She pulls a seaweed rope from a hook next to the door and loops it around Ecgbert's horn. "We can talk on the way."

As he swims with Chantara and Ecgbert through narrow, winding streets, anxiety gnaws at his gut. Every meeting with a person who seems a stranger, but who looks at him with an expression full of recognition, has been an ordeal, but this will be different.

Far too soon, Chantara stops outside the battered driftwood door of a tiny sandstone house. She loops Ecgbert's lead around a hook protruding from the wall and raps on the door.

It creaks open slowly, as though whoever is on the other side is struggling to maneuver it. Looking down, he sees a small boy with dark blue hair, the same shade as Locklyn's, gazing up at them. "Mum, it's Auntie Chantara," the little one bellows, before his eyes find Darin. For an instant, confusion wrinkles his small face, replaced in the next second by mad delight. "Uncle Dar! You're back!" And he throws himself forward, wrapping his small arms around Darin's waist in a squid-like hug.

Unable to help himself, Darin tenses against the child's embrace. The boy looks up, and the confusion and hurt on his face cause Darin to stiffen even more, and the boy backs away. Two other little boys hurtle down the hallway with delighted cries of their own.

At Darin's expression, the merchildren slow to a stop. The shattered looks on their faces almost make him turn and swim away through the darkening streets.

"It's alright, boys. It's alright," Chantara has moved forward, her presence a shield between him and his nephews. "Uncle Darin isn't well." She shepherds the children ahead of her into the hall, but as he starts to follow, she turns, the forbidding expression on her face reminiscent of Locklyn. "Darin, you need to stay here."

The door clicks, and he slides down the sandstone wall. Ecgbert darts forward, nuzzling against him, but he shifts out of reach, anxious as to what is before him.

Minutes slip by and he stays there, ignoring Ecgbert's increasingly insistent whimpers for attention.

Finally, the door creaks open. "Darin?"

He looks up into the face of a wispy Merman with a dull, blue-green tail and eyes so pale they are almost translucent. The Merman closes the door and moves toward Darin.

"I'm Beck. Chantara told us," he adds and sits down beside Darin.

Beck.

My brother.

He waits for Beck to say more. To ask questions. To berate him for frightening his sons.

But Beck does none of these things. He simply sits in silence.

"I'm sorry. About the boys," Darin says.

"They idolize you."

"Maybe not after this."

"Nothing has changed," Beck says simply.

"Except the fact that I can't remember any of you," Darin says in frustration.

"Memory does not change reality," Beck says quietly. "If I were to forget Amaya, she would not cease to be my wife. You are still my brother. My children's uncle. As I said before, nothing has changed. Nothing material."

"But I've changed." His voice rises, and he steadies it. "I feel strange to myself. I struggle with anger constantly."

Beck turns his pale eyes on him. "When we were young, I was mocked by the other children for my smallness, my paleness. You would defend me, and I both loved and hated you for it, despising my own weakness. One night, I lashed out at you, telling you to let me fight my own battles. When I came later to apologize, I admitted I was ashamed of my anger. But you told me to take my anger and harness it. To let it drive me to become a person who would always protect others from the attacks of the ignorant and cruel. To use it as a fire to help me stand against those who hated the person the Wave Master created me to be." He pauses. "Don't let the amnesia take your life from you, Darin. Use the anger. Fight back."

We'll make new memories. Memories for both of us.

Darin drags in a gulp of salty water. He might not remember Beck, but he feels at home with him. "I haven't seen Avonlea yet. Or Amaya."

Beck pushes upward, opens the door, and motions to him. Darin follows his brother into a small living area, with stools grouped in a loose circle around a clay pot of magma. Chantara is perched on one of the stools with the smallest boy in her lap, telling him a story, while the other two are sprawled on the sandy floor, playing a complicated-looking game with a set of bright orange shells. Gathering his courage, Darin drifts to the sand next to them. "What are you playing?" he asks.

The older boy speaks without looking up. "Concentration. It's a game we invented."

"You brought us the shells, Uncle Dar," the younger one says timidly.

The hesitation in the child's voice pierces Darin's heart. "Will you teach me to play?"

"It's complicated," the older one says coolly.

The boy's lack of sympathy is oddly refreshing. "I think I can handle it," Darin says, looking into the merchild's eyes, pale and translucent like his father's.

The boy gives a reluctant smile, a dimple popping out in his cheek. "All right," he says, but just then, a shadow falls over the pieces.

"Darin? I think I'm the only one who hasn't gotten to say hello."

He looks up, and his heart gives an odd jump as he gazes into a pale, heart-shaped face that is slightly rounder than Locklyn's, but with the same shifting, blue-green eyes. Amaya's body bears signs of the four children around her, but she is still lovely, and he can see in her the way Locklyn will look one day.

"Amaya," he says, rising up from the floor. She reaches out, wrapping the arm that isn't holding a small Mermaid with spiky, light-blue hair around his waist and squeezing.

"I'm so glad you're back," she whispers.

The baby seems less sure, staring at him distrustfully with a pair of deep purple eyes. When he reaches tentatively toward her, she shrinks back against her mother, squinching her small face into a forbidding scowl.

"Avonlea," Amaya scolds, but when she tries to move her daughter closer, Avonlea begins to squeal in protest, thrashing her aquamarine tail. "I'm sorry," Amaya apologizes. "She just doesn't remember you."

A smile spreads across Darin's face. "Finally," he says. "Someone who remembers as little as I do. I think we're going to get along just fine."

20

LOCKLYN

"FINE." THE WORD IS A FRUSTRATED sigh, but there is softness in Ginevra's face as her eyes flicker to Michal hovering behind us, her one good eye studying the entrance to the reef with interest. "You're lucky we're early. You've got one hour."

My tail whips the end of her sentence away as I dart into the reef, flying through the twists and turns my body remembers effortlessly. As I pass the offshoot leading to my house, I pause for the barest fraction of a second before hurtling on. If I had time, I would stop to see Darya and my dugongs. But, as it is, I will barely get the chance to see my sister and brother-in-law. My nephews. Avonlea.

And I need to bring Darin back with me. Orwell revealed that their trip to Aquaticus had been exciting because Darin was kidnapped by a pair of rogue Schatzi while out for a swim–then he was taken to see Malik. "We nearly went crazy searching the area for him when he didn't return," Orwell had said. "But when we finally reached Aquaticus, we found him at his brother's. That's where he is now."

Now, the open gates to the city fly past me. Dark memories bubble up in my mind.

A pale, twisted face marred by an ugly, puckered scar.

Pain lancing through my arm with every movement.

The wide, pitiless eyes of tiger sharks appearing with deadly suddenness.

Clouds of scarlet filling the water with the metallic scent of blood.

I swim faster, the strength of my new tail propelling me through the streets at breakneck speed. As I enter the square, the crowds of shoppers examining the booths arranged along the edges slow my pace. The owner of the cheese stand, who used to buy my dugong milk, catches sight of me and does a double take, his eyes ricocheting up and down between my face and my tail.

I try to speed up, feeling no desire to explain the absence of my legs. In my haste, I bump into someone swimming the other direction. "I'm sorry," I start, but the words trail away into bubbles as the full impact of what I am seeing hits me.

It is impossible to tell whether the Merperson I collided with is male or female. A billowing black cloak shrouds them from head to tail with only a pale, dead-looking fin protruding from the bottom. A hand whose skin is red and bubbly with scars reaches up and fumbles with the hood of its cloak, which slipped when we collided. The neckline of the garment shifts, revealing a flash of silver. A locket.

In the next instant, the cloaked figure pushes past me and darts away through the crowd. I spin, staring after it. Foreboding spreads over me.

What was that? Is it possible Llyra's locket was around its neck?

Another passerby bumps my shoulder and snarls, breaking my trance. I attempt to follow the hooded figure as it heads toward an alley. But by the time I reach it, there is no one there. After searching the nearby streets without success, I turn back in the direction of Amaya's house. The stranger has vanished. The hour Ginevra allotted me must be nearly half gone. My heart quickens. If I don't go to Amaya and Beck's now, I won't get to see them at all.

The sight of their reddish house sends warmth pulsing through me. Darting up to the front door, I open it to see Darin right inside.

He turns and his eyes light up. "Hey," he smiles.

My heart somersaults inside my chest.

"Would it be out of line to hug my best friend?" he asks.

Not wanting to seem overeager, I fight the smile tugging at my lips and raise my eyebrows. "I suppose."

"Do you know that is exactly the expression Avonlea has every time she looks at me?" he says.

"Not your biggest fan, huh?" I say, trying desperately to ignore the feeling of his arms now around me.

"I think she hasn't decided yet. Come on," he says. "They'll all go crazy when they see you." Darin seems almost his old self as he speaks.

After a month of open sea and enchanted wrecks and brushes with death, the cramped interior of Beck and Amaya's house feels dreamlike, unreal. I struggle to shake a strange sense of homesickness.

"Look who decided to show up," Darin announces and quickly darts to the side as my sister hurtles toward me, tears in her eyes.

"Locklyn," she whispers as we embrace each other. A lump comes to my throat as I realize this moment is a greeting and farewell mixed into one. "Darin says you two are leaving again."

"In less than an hour," I say.

She moves back. "Locklyn." Her eyes darken to a stormy gray-green.

"What?" I say, my defenses rising.

She sighs. "Why do you have to be involved, Locklyn?"

I turn to Darin, who gives me a slight shrug, shaking his head. "Did Darin tell you?" I say. "About the locket? The monster? About Circe, who is the reason he can't remember anything?" Amaya gives me a pointed look, as though I had just said something highly insensitive. "What? There's no point swimming in circles around it, Amaya. Darin can't remember his entire life because of Circe. And we have to find her and change that."

Amaya purses her lips. "I don't see why he has to go either." Flabbergasted, I open my mouth, but she raises a hand. "Hear me out. You don't know that you'll be able to find Circe, and even if you do, you don't know you'll convince her to give Darin's memories back. It's far more likely that she'll kill both of you. If you stay here, you'll both be safe. And there might be other ways. Maybe his memories will return in time. Or maybe Chantara knows of an herb."

I draw in a lungful of water, counting to thirty as I exhale it. "Amaya," I say steadily, "even if it is possible for Darin to regain his memories without finding Circe—which I highly doubt—that's not the only reason we have to go north. If Circe is able to use Llyra's locket to release and control the monster trapped in Loch Ness, she will be able to devastate the entire North Sea."

"The North Sea is a long way from here."

I stare at her, stunned. "Do you hear yourself? There are children there, Amaya. Mermen, Mermaids, families, entire communities that will die horrific, fiery deaths. Mind you, I'm not convinced Circe will be content with wiping out the North Sea. The Mediterranean might be next. But even if it's only the North Sea she is planning to target, that doesn't make it any less important to stop her."

"But it doesn't have to be you who stops her, Locklyn!" Her voice is full of tears. "Do you know what this past month has been like? Not knowing where you two were, not knowing if you were dead, not able to do a thing except wait and wait and wait. And now you're back, and even if Darin's memory is gone, at least you're both alive." Her voice breaks. "Let someone else save the world."

The front door bangs, and I turn to the chatter of children's voices. Zale comes pelting down the short hallway, swinging a posidonia-fiber shopping bag over his head like a morning star. At the sight of me, he lets out a yell.

"Aunt Wyn! You're back!" Tossing his bag heedlessly onto the floor next to the magma pit, he wraps his arms around me in a tight hug. "Uncle Dar says you met the Sea Enchantress! What was she like?"

Before I can answer, Ren and Fisk dart into the room followed by a harassed-looking Beck, struggling with Avonlea and a mountain of shopping bags. My younger nephews let out excited whoops and fling themselves onto me as well, Ren hugging my side and Fisk clinging to my back like a baby dolphin.

"Tell us about the giant crab! Uncle Darin can't remember exactly how you killed it!"

Apparently they listened freely to all the grown-up talk that must have taken place. I can't help but smile. Fisk's arms are so tight across my windpipe that I gargle. Darin gently pries my youngest nephew off me, as Amaya wipes her tears and goes to help Beck with Avonlea. My eyes find the small hourglass perched on the stone ledge that serves as a counter, which is set to mirror the giant hourglass outside the city gates. I gasp.

"We have to go, Darin. Ginevra said to meet them outside the reef and it's almost time."

My nephews let out howls of protest.

"You just got here!"

"You can't leave again!"

"Don't go!"

"Listen." The word is quiet, but the tone of Darin's voice quells the rising clamor, and all three of the little boys' faces turn toward him. "There is only one thing your aunt and I want more than to stay with you right now," he tells them. "And that is a safe ocean for you boys and your sister. We don't know that we will be able to stop the Sea Enchantress. But as long as there is a chance, we have to try." His eyes flicker over Fisk's head to meet Amaya's tearful gaze.

I reach down, wrapping my arms around Zale and Ren, squeezing them tightly. "I'll bring you both something back from Atlantis," I promise. "You too, Fisky. And I'll miss you every second I'm away."

As the boys turn to latch onto Darin, I move toward my sister. The lump in my throat swells at the sight of the tiny girl now in her arms. Avonlea is twice the size she was when I saw her last. I swallow painfully as I gaze at her aquamarine tail.

It's for the best.

"I'm your auntie, sweetheart," I whisper, reaching out to her. To my surprise and delight, she begins to squirm in my sister's arms, and when Amaya releases her, she swims toward me, immediately dropping in the water and charting a wobbling, unsteady course. I stretch out even further, catching her small body and drawing her close. The slender lines of her face remind me of her mother, but her spiky, pale blue hair and violet eyes are all her own. "Hi, little Avonlea," I say, smiling down at her with moistened eyes. "You've gotten big."

Darin huffs behind me. "I see how it is. I've been here three days and I still have to bribe her with pieces of dugong cheese to get her to look at me."

I give him a saucy grin. "She's got good taste."

"She's probably just in a good mood. Here, give her to me." When he tries to take her, Avonlea wails, clinging to me. "Come on, you little wunderpus." I detach Avonlea's clinging fingers and watch Darin toss her toward the ceiling until her wails turn into reluctant giggles. For a mad instant, the scene morphs in my mind, and I see him tossing another baby, a baby with golden hair and changing eyes. But I'm still there, beside him, my laughter mingling with that of the phantom child.

"So long, small one," Darin's murmur draws me back to the present as he nuzzles his nose gently against Avonlea's soft cheek before holding her out to her mother. Beck silently grasps his brother's hand as I wrap an arm around my sister, unable to speak as she turns her face away, her shoulders shaking with the strength of her grief.

I murmur to her, then take a deep breath.

"Let's go," Darin says. I hug Beck and Amaya once more, and then we exit through the driftwood front door. For a few moments, we swim in silence, but as we enter the square, which has emptied since I last passed through, memory stirs.

"I saw the strangest thing on the way here," I tell him, scanning the crowds for any sign of the cloaked stranger.

"It didn't happen to be Igor, did it?"

I turn to look at him. "That's actually an idea," I say slowly, conjuring the image of the mysterious figure. "But no . . . I'm almost sure I saw a fin at the bottom of the cloak."

"Cloak?"

"I bumped into someone in a long black cloak on my way through the square when I was going to Amaya's," I say. "Undulae don't wear cloaks. They're so impractical for swimming."

"Obviously whoever was under the cloak wanted to hide," Darin says. "Did you notice anything else?"

I close my eyes for an instant, then open them quickly. "The fin I saw sticking out of the cloak looked . . . like it had died or something. It was weirdly pale and flakey-looking. I did catch a glimpse of hands, which were bright red, with a bunch of bumps, like scar tissue. Or a disease."

We're leaving the city now, swimming through the tortuous twists and turns of the reef.

"Here's an idea," Darin says after a moment. "Could the fin you saw have been fake? Paired with the cloak to hide legs?"

"But why would Igor be here?" I ask, veering around a coral outcropping and brushing close to Darin. "It's in his best interest to reach Atlantis before we do."

"Maybe he's waiting to catch the next blue whale out of here. There's no way he'll beat us to Atlantis swimming."

"But I haven't told you the oddest part yet," I say. "I think the thing in the cloak was wearing a silver locket."

He swivels his head to me. "Are you sure?"

"I definitely saw something silver around its neck."

We've reached the end of the reef, and the shape of the submarine is hovering a bowshot to our left, its propellers already spinning. I turn to Darin, wanting to get his opinion before unnecessarily frightening the others.

"What do you think?"

He reaches up to run a hand through his blond hair, his face troubled. "I think there is no good reason for Circe to be in Aquaticus."

"We don't know it was her," I reply in a small voice.

"No," he agrees. "But we don't know that it wasn't, either."

"Aalto! Adair!" Ginevra is at the door of the submarine, arms crossed, pique written all over her face. "Last time I checked, this was a time-sensitive mission. You two will have plenty of time to talk on the ten-day trip to Atlantis."

I glance at Darin and then look quickly away again, choking down an unholy desire to laugh. "We're coming."

As I follow Darin into the submarine, movement catches my eye and I pause, certain for a moment that I had seen a shadow dart along the bottom of the submarine. I am about to head down to check when Ginevra barks, "Locklyn!"

Probably just a manta ray.

Besides, Ginevra is right. We don't have time to waste.

21

DARIN

"WANT A BREAK?" HE ASKS CONWAY. The prince looks away from the submarine's controls, then glances over to where Locklyn is playing High Tide with Ginevra.

"I wouldn't be welcome over there, and everyone else is sleeping or talking about dolphin husbandry." Conway rolls his eyes toward Kai, who is sitting next to Michal, talking animatedly. "So I might as well keep steering. Thanks, though."

After Conway's apology when he and Orwell found Darin in Aquaticus, and after seeing the prince's father, he was less inclined to be put off by the other's prickly demeanor. A tentative cordiality exists between them now.

Darin glances at the High Tide players, then lowers his voice and says, "Don't tell me if you don't want to, but what is the deal between you and Ginevra?"

"The deal is that she wants a marriage alliance between Undula and Nebula," Conway says shortly.

"Because it would be advantageous for Nebula?"

Conway groans, then glances back quickly to make sure everyone else is still occupied. "You're not the only one who can hook a Mermaid's heart unintentionally, Aalto."

Darin just looks at him, nonplussed. "I don't understand."

"She's in love with me, you fringehead."

"And you don't care about her."

"I do care about her." Conway gives the steering pole an impatient twiddle. "We've been friends since we were kids."

Darin glances over his shoulder again at Locklyn and Ginevra. Locklyn says something that makes Ginevra laugh, throwing back her magnificent silver mane of hair.

"I'm still not sure I understand," he says, returning his gaze to the black water rushing past the front viewing port. "You've known her for years. You care about her. She's clearly taken enough by you to want to disembowel you for rejecting her." Conway snorts and Darin grins. "Is she not your type or something?"

Conway glances back again also, and his gaze flickers between Locklyn and Ginevra, expression unreadable. When he returns his attention to the viewing port, he is silent for a long time. Finally, he says, "What I feel for Ginny isn't the real deal, Aalto. I know, because I have felt it. But for someone else."

His black eyes meet Darin's squarely, and now that the subject has been broached, Darin makes it plain. "Locklyn."

Conway's lips tighten. "You know I regret the things I said before, Aalto. But"–he hesitates and then goes on–"I'm not going to let you stand in the way of me pursuing a future with her. And you shouldn't let me stand in yours. It's Locklyn's choice."

The prince's bluntness is almost a relief. "For what it's worth," Darin remarks, "the things you said about me being a fool for not pursuing her during the four years I had the chance were true. So if she picks you, I won't blame her. Or you. Because I'll know who messed up his own chances."

Conway quirks a grin. "Well, for what it's worth, your arrogance and bullheadedness have come a long way, Aalto."

They hover in companionable silence that is shattered as the submarine suddenly shudders, sending Darin sloshing backward. A High Tide piece strikes his left ear, and he turns to check for more flying pieces. Then Ginevra screams, pointing past him, and he whips back around to see the entire viewing port obscured by two gargantuan, sucker-studded tentacles.

"Wave Master, save us," Conway mutters, yanking at the steering rod, which appears to have become immobile.

A single word slips past Kai's lips, "Kraken."

Locklyn tries to shake Orwell awake, but as he stirs, there is a splintering sound and a web of cracks appears along the viewing port. A clang reverberates through the ship's interior, and Kai drags Michal away from the wall just as a colossal, beak-shaped dent appears in the submarine's door.

"We have to get out!" Darin shouts, darting to seize Ginevra's trident, lying abandoned in a corner. "Or we'll be crushed!" But as he raises the shaft of the trident to smash the nearest porthole, a sound fills the submarine's cabin, immobilizing his arms.

The most beautiful voice he has ever heard in his life is singing in a language he doesn't recognize. But the music is a push, a send-off, and he finds himself wanting to fling open the door of the submarine and swim away into the open ocean, with no destination in mind.

"Don't." The whisper is Locklyn's, and he turns to see her hovering before the submarine's door with her arms spread wide, blocking Kai and Conway, who both seem to be feeling the same pull tugging at him. "It's not for us. See?" She points toward the viewing port, and everyone watches, dumbstruck, as the tentacles peel slowly away, vanishing with only a sticky residue left in their wake.

He finds Locklyn's eyes, raising his eyebrows in question as the music continues, finally fading away into nothing. Her face is white. "I've heard that voice before," she says shakily. "That's Llyra's voice. Circe's here."

Dread wraps around his insides, squeezing like the Kraken's tentacles. "Why would Circe be here?" Ginevra's voice is tinged with fear.

"Why isn't she already halfway to the North Sea?" Orwell's rumble contrasts sharply with the timbre of the Nebulae queen.

"And why would she save us?" Darin adds, his eyes still on Locklyn's face. Coming after her encounter with the hooded stranger in Aquaticus, this second incident feels almost sinister.

"What are we waiting for?" Conway's voice is sharp. "The whole point of this trip is to stop her, isn't it?"

"Don't open that door!" Arledge's normally soft voice is edged with panic. "What if the Kraken comes back? We should go!"

Conway makes a derisive, scoffing sound as he reaches for the door handle, but Locklyn's fingers close around his wrist.

"Arledge has a point," she says. "We're not prepared to face Circe. Or the Kraken, which she can clearly control. We need to move quickly. Our best chance of stopping her is to get reinforcements in Atlantis."

She looks to Orwell for confirmation, and the giant Merman nods. "My heart is with the prince. But most of my failures throughout the years have been a result of zeal without discretion."

Conway glares at them all, then gives in. "Atlantis it is," he says, heading back toward the steering rod. It sticks as he jiggles it, then finally scrapes forward enough to send the submarine moving slowly through the water. Conway's eyes dart to the crushed-in door and then back to the viewing port, now webbed with cracks, making it difficult to see through. "Let's hope this battered old tub can make it another three days."

22

LOCKLYN

"DID I KNOW THAT SONG?"

My quiet crooning immediately stops as I turn to glance at Darin. We are so close together that I can see the faint smattering of golden-brown freckles on his nose, and my chest aches as I remember how embarrassed I was at fourteen when Amaya let slip to Darin that I had said I found freckles attractive.

"Yes," I say, keeping my voice as casual as possible while my fingers twist together in my lap.

"Did I like it?" he asks.

"You liked all my songs," I say, before I can stop myself.

"Maybe I envied my best friend for being Vocalese."

I shake my head. "The ability to sing came with the legs that got me abandoned in the reef. I don't think anyone envied me, least of all you."

"Why least of all?" he asks anxiously, and I can feel his eyes on my face, so intent they are almost a physical touch.

"You were the one people envied. You had it all, Dar. The money, the fame, the looks–"

"My looks?" he interrupts, and the mischief in his tone causes my cheeks to heat instantly.

I force myself to glance up at him dispassionately. "In a beauty contest between you and blobfish, I suppose I'd pick you."

His lips curve up, and I turn quickly away, so that he won't see that he only has to smile at me to reduce my insides to blubber. "I get it. Without blue hair and changing eyes, I wouldn't pick me first in a beauty contest either."

The warmth inside me is expanding. "I didn't know you had a thing for blue-haired Mermaids."

"Well, you know now," he says, and a flicker of joy shoots through me.

Is it possible that losing his memories broke down whatever wall separated our friendship from anything more?

Before either of us can say another word, a shout echoes through the cabin. "Look!" Michal's face is pressed against one of the portholes. Questions rebound through the cramped space.

"What do you see?"

"Is it another Kraken?"

"What's wrong?"

"Stop the submarine!" Michal cries out, moving away from the porthole.

"Michal, what is it?" Ginevra places a hand on her sister's shoulder.

"Evrie, it's Hugo!"

"What?" The pitch of Ginevra's voice rises a notch. "Stop the submarine."

Conway glances away from the controls, his brow furrowed. "Who is Hugo?"

"Did you not hear me, Struan? Stop the submarine."

"Excuse me, *Your Highness*, but I thought we were in something of a hurry."

Ginevra pulls herself to her full height, her eyes flashing with fury, but Orwell moves between her and Conway. "Ginevra would not ask you to stop the submarine flippantly, Conway. And I am sure she will be happy to explain her reasons as soon as we have retrieved this Hugo."

Conway pulls the silver lever beside him, and the submarine has barely shuddered to a halt when Ginevra seizes the door handle and heaves. It opens slightly before sticking, the bent metal from the Kraken's attack hindering smooth motion. Before anyone can help her, Ginevra throws her weight against the handle again, and the door scrapes open another few inches. A familiar little man with an eel's tail darts inside, a glass tube clutched in his hands.

Michal holds out her palms, and he swims immediately into them, curling himself into a semicircle and emitting a throaty rumbling sound. She raises her hands to her cheek, gently rubbing her nose against his small head. "How did you find us, little one?"

"Michal, the message." Ginevra's voice is taut. Michal reaches down and wriggles the glass bottle free of Hugo's grip. She drifts it to her sister before returning her attention to the mulciber.

"How did you find us, Hugo?"

The mulciber squirms and Michal releases him. To my shock, he swims over to me and latches onto my right hand.

"What . . . ?"

Michal stares at the band of silver encircling my pinkie finger and her eyes widen in understanding.

"Undula has attacked Nebula."

At Ginevra's words, Conway explodes. "What?"

But Ginevra does not look at him. She only stares helplessly at Michal, clearly on the verge of tears.

"It's from Rihanna," she says, the scrap of parchment fluttering in her shaking fingers as she holds it up. "She writes that Malik attacked as soon as news reached him that she had been made temporary regent." She takes a deep breath. "Imber is under siege. Malik hired mercenaries from the Red Sea."

"He drained Aquaticus's treasuries again?" Conway looks wild.

Ginevra's eyes are fixed on the message in her hand. "She says that the General found someone named Brosnan putting a bottle with another treasonous message onto the wreck. He's been arrested." I hold back a gasp. Ginevra lifts her eyes. "One thing to thank the Wave Master for, I suppose."

"Brosnan?" Michal asks, horrified.

"You know him?"

"Rihanna's in love with him, Evrie."

"Oh. The scullery boy." Ginevra skims the remainder of the missive. "She claims he's innocent–that he was set up. She says she doesn't know what to do." She lowers the note. "This is my fault," she says almost inaudibly.

Michal swims to her older sister and puts an arm around her, her voice as calm and soothing as always. "We're only a day's journey from Atlantis. Should we leave the others there and go back?"

"We couldn't get into the city." Ginevra's voice is flat. "Unless . . ." Her head rises from Michal's shoulder. I follow her burning gaze across the cabin to where Conway hovers next to the controls. "Unless we had a hostage."

Horrified exclamations fill the submarine.

Ginevra's furious voice pierces through the tumult. "His father is attacking my kingdom! My younger sister's life is in jeopardy because of his family! His nation!"

"Ginevra." Conway moves away from the submarine controls, through the group that has moved between him and Ginevra, and stops, face-to-face with the Nebulae queen. "What my father is doing is wrong," says the crown prince of Undula. "So if you think it will stop the war, I place myself in your custody. Willingly."

They stare into each other's eyes for a long moment before Ginevra bursts into tears. Conway moves forward, drawing her out of Michal's arms and into his own, holding her as steaming, green tears pour down her face.

"I didn't mean it." The words are blurred through her crying.

"I did, though."

"She's my baby sister . . ."

"I know," he says quietly. "I know."

A pang of panic shoots through me. Undula's standing army is not large. Even with the help of mercenaries, they are almost certainly drafting able-bodied males for a campaign as extensive as this. Has Beck been forced to leave his family? Is Amaya alone, her grief over my participation in a dangerous mission compounded by uncertainty as to whether she will ever see her husband again?

My eyes find Darin's and he raises an eyebrow, clearly questioning my distress. He would have no memory of Undula's drafting laws. No idea of the danger his brother is in.

As Ginevra's sobs subside, she pushes out of Conway's embrace and draws herself up. "Can the submarine make it back to Imber with the damages sustained from the Kraken attack?" she asks, her voice cold and formal once more.

Conway's tone lacks its usual cynicism as he says, "I don't think so. Even if it could limp all the way back–which is unlikely–you would be looking at a much longer trip. The Kraken ripped one of the fins off the propeller, and we've been going at about half speed ever since."

Ginevra's lips tighten. "Can you teach me to drive the submarine before we reach Atlantis?" When Conway looks confused, she says impatiently, "I can find someone to repair it there. Then Michal and I can go back to Imber while you all continue north."

I interrupt. "But, Ginevra, if the Council won't help us, we'll need this submarine to take us north."

I expect her to bite my head off, but Ginevra's voice is surprisingly calm. "Then I'll beg, borrow, or steal another if necessary. My sister needs me."

"I can teach you to drive it," Conway breaks his silence.

"What are we waiting for?" She streams toward the front of the submarine. "We all need to get to Atlantis. Let's go."

23

LOCKLYN

I HAVE DREAMED OF THIS PLACE.

But it is not often that a place is the stuff of dreams.

The walls of Atlantis rise above us, pushing toward The Surface from which they came, soaring upward like the peaks of the Rayan Mountains, elevated on the mounded base that was once an island floating on the waves of the Atlantic.

The ancient appearance of the walls somehow adds to the grandeur of the fabled city–a visible reminder of its age and centuries of uncontested power. No dome rests on top of the walls, and I am about to remark on this when I catch sight of something that shrivels the words in my throat. A school of rainbow fish swimming toward the walls suddenly begins to fall like rain, their tiny bodies sparking with electrical energy from an invisible barrier. A shock thrills through me as though I too am touching the electrical obstacle, and my eyes travel downward to the main gate of the city. A tunnel, made of what appears to be droplets of oil suspended in the water, extends from the gate to the electric field, where I can barely make out a checkpoint. A long line of submarines, blue whales, and Merfolk travelers extends away from the city, winding across the sandy plain surrounding Atlantis.

"We must leave the submarine," Orwell says, and I turn from

the porthole. "It has been more than a hundred years since I was last in Atlantis, but at that time, every Atlantean-made submarine had a serial number, which was tied to the rightful owner in a massive database. Unless they have changed their system, the craft will be linked to Igor, and even if he has not yet reported the craft stolen, none of us will be able to pass ourselves off as a Crura." He gives me a slight smile, which I return.

Who would have thought? A moment when legs would have been handy.

"Even if we leave the submarine, if Igor has already arrived, we will definitely have problems," I say. "He will have given our descriptions to the guards at the checkpoint."

"Is there any other way in?" Michal asks.

I know the answer without Orwell's shaking head.

Conway gives a half-hearted laugh. "We could coat ourselves in oil and sneak over the walls."

"The tops of the walls are equipped with machines that sense movement and shoot projectiles at anything that comes within their range," Orwell informs us. "Not to speak of the guards."

"Then we should go now." The tone of Darin's voice is one I remember–the tone that made Schatzi crews follow him without question. "The longer we wait, the greater the odds are that Igor will return and initiate security measures against us."

"Should we split up?" Ginevra asks. "We're not exactly an inconspicuous group."

Darin looks at Orwell, who scratches his beard before saying, "I think the risks of splitting up outweigh the possible benefits. If certain members of our party are captured, the others will face a decision whether to try to find and free them or continue alone, whereas if we are all taken into custody together, we will at least know where everyone is and be able to work together to free ourselves."

"If we make it into the city," Conway questions, "what then?"

"Then I secure an audience with the Council. Even after a

hundred and fifty years, I believe my name will still command enough respect to accomplish that much."

"And if the Council refuses to listen?" Arledge wants to know.

"Then we use what remains of our treasure to purchase another submarine and replenish our supplies, and we head north alone," Orwell says. He surveys the group, eyes grave. "I will not lie, this is by far the most likely outcome. For centuries, the Council of the Guardians has maintained a tenuous sense of peace and security by ignoring unpleasant situations. They will not want to hear what we have to say."

There is a strained silence before Ginevra says brusquely. "Why wait? Grab what you can carry. Everything else must be left behind."

I drift back against the wall as the others break into motion around me, gathering scattered belongings. I rotate the ring on my pinkie finger, staring down at my own neatly packed bag.

I can't believe I finally made it to Atlantis.

"Pack last night?"

Michal, her slate-colored hair pulled into a low bun at the base of her neck, swims to my side. Unwillingly, my eyes focus on the raised scars disfiguring her left cheek beneath her eye patch. I've never seen their extent before, since her hair is usually down, and my stomach clenches as my mind transforms the vermilion bumps and craters into a gaping hole surrounded by bleeding ribbons of charred flesh. The kind of wound that could cause scarring like that must have been dire.

I catch Michal's good eye and my stomach drops at the knowing look glimmering there. "I'm sorry," I say quickly, heat rising up my cheeks. "It's just, I–I can't imagine how much pain you must have been in . . . after the explosion . . ."

"The Wave Master was kind." A rueful smile accompanies Michal's voice. "The physical discomfort became bearable soon after I returned to consciousness." She pauses. "The real pain came later, anyway."

"The people?"

Michal's face twists. "I hadn't realized how many of my friendships depended on my ability to shoot a bow."

On an impulse, I reach for her hand. I know Ginevra wouldn't tolerate such a gesture. But I have a feeling Michal won't mind. "At least you know who your real friends are now," I say. "One of the benefits I never fully appreciated about being born with legs was that I always knew exactly who my true friends were. People didn't feel the need to pretend. And in some ways, that made everything a lot simpler."

Michal's fingers tighten around mine. "And the people who leave aren't worth missing?" she says, the corner of her mouth tipping up.

In my mind's eye, I see a Merman with my changing eyes, navy blue hair pulled into a ponytail like Darin's. The Merman has an arm wrapped around a small Mermaid with an amethyst-colored tail. My mental picture of the parents I have never seen. Will never see. "Probably not," I say, swallowing around the lump suddenly clogging my throat, "but that doesn't mean you won't miss them just the same."

"Michal! Locklyn!" Our names fly from Ginevra's tongue with the sharpness and speed of arrows. "Are you two ready?"

"Only for about the last hour," Michal says good-naturedly, pushing off the wall and scooping up her pack.

I laugh, reaching down for my own bag. "Don't look at me. I didn't say anything." As I come back up, my eyes catch Conway watching our exchange. His smile widens as our eyes meet, and he jerks his chin, a clear invitation to come over.

"I barely recognize your face," he greets me as I join him at the back of the group slowly exiting the submarine. "Because I haven't seen it in so long," he continues seriously at my bewildered look.

"Conway, we've been cooped up in the same submarine for the last ten days."

"During which I've been steering, and you've been spending every spare minute with Ginevra. Avoidance tactics?" His tone is light and teasing, but I see a serious question in his eyes.

I force myself not to look away, meeting his gaze squarely. “Mostly it’s because I like Ginevra,” I say. “But I wasn’t entirely sorry that you were driving, either.”

“And why is that?” His tone is still light, but I can hear the tension underneath. It takes everything I have to continue looking into his face and say the words I know must be said, rather than one of the million snarky responses flitting through my mind. Responses that would return us to the familiar and comfortable place of banter.

“Because I’m too vulnerable.” The words come quickly, more raw than I intend. Conway’s fingers, long and slender, close around my wrist, pulling me to a stop. I watch as the distance widens between us and the rest of the group. “Conway . . .”

“They don’t need to hear this,” he says quietly, fingers still holding my wrist, but more loosely now.

I look up into his black eyes, pain swelling inside that makes me want him to wrap his arms around me, pull me close like he did when we first found Darin. “He doesn’t know me,” the words come out jagged and jumbled, tumbling over each other. “I’ve lost him. And I . . .” The heat of his fingers seems to be creeping up my arm as I stare at him, willing him to understand. “I’m scared of . . . of falling into your arms, not because I truly want to, but because I miss him.”

I expect him to pull away from me, but instead he moves in, his fingers around my wrist drawing me closer until our faces are inches apart. “You know,” he whispers, the bubbles of his words brushing my cheeks, “if you ever fall into my arms, I don’t think I’ll be questioning why.”

I swallow hard, staring into his handsome face. His dark hair has grown longer over the weeks of traveling, and my fingers itch to brush the flopping strands aside. I imagine myself reaching up to cup his slender face in my hands before our lips meet. But then the imaginary me pulls back, because that kiss would be a wish to forget something, not a wish to remember this moment and every other like it.

And I know–finally–that I will never be able to care for Conway that way. Because behind every moment, every touch, would be a wish for someone else. Until the day I die.

I move back, withdrawing my wrist from his grip. "I'm not over him," I say. "And I don't think I ever will be." His lips part, and I see that there is still hope in his eyes, fueled by the moment of closeness. "Don't wait for me, Conway." I turn away from him, starting to follow the rest of the group. Over my shoulder, I say, "I know this other girl. And, Wave Master knows why, she's crazy about you. Think about it."

A flick of my tail sends me shooting away from him, toward the walls of Atlantis.

24

DARIN

AFTER HOURS OF WAITING, SMALL TALK between members of the group dies out and tension grows as the checkpoint to Atlantis draws nearer.

"Is there anything we should know to say?"

"Nothing," Orwell answers Locklyn. "I will explain to the sentries that I am Lief Orwell, sea-renowned Schatzi and explorer, and my purpose in entering the city is to address the Council of Guardians on an urgent and confidential matter."

"This might sound odd"–Locklyn's voice is hesitant–"but why would they believe you?"

Orwell's laugh booms. "The answer is that they will believe me because I have identification."

"Identification?"

Orwell removes the emerald-encrusted buckle of his belt and hands it to Locklyn.

"Leviathan Tamer," she reads slowly. Her eyes flicker up to Orwell's face. "The Council must have given it to you after . . ."

"They gave it to me as an honor." His words are precise, firm. "And I have worn it every day for one hundred and fifty years so that I would never forget my shame."

Darin's eyes go back to the area. No amount of belt buckles could help him remember his past.

As he idly watches, the submarine two groups ahead reaches the checkpoint. He becomes more attentive as a pair of guards–Mermen with vivid green tails who clutch unfamiliar, L-shaped weapons–beckons the submarine's passengers to exit the vessel. As one of the guards enters the submarine, presumably to conduct a search, the other swims between the passengers, examining and questioning, while attaching a thin, metal bracelet to the wrist of each one.

The submarine's passengers reboard, and the ship slides into the iridescent tunnel and whirs away. Darin prepares to move forward, but a couple directly in front of them, a Merman and Mermaid riding harbor seals, has come to a standstill. The seals have sunk to the sandy ocean floor and appear to be trying to take a nap, ignoring all attempts to chivvy them onward to the checkpoint. He can see the guards' irritation growing as the couple tugs the harbor seals' leads, alternately threatening and cajoling.

Restlessness spreads up the line as people lean forward, attempting to see what the holdup is. Several young Mermen from a group further ahead begin to heckle the poor couple.

"Outsmarted by a pair of harbor seals–your noggins must be full of fish guts!"

The Mermaid's obvious distress as she redoubles her efforts to induce her harbor seal to move causes something inside Darin to snap.

"Hey!" He whirls to face the youngsters behind them. Suddenly he remembers Beck's advice about channeling anger for good. "Since your brains are clearly *not* made of fish guts," he says, "show us how it's done." He gestures invitingly toward the harbor seals. "We all have places to be. I'm sure these fine people would be grateful for your help."

The teens fidget nervously, glancing at each other and avoiding making eye contact with him.

"We didn't mean anything . . ." one mumbles.

"We were just having a laugh," another protests.

"They don't need our help," the ringleader says and points behind him. "Your pretty little friend seems to have it all under control."

Darin hears it before he can turn–the soft notes of a merry melody. And even though he can't remember ever hearing it before, he feels the tug of the music.

"Come," it says. "You still have energy. Imagine what's in front of you if you only start to swim. Come."

He watches as the harbor seals rise from the sand, lumbering upward in the water. Locklyn continues to sing under her breath as she moves in the direction of the checkpoint, only stopping and gliding back to the group when the harbor seals are nearly to the mouth of the tunnel, inclining her head at the effusive gratitude called after her by the Mermaid.

Darin's heart stills. The guard with the bracelets has his eyes fixed on Locklyn's back; the expression on his face is as if a crucial puzzle piece has just been discovered. This guard was obviously told to watch out for a group with a little, blue-haired Mermaid who happened to be a Vocalese.

The harbor seals are moving forward into the oil tunnel.

Their group is next.

He sends up a prayer to the Wave Master.

I don't remember You. But maybe, like Beck said, that doesn't change who You are.

Help us.

25

LOCKLYN

I HADN'T PAUSED TO CONSIDER BEFORE helping the couple with the harbor seals. The youths' insults triggered memories of similar scenes where the cutting words had been aimed at me.

Then I notice the eyes of one of the checkpoint guards, and his expression creates a jolt of fear. I suppress an urge to hide behind Darin, drifting to the middle of our group instead of hovering conspicuously in front. But there would be nothing inconspicuous about diving behind Darin.

So I will my eyes to be a steely, pale blue, cool and unafraid, staring down the guard, waiting for him to speak first.

"Na-ame?" the guard asks, his drawl stretching the word into two syllables.

I swallow, mind racing.

Should I give him my real name? Does it matter? Why didn't I think about this before now?

I feel Orwell's solid presence at my right shoulder and breathe a sigh of relief when he speaks. "My name is Lief Orwell."

The guard's eyes flicker and his expression changes. But the change is not what I expect. I expected surprise, admiration. Maybe fear. What I see is . . . satisfaction?

"And what is your business in Atlantis, Mr. Orwell?"

"I am seeking an audience with the Council of the Guardians," Orwell declares. "My business with them is urgent. My companions," he gestures to the rest of us, "are here to corroborate my story and to offer their services to the Council when a course of action is decided upon."

I turn my head a fraction to glance at Darin. His eyes are narrowed, and when he catches my gaze, his fingers flicker down, tracing across his midriff. A belt buckle. His unspoken question causes my stomach to drop.

Why didn't they ask for his identification?

"Locklyn." At Orwell's mention of my name, my gaze goes back to the thin metal bracelets being held out toward me.

"What is that?" I ask guardedly, not extending my arm.

The guard's expression sours, and I wonder if he'd just explained to Orwell and I missed it. "It is a mulciber-wrought identification bracelet," he says stiffly. "Not only does it allow our patrolmen to know at a glance whether an individual has gone through the checkpoint to enter the city, but the mulciber magic with which they are imbued allows us to find any undesirables who manage to sneak through our security."

"Mulciber magic?"

"My role is not to explain the intricacies of undersea enchantment to the ignorant. If you wish to enter the city, you must accept a bracelet. If you do not wish to enter, move aside. You are holding up the line."

I notice the silver encircling Orwell's left wrist, so I slowly extend my arm. The guard catches hold of my wrist and slips the circle of silver around it. Instantly, searing heat near the inside my wrist makes me attempt to jerk my hand away, but the guard's fingers are like shackles. I look down to see red-hot tongs clamped around the cut edges of the metal, welding them together. When the guard pulls the tongs away, I see a tiny 113 etched into the bracelet. The tongs must contain a stamp of some kind.

"Next," the guard raps out, gesturing me impatiently to the side.

I slowly join Orwell, trying to wiggle the bracelet so that the freshly welded edge is not touching my skin. The guard has welded the bracelet so small, it is impossible to remove without cutting it.

"What is mulciber magic?" I ask Orwell as Ginevra submits to a bracelet, her back spear-straight.

"Mulcibers have the ability to know the location of every object they have ever created," Orwell replies. "No one knows how–it is simply a magic inherent to the way the Wave Master created them. This makes them invaluable as trackers. If you know a person carries a given object on their person and can find the mulciber that created that object, the mulciber will be able to lead you to that person."

Ginevra joins us, her lips pursed, most likely less from the pain of the searing metal and more because of the guard's attitude. The irony of her being annoyed by someone else's attitude makes me bite back a smile.

"It's amazing," she says loudly as the guard clamps a bracelet around Michal's wrist, "that people who can create the most advanced technology under the sea have yet to master rudimentary politeness."

Orwell's beard twitches, and I look quickly away, sure that I will burst out laughing if I catch his eye.

Michal moves in beside us, rubbing the red skin on the inside of her wrist. "This is good, right?" she asks hesitantly. "At least they're letting us in."

Orwell's shoulders rise and fall in a noncommittal shrug.

"Somehow it almost feels too easy," I say. "And it worries me they didn't ask for any sort of confirmation that Orwell was who he claimed to be."

"That could just be laziness though, couldn't it?" Worry tinges Michal's voice.

"It could be." Orwell waves the question away. "But now is not the time to discuss it. We have no choice but to hope for the best."

Darin, Conway, Arledge, and Kai join us one by one. The guard with the tongs gestures to the mouth of the tunnel. "You may proceed. I have sent word ahead. There will be an escort waiting for you."

An escort?

"Ready?" Orwell's eyes sweep the group. At our murmurs of assent, Orwell turns and dives into the tunnel. We dart after him.

The sensation that follows is completely strange. It is as though there is a current trapped inside the oil droplet tunnel. Rainbow shimmers flash past my eyes as the walls zip past, the water propelling us irresistibly forward. The words of *Rainbow Sheen* dance through my mind, along with memories of the night around the magma pit as we traveled toward Circe, sand trickling through Darin's hands.

But, look closer, sweetheart
I'm wearing my heart on my sleeve
The love I've always had for you
That, dearest, is the rainbow sheen

Soon, we burst out of the tunnel, into the heart of the Paradise of the underwater realm. A million sights and sounds seem to erupt from nowhere and separate us a space.

A market square swarming with Merfolk and Crura.The smell of unfamiliar spices assaulting my nostrils. Tiny, open-topped submarines built for one zooming through the crowds. A choir of

Vocalese singing in the corner of the square, accompanied by a group of Mermish folk playing instruments I have never seen before.

But one sight pushes all the others out of my mind.

The sight of a white-haired, scarlet-eyed Crura, incisors gleaming with jewels as he leers at me, surrounded by viridescent-tailed guards, two of whom are supporting an unconscious Orwell, three finned darts protruding from his neck.

"I heard tell that there was a little, blue-haired songbird outside the gates," he grins, lifting his blowgun to his lips.

26

LOCKLYN

I THINK IT IS THE SILENCE THAT AWAKENS me. For the past ten days, there has never been complete silence, so now the stillness presses on my consciousness, forcing me out of oblivion.

My eyes open into a darkness so deep, I can feel my pupils dilating, straining to pierce the impenetrable blackness. I grope outward, and my fingers find rough stone. Pulling myself up, I begin to swim slowly, my fingers tracing the contours of the room. It is tiny, smaller than my hut in the reef, and completely empty. Stone walls. Stone floor. Claustrophobia grows as my fingers fail to find hinges.

Is there no door? How did I get in here?

Something twinges at the base of my neck, and I reach up, brushing at the swollen pinprick just above my collarbone. That bump beneath my fingertips sends a flood of images into my mind.

The look of satisfaction on the checkpoint guard's face.

Igor waiting at the mouth of the tunnel.

Orwell unconscious in the water.

The blowgun.

Questions follow quickly on the tail of the memories.

Is each member of my group in a separate cell, or am I the only one in solitary confinement?

How long have I been here?

What is Igor going to do with us?

Hunger nips at my stomach, and I allow myself to sink to the cell floor. I ought to conserve energy since I have no idea when or if food is coming. My thoughts swim in circles, searching for a means of escape. But every circle ends in the dead end of my ignorance. I don't know where the door is. I don't know whether there are guards. I don't know when or if I will be checked on.

I need to wait to make a plan until I've been awake long enough to tell if there is any sort of routine to plan an escape around. My thoughts spiral down blenny holes, speculating where the others are, trying to comprehend mulciber magic, pushing away memories of Amaya and her children, listening to snatches of song lyrics playing on repeat in my mind.

Suddenly, a strange blue light fills the cramped cell. A scream catches in my throat.

Please let this be a nightmare.

"Why, dearie, you don't look a bit pleased to see me." Circe's voice is teasing as she drifts above me, the blue light seeming to emanate from her lithe, aquamarine tail.

I gather myself. "You took Darin's memories."

"I did not force him to do anything. It was his choice to drink."

"You tricked him!" I push up from the floor so that I am hovering across from her. "He was disoriented. And you took his life from him. His identity. For no reason."

"Everything I do has a reason." The flawless beauty of her voice grates on my nerves.

"Then why?"

Circe sighs, the sound light and delicate as the bubbles it elicits. "You are asking the wrong question, my sweet. The correct question is, why not?"

Nausea churns my stomach. "All the memories you erased. You

did it just because you could? You took their identities and lives away for the pleasure of seeing your own control?"

"Oh no, dear." Circe's voice is as sweet as ever, but her eyes cause goosebumps to erupt on my arms. Those eyes are glassy, dead-looking. "I did it for the pleasure of destroying their lives." I swallow at the cold, matter-of-factness of the words. Then, with a return to her sparkling lightness, Circe says, "But I'm not here to discuss myself."

"Why are you here?"

But I already know.

"I've come to free you." Circe smiles, but the pit in my stomach expands. When I say nothing, her full lips compress into a pout. "I know you never had any bringing-up, but I hadn't realized basic civilities were foreign to you."

"Why?" I look at her blankly.

"On second thought, perhaps you ought to stay here a while longer." Circe's face hardens as she begins to turn away. "Other than the allergic reaction induced by Igor's darts, Michal is doing well. Ginevra's fingernails are nearly gone from trying to pry stones from the ceiling, but they should grow back in time. The guards think Darin Aalto is going mad—muttering in his cell—but since his memory is already gone, I doubt he can get much worse. I'm sure a few more weeks here won't do any of them lasting damage."

She drifts toward the ceiling, and I see the stones above her begin to move, whether through magic or a bribed guard on the other side, I can't tell. But it doesn't matter.

I grit my teeth. "Thank you."

Circe pauses, a smile twisting the corner of her mouth. "What was that?"

"Thank you," I grind out again, the words sand on my tongue.

"Why, you are most welcome," Circe says sweetly, drifting back down toward me, her white hands performing a complicated motion in the water, causing the trapdoor in the ceiling to settle back into place. "I am delighted to do it. Especially because that little favor you owe me will be difficult to accomplish while locked in the caves under Atlantis."

There it is.

Somehow, now that the words are out, the demand made, calm settles over me. "And what exactly is this task that will release me from the dungeons of Atlantis?"

"It's the easiest thing, my dear. Barely a favor at all. I need you to take this." My eyes widen as she reaches to pull the chain of the sapphire and moonstone-studded locket resting against her collarbone over her head.

"I don't understand." My fingers reach tentatively for the necklace dangling from Circe's fingers, expecting her to yank the trinket back at any moment.

"This locket is dangerous," Circe warns.

The coolness of the chain settles around my fingers, as the weight of the oval-shaped pendant presses against my palm. My eyes search Circe's face, mind racing. *Why is she giving this to me? Could we have been wrong about her?*

"Yes," I say slowly, my eyes locked on hers. "It is."

Circe leans toward me, and I resist the urge to back away. "You know what is in the north?" she says.

I bite my lip, fighting a strong urge to lie. "In a Scottish lake?" I say, wanting to make sure I am not somehow giving her information she doesn't already know.

Her eyes never leave mine as she nods. "The locket is its key. You understand me, Locklyn." Her hand darts out, and shivers rack my body as her fingers stroke my throat. "If it were to be released, the results would be catastrophic. But no one would release it without a means to control it." The hand with which she stroked my throat drops. "I want that means destroyed."

My eyes widen as I raise the locket clasped in my hand. "You want me to destroy this?"

Her clear blue eyes stay on me. "There is only one way to keep it from falling into the wrong hands. You must go to the North Sea, to the city of Svengd, where the River Ness meets the sea. It is there that the caretakers, the feeders of the monster, dwell. Every month, on the first day of the month, the corpses are collected and brought up the Moray Firth."

"Corpses?" I manage.

Her eyebrows constrict. "There is no longer any life in Loch Ness. And there is speculation that if the monster grows too hungry, its desperation will provide enough strength for it to break through the gate."

"But do you mean corpses of Merfolk?" Bile is rising in my throat, and I swallow convulsively.

"From the rumors I hear, they are not Isja youth," Circe says. "You must go with the corpses. Before the hatch is opened, to deposit the food into the lake, put the locket around a corpse's neck. But not before reaching the gate. We cannot risk anyone finding and removing it. The beast will not notice a trinket around the neck of a piece of fodder. And in its magma-filled belly, the locket will melt into oblivion, destroying the threat it poses."

The silence that fills my cell after her words seems to pulse like the faint, blue light surrounding us. I struggle for understanding. "But why did you take the locket in the first place?" I finally dare to ask.

Circe's voice is soft, gentle, reasonable. "You heard Llyra's voice, Locklyn. You felt the beauty. The persuasiveness. The kind of power that comes with music like that. Who wouldn't want to wield it? I was tempted. I admit it. I was born a Vocalese like you and Llyra, my dear. But I can sing no longer. There was an accident, years ago. The scar tissue in my throat prevents me from singing." She sighs. "As you know, I have found other kinds of magic. Potions. Spells. But I longed for the magic of music again. That is why I acquired Llyra's locket."

"For the favor I owe you, you want me to take Llyra's locket to the North Sea and sneak it onto a corpse, so it can be eaten by the monster and destroyed? Once I've done that, our bargain will be fulfilled?" It sounds incredible in my ears just to say that, much less actually do it.

"Only one other thing." Circe nods, like it's an afterthought. "Bring one of your companions with you to the gate. If anything were to happen to you, the mission must still succeed."

If anything happens to me?

"Enough talk." Circe raises her hands toward the ceiling again. "Your trial is set to begin in a few hours."

"Wait!" The trapdoor is beginning to rise. "How are we supposed to get out of the city without being recaptured?"

Circe laughs, the bubbly sound jangling against my taut nerves. "Dearie, I'm not going to do *everything* for you. You made it past an Anakite crab, a giant stonefish, a sorceress, and a siren to reach Llyra's Treasure. I think you can make it past a few guards to get out of Atlantis."

She rises with the water she manipulates to push the trapdoor open. As her head and shoulders disappear through the opening in the ceiling, I want to shout more questions after her. But that would serve only to attract the attention of the guards.

I watch her glowing, aquamarine tail recede through the trapdoor until only her fins are visible. Then they are gone and her face appears in the opening above me. "I almost forgot."

Something falls through the water, gleaming in the darkness. As I reach out a hand to catch it, I see it is a knife, not coral like the ones I have always used, but a metal so sharp, I wonder if it could slice through scales.

"The power of the locket poses the greatest threat the Undersea Realm has ever faced." Circe's words linger as she disappears. "Don't fail me, Locklyn."

27

ONE HUNDRED FIFTEEN YEARS EARLIER

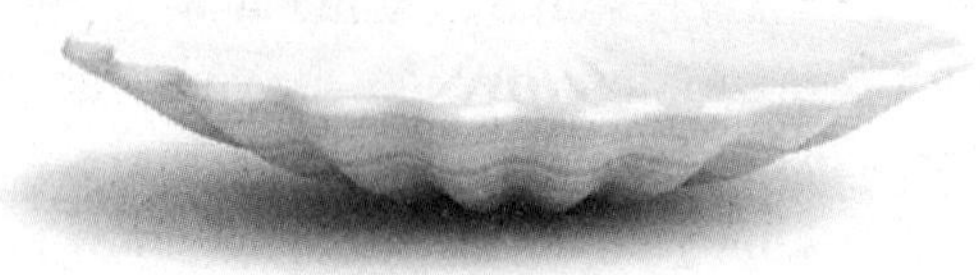

CIRCE LOOKS INTO THE MIRROR propped against the cave wall. Her appearance is flawless. She has grown adept at using spells and potions to hide her scars. Before Morrigan died, she had said, "You've surpassed me, child. You are the greatest sorceress under the sea."

In the mirror, she notices a damselfish swimming through the entrance of the cave. Turning, she tries to sing to the creature. The sound that escapes her throat is more of a growl than a musical note. The damselfish turns and swims away.

She has tried every elixir and incantation imaginable to repair her damaged vocal cords, but nothing has worked. This magic of music remains out of her reach.

Hatred toward Orwell resurfaces. She longs to avenge herself. If she still had her voice, she would go north, gain control of the monster, and command it to attack Orwell.

A sound reaches her from outside the cave. Someone is singing. The voice is pure and sweet, unlike anything Circe has ever heard before.

The singing stops. "Circe?"

Circe rises and swims to the cave's entrance. "Who are you? What business have you with me?"

A red-haired Mermaid with a green tail hovers outside. "Are you the enchantress Circe?"

"I am. But you still haven't said who you are."

"I am Llyra, the youngest daughter of King Triton of Aquaticus."

"Aquaticus? That is fifteen days distance from here."

"I know. My father thinks I am visiting my cousin in Ondine. I told him I wouldn't be back for a month."

"Your father lets you roam the seas alone without an escort?"

"Oh, I'm not alone. Morissey is with me." Circe looks further out and sees a hulking Merman with silver-streaked hair, holding a trident. "He won't tell my father about me coming here. But the open ocean isn't that dangerous for me anyway. I haven't met a sea creature yet that doesn't respond to my singing."

The young Mermaid is certainly chatty. "Why are you here?"

Llyra looks uncomfortable. "May we speak inside?" Circe leads her deeper into the cave. "I want legs."

"Legs would make life under the sea difficult, dearie."

"I don't want to live under the sea anymore. I want to live on land."

"Why?"

"Because I've fallen in love with a human."

"You want to give up your tail for a man?"

"I want to be with him," Llyra says. "There's no other way."

"No man is worth what you are trying to do."

"You're wrong," is her reply. "Please. I came here because I've heard that you are the most powerful enchantress under the sea. I'll give you anything you want if you'll make me a potion that will turn my tail into legs." She withdraws a pouch from under her cloak. "Here are two hundred moonstones. If that isn't enough, I'll bring you more."

"I have no need for money."

"What do you want?"

"Nothing that you can give me, dearie."

"Please." The Mermaid is desperate. "I'll do anything you ask."

An idea begins to form in Circe's mind. "Anything?"

"Anything,"

Circe takes the locket from around her neck. Once it had symbolized Orwell's love for her. Now it symbolized her hatred of him.

"I want your voice."

The locket Orwell had given her would become her means of avenging herself.

28

DARIN

HE TAKES A DEEP BREATH AND EXPELS IT in a groan that reverberates around the walls of his cell.

Heaving in another gulp of water, he begins a series of retching noises.

The trapdoor above his head stirs. "Pipe down!" a guard's voice commands tersely.

"I think I've been poisoned," he moans, clutching at his stomach and performing a slow, drunken somersault in the water.

"Or you have the stomach of a little Mermaid," a different voice snickers.

Two guards. At least.

Darin darts toward the corner of his cell, bracing his hands against the walls as he convulses, pretending to expel the contents of his stomach. He counts on the dimness of the cell to keep them from noticing the lack of evidence in the water around him.

"Do you think he really is ill?" one of the guards mutters. "Igor's only stipulation was that they all be upright for the trial."

Darin crumples to the sea floor.

"Perhaps we ought to fetch a doctor."

"He's just trying to get attention," the first guard snaps. "Oy, you! Stop it! Your stomach would have to be full of worms to warrant this kind of exhibit. Have some respect for yourself!"

In answer, he rolls onto his side and pretends to retch again.

"I'm going for the doctor," the voice of the worried guard says, and the trapdoor clicks, shutting out the other guard's snort.

Darin immediately rockets upward and plasters himself in a corner of the ceiling. To anyone looking straight down, the cell will appear empty. Minutes slip past, and his hope begins to trickle away.

Either the guard thought better of fetching a doctor, or his compatriot persuaded him that I was fine.

Then, just as Darin is about to give up and sink back down to the bottom of the cell to begin fake-heaving again, stone scrapes on stone. His body tenses as he watches the opening in the ceiling widen.

"Guard?" the doctor's voice is querulous. "I believe you have brought me to the wrong cell. This one appears to be unoccupied."

"What?" The voice of the skeptical guard. It is clear he is looking down when a string of profanity that could remove barnacles explodes from above. "Where is he?" The guard's face appears upside down in the hole, and Darin throws himself forward, driving his fist into the Merman's temple. The guard collapses onto the cell floor, and Darin speeds out into the corridor above. He whips his tail into the stomach of the other guard so that he falls back, bubbles ballooning from his mouth.

"Sorry," he says, grabbing the guard by the scruff of the neck and heaving him into the cell after his friend. The doctor turns to escape up the passage, but Darin is quicker. Darting past, he braces his hands against the walls. "You can swim into that cell or I can throw you in. Your choice, Doctor."

The raised eyebrows that meet the physician's dying-dugong look send the doctor scurrying for the trapdoor. The dull thunk of its closing causes Darin to glance quickly over his shoulder before sliding the deadbolt into place. With no clear idea of where to go, he swims slowly up the corridor, hugging the wall and examining the floor for other trapdoors, ears straining for the sound of anyone else's approach.

The walls and floor of the passage he follows are smooth, yet uneven, clearly formed by the movement of time and water, rather than Atlantean technology. The realization surprises him after his brief glimpse of the city. Everything he saw before being captured bore the stamp of originality and innovation–from the fried shrimp dispenser in the market to the rust-proof metal and glass out of which the buildings are constructed.

A noise makes him press against the wall, although aware camouflaging a shiny, copper tail is impossible. His ears strain to catch the sound of shifting water. Whoever is coming is working hard to move quietly. His fingers curl into a fist, and he waits as the waves of movement draw nearer. A split second before the newcomer rounds the corner, he throws himself around it, his right hand closing around their throat as his left swings back to strike.

Then pain explodes up his forearm, and his fingers go slack as a knife pommel chops at his wrist. His attacker darts behind him, and an arm hooks around his neck. Bubbles whoosh from his lips as the arm cinches tight, and the point of a knife pricks his skin.

"How often have I told you," a voice says in his ear, "not to get close enough to someone to allow them to grab you?"

Relief, warm as sunlight dancing on the waves of The Surface, surges through him. "Why are you asking me?" he says. "As far as I know, this is the first time you've told me."

"As a matter of fact, you're right about that." She swims around to face him. "How did you get out of your cell?"

"How did you get a knife?" he counters. When her eyes narrow, he answers, "Feigned sickness. When my guard opened the trapdoor for the doctor, I pulled him in."

Her lips twitch toward a smile. "Well, now we need to go find the others."

She heads down the tunnel in the direction he came from. "The cell they were keeping me in is just around that corner in a dead end," Locklyn says. "My guard is lying there unconscious. Circe must have given him some kind of potion."

"Circe? Circe was here?"

"She helped me escape," Locklyn's voice drifts back as they move past his trapdoor, from which muffled shouting emanates. "So I can be free to complete that favor I promised her."

"Which is?"

"Extremely strange," is all she says, before halting at the next bend in the passageway to peer around the corner. "All clear. I guess you and I must have been high priority prisoners. Or else this cell's guard needed a snack break."

"Maybe he went to visit my guard," he says, slipping downward in the water and sliding the deadbolt aside. "That would explain why there were two guards outside my cell."

"You'd probably better stay back," she advises as he reaches to open the trapdoor. "If Ginevra's in there, she's going to be hopping mad."

"Good point."

29

LOCKLYN

"THE DUNGEONS ARE LOCATED BENEATH the Halls of Knowledge." Eyebrows raise at Conway, who shrugs. "I've always been interested in Atlantis."

We're hovering beneath a round, mirror-like trapdoor in the passage's stone ceiling. Everyone from our group is here, and unconscious guards are strewn along the passageway behind us. The first trapdoor Darin and I found was Ginevra's, and every fresh addition to our party made the demise of the next guard easier.

"And the Halls of Knowledge are?" Impatience clips Ginevra's words.

"The building where the Council meets," Conway replies. "It used to be the palace when Atlantis was an island on The Surface. But there's no monarchy here now."

"We must move," Orwell states. "The longer we wait here, the greater the odds that we will be discovered and recaptured. None of us know the layout of the Halls of Knowledge, so we have nothing to gain by continued discussion."

I am the only one who notices Arledge's attempt to attract the group's attention.

"What is it?" I say, moving close to him as the rest of the party follow Orwell's instructions to gather into a loose formation. Arledge's eyes flit up to mine and then to the stone passage floor.

"I know the layout of the Halls of Knowledge."

I stare at him, certain I must have misunderstood his barely audible words. "You do?"

He nods. "I found a map in the submarine. Among Igor's things."

Without hearing anything more, I shout out to the others. Everyone spins around, some fingers pressed to lips. "Arledge knows the way out of the Halls of Knowledge," I say in a quieter voice. I wait until they're closer. "He should be the one to lead us."

"Son, the Wave Master must have sent you to us." Color floods Arledge's face as Orwell claps him on the shoulder before gesturing to the trapdoor. "Lead the way."

Arledge hesitates before swimming upward. As he reaches the trapdoor, he glances back at the rest of us. Darin leans toward him, hand on his shoulder, as he whispers something in Arledge's ear. Arledge nods, and then he and Darin move together, throwing their shoulders against the trapdoor.

There is an echoing clang. Darin and Arledge fall back, grimacing and rubbing their shoulders, which I'm sure will be nicely bruised by tomorrow.

"It's locked?" Michal asks.

"And there's no lock on this side," Darin says tersely. "But there must be some way for guards who want to get out to alert the guards on the other side to open the door."

"Look." Arledge points.

The trapdoor slowly rises. Darin exchanges one glance with Orwell before launching himself upward. His golden tail whisks through the hole in the ceiling, followed immediately by a grunt and the thwacking sound of flesh on flesh.

I breathe in a sigh of relief as Darin's face appears in the hole. "We need to go. There'll be more guards any minute."

Arledge propels himself through, and the rest of us follow. In the hallway above, he turns to the left, past the unconscious guard, and the rest of us veer with him. Bubbles hitch in my throat. The floor beneath us is the most exquisite mosaic I have ever seen. But what truly makes it difficult to breathe is the scene it depicts.

A beastly, slate-colored monster with flashing orange eyes spews a stream of magma onto a cluster of cottages. Inhabitants flee, terror etched onto their faces. The scene looks so real it unnerves me.

"They started this the week after we returned from the north," Orwell tells us. "They said they never wanted to forget the devastation the monster had caused. Or the importance of keeping it caged."

My stomach turns as we swim over the depiction of a pile of corpses with charred white tails and blistered, angry red skin. Arledge rounds another corner, and the mosaic on the floor beneath us changes. Now it almost looks like a family tree, with a stream of Crura depicted one after another, each one clutching the heel of the Crura above them. A pang of nostalgia for my legs hits me when the sight of something on the floor below draws my breath away.

The family tree ends with a branched top—a row of seven Crura with linked hands. They are beautiful—their bodies lean and toned, surrounded by billowing waves of blue-purple hair and piercing, gray eyes. But at the very end of the row, where I would assume the youngest in the family would stand, is a picture of a Merman with skin depicted by snow-white pearls, lank strands of pale hair floating around his face. The rubies that represent his eyes sparkle up at me and I swallow hard, pointing down.

"Look."

Conway gives a low whistle. "So, Igor is one of the Souverains?"

Ginevra scowls. "What does that mean?"

"The Council of Guardians has had seven members since it was formed centuries ago," he says. "Traditionally, one representative came from each of the Seven Seas—one of the Isja people for the North Atlantic, one of the Jumu people from the South Pacific Ocean, and so on. In the past, the representative for the people of the South Atlantic has always been a member of the Atlantean royal family, the Souverains."

He pauses, and Arledge intervenes. "I don't mean to be pushy, but . . ." He gestures down the hall.

"Haste is of the essence, as you say, Arledge." Orwell's voice is kind. "Conway, what is the importance of this?"

"The year my grandfather took the throne of Undula," Conway says, his voice quickening, "sextuplets were born to Asita Souverain, the Atlantean representative on the Council. The next year, she gave birth to another son–seven children in all. Fifteen years later, on the night of the sextuplets' coming-of-age, Asita and her husband threw a massive party. All of the other Council members were invited. At midnight, as a toast was given, the six other Council members mysteriously dropped dead." Seemingly unable to help himself, Conway pauses dramatically. "The next day, the sextuplets joined their mother on the Council, nominally as interim Council members. But, by the time word of their delegates' death reached their kingdoms, the interim part of the title had been dropped. On his sixteenth birthday, the youngest Souverain brother joined his siblings on the Council, replacing his mother. In the years immediately following the takeover, anyone who dared to challenge the Souverains mysteriously disappeared. None of the other kingdoms had the military might to mount an offensive against the technological capital of the Undersea Realm. So for the past fifty years, the Council of Guardians has been dominated by the Souverains."

"Why have I never heard any of this before?" Ginevra's tone holds a hint of accusation.

"The whole purpose of the takeover was to do it as quickly and quietly as possible, to minimize the chance of backlash from the rest of the Undersea Realm," Conway replies. "And since the Mediterranean is considered part of the South Atlantic, there were never any representatives on the Council from Undula or Nebula."

"So, this tells us"–I gesture to the mosaic beneath us–"Igor is the seventh Souverain son. Which brings up the question–why was one of the rulers of Atlantis roaming the Mediterranean with a bunch of scavengers?"

"Exactly." Conway's eyes meet mine for a beat before sliding away.

"Did you hear anything about Igor from the scavengers, Arledge?" Darin's question causes the pale Merman to start.

"Only . . . only that Pike and Kelby kept saying he would be disappointed because they didn't have more information for him."

Michal speaks up. "If Igor is on the Council, along with his six siblings, am I the only one who thinks we should be going in the opposite direction of the Halls of Knowledge?"

There is a moment of stunned silence. Then Conway whistles again. "Michal, I don't know why a genius like you is traveling with a bunch of fringeheads like us."

"She's always been the smart one in the family," Ginevra says, and I see a hint of smile pass between her and Conway.

Orwell shakes his head. "This Schatzi has clearly been a hermit in the mountains too long. Michal is right. Arledge, did you see a way to exit the palace on the map? We need to get out of the city as quickly as possible."

Arledge's eyes blink with uncertainty. The quick change of plans appears to have rattled him. "I . . . yes, of course. This way."

We all turn, following Arledge back along the passage. I try to keep my eyes trained ahead, but the monster on the floor seems to drag my eyes down, and I am unable to suppress thoughts of Talia, covered in burn wounds, watching as Orwell slammed the gate to Loch Ness, leaving her trapped inside with the monster.

How could he? What kind of coward leaves someone they love to die?

Stop it, I tell myself. *It is an endless pain to him.*

"This way," Arledge's voice says, and I glance around to see him leading the group through a door into another passageway. I speed up to swim next to Darin and nudge his arm.

"Is it just me, or is it strange that we haven't met anyone since the dungeons?" I say softly.

He turns his head slightly, eyes narrowing as he considers my question. "We don't know what time it is," he responds. "It could be the middle of the night."

I purse my lips, considering, as we turn another corner. "Does Orwell have a plan as to how to escape the city once we get out of this castle?"

"Right now, the best idea we have is to try to commandeer a submarine."

"But they search every submarine that leaves the city," I point out. "And we're all definitely fugitives by now."

"The plan doesn't really involve stopping at the checkpoint." He grins at my confusion. "It's quite simple, Locklyn. Most Merpeople wouldn't be foolish enough to jump in front of a submarine going at swordfish speed."

My mouth opens slightly. "Your plan is just to rocket past the guards at the city gate and out through the tunnel before they can stop us?"

"You've put it in a mollusk."

"But that seems too easy. You really think they won't have any precautions against that?"

"They didn't on the way in."

"But we can't go out the same way we came in," I persist. "The current in the tunnel only flows one direction."

"There's an almost identical exit tunnel on the other side of the city. Orwell claims the security is less stringent there."

Before I can pick another hole in his plan, Arledge's voice floats back to us. "We're here."

Our group drifts to a stop in front of the closed door before which Arledge is hovering. Every eye turns to Orwell.

"It is difficult to formulate an escape plan with so many unknowns," he observes. "Since what we do know is that there is no possibility of protection from the Council of the Guardians, our top objective is to avoid drawing attention to ourselves. This will be extremely difficult with the size of our group. So our second objective is to find an unattended submarine as quickly as possible." His lips twist into a wry smile. "Normally, I would hesitate to encourage stealing, but in this instance, I would say that our end justifies almost any means."

There is a moment of hesitation. Then Kai's gravelly voice scrapes through the water. "Wave Master, go with us."

"Wave Master, go with us," we echo.

All except for Arledge, who reaches for the door. In the split second before he opens it, I know something is terribly wrong. But the rest of the group swims forward, sweeping me through the door. It clangs shut behind us.

We aren't outside the palace. We are in a hall with high, vaulted ceilings that appear to be made of glass. White light floods from the glass boxes embedded up on the walls, which are lined with statues of Mermish warriors, each holding a fragor sphere in one hand and an L-shaped metal weapon in the other.

"What's going on?"

"Arledge?"

"Where are we?"

"What is this place?"

Our questions jumble in a cacophony of voices through which Orwell's rises in a shout.

"We've been betrayed! Go back!"

I dart for the door, rattling at the handle, but it won't budge. "It's locked!" My eyes find the keyhole. Without a key. "We have to find another way out!"

"Let's use the fragor!" Conway points at the spheres in the hands of the statues lining the walls, and my heart leaps.

"No need." Orwell's voice is deadly quiet. One of his massive hands is locked around Arledge's throat and in the other, he is holding a small golden object that he has clearly just attained. "This scum has the key."

For an instant, hope that we will still escape swells inside, and a bubble of optimism courses through my veins.

Then the bubble explodes as a familiar voice rings through the hall. "Well done, Arledge. I didn't think you had it in you."

30

DARIN

IT IS INSTINCT THAT MAKES HIM LUNGE toward the nearest statue, hand covering the glass ball in its grip. Because the sound of that voice awakens something primal in him that says, "Show no mercy."

But as his fingers close around the sphere, his heart skips a beat.

Because instead of touching carved, stone fingers, he feels flesh. A split second later, pain explodes through his head as a thin stream of pressurized water zeroes in on the acupoint inside his ear.

Darin's cry mingles with the horrified screams and gasps of his companions as the statues along the wall come to life, surrounding them, metal water shooters targeting each individual member of the group.

Except one.

"Igor." Arledge's voice is a pitiful squeak through the unrelaxed pressure of Orwell's fingers.

Darin's eyes rake the room, scanning for a sign of the achromos. The room is empty apart from the dozens of guards.

"Igor," Arledge whimpers again.

"Really, Arledge." Igor's lazy voice fills the room, and for a mad moment, Darin wonders if the Atlanteans have found some way to transmit a person's voice without their presence. "Try to have a little backbone. You're embarrassing me."

Darin's eyes search upward, drawn in the direction of the sound.

First, he sees webbed feet, waving lazily. Then legs, swathed in white trousers. Then torso and arms, one hand twirling the signature silver rod.

And finally the face, jewels sparkling from incisors bared in a leer, red eyes glinting, as Igor drifts slowly down from a small balcony embedded in a corner of the room, directly below the vaulted ceiling.

The perfect place for spying.

Igor lifts the blowgun lazily to his lips, and before Darin can react, the projectile is flying toward its mark.

It sticks in the back of Orwell's hand, finned head thrumming.

Orwell reaches across his body with his other hand and plucks the dart from his skin, tossing it away. He growls, "You, of all people, should know it will take more than one of those to have any effect on me. How many did it take last time? Seven?"

Igor clicks his tongue. "Oh, but, my friend, you don't suppose I only use one concoction on my darts? No, no, no. Weaponizable elixirs have always been rather a specialty of mine."

"Weaponizable elixirs?" Locklyn repeats. "In other words, poisons."

Igor clicks his tongue again. "Ah, but, sweetheart, the word poison is so crass. So misunderstood. The use of poisons is seen as underhanded. Cowardly. But weaponizable elixirs? They are–as the name implies–simply tools. You see?" Igor's languid gesture sends Darin's eyes from Locklyn to Orwell in time to see the giant release Arledge. Darin's stomach turns as he catches a glimpse of Orwell's hand. The back of it is now covered in an eruption of scarlet bumps, each tipped with a throbbing purple pustule. Orwell rakes his fingers across his infected hand, clearly trying to dispel the itching. Four or five of the bumps burst, oozing purple streaks which immediately begin to swell into more bumps, layering on top of the first rash. "This particular elixir precipitated my little snitch's release," remarks Orwell.

"You've been working for him?" The look on Ginevra's face ought to make Arledge fear for his life. "All this time?"

"You mean since he joined your group?" Igor's voice is gleeful as he stares down at Arledge, who is blinking rapidly while a dull red flush creeps up his face. "Oh, no. He and his beloved sister were pure little idealists, wanting nothing more than to help the heroes who had rescued them from the scavengers. But then there was an incident. A nasty, bloody, snipping, shearing incident. And, well, beloved little sister was no more."

There is soft, calculated cruelty in each word, digging and prodding, searching for the nerves that will inflict the most pain.

"And that is when I had the great good fortune to meet Arledge," Igor's voice continues, smooth and unctuous. "Onboard a submarine where I happened to be a prisoner. And I was sympathetic, wasn't I, little snitch? I listened to your pathetic sob story. I commiserated. Night after night, when I could have been resting, I sat up with you, murmuring comfort to your tedious, never-ending sniffling. But, in the end, it all paid off."

The smooth sweetness of Igor's voice is morphing, the edge of cruel mockery sharpening. "Because you were desperate," he continues. "And desperation makes people foolish. Such a useful idiot. When I told you I had the recipe for a potion that could bring your little sister back from the dead, you believed me. When I told you I needed to escape from the submarine to go to Atlantis and start preparing the elixir, you loosened my bonds outside Imber. When I told you that if you brought your companions to the Halls of Knowledge in the dead of night, I would have the potion ready for you, you took the keys I offered like an obedient little dugong and led them all here."

During the last part of Igor's speech, Arledge has been attempting to interject, choked gurgles erupting periodically from his lips. Now the words burst forth, high-pitched and panicked. "I did it! I did what you asked! Please, let me have it now!"

They all stare at Arledge in disbelief, Darin in disgust.

The jewels in Igor's teeth flash, rainbow sparkles flickering in the water. "Here, snitch." He reaches into his pocket and a bottle slips through his fingers, falling toward Arledge, who staggers forward to catch it. "Drink it," Igor purrs. "You'll see your little sister again."

Dismay and pity now join with the disbelief and disgust as Arledge wrenches the diamond stopper out of the bottle. The jubilation twisting his features is almost grotesque in its intensity. A sick certainty sends Darin hurtling through the water to knock the bottle away, but Arledge lifts it and tosses the contents down his throat.

Darin collides with the Merman a split second later, knowing he is too late, even before the other's body begins to spasm in his arms. Screams and gasps from his companions are dulled in his ears as he locks his arms around Arledge from behind, pressing upward against the youth's stomach again and again.

Arledge's eyes roll back into his head, blood-streaked foam staining his lips. Darin pauses, fingers pressing into the side of his neck in a practiced gesture he has no memory of learning. No matter how hard he seeks, there is only stillness beneath his fingertips. He lowers the young Merman gently to the floor.

Be his tomorrow, Wave Master.

Locklyn's eyes brim with tears. Ginevra's voice breaks the stillness. "You're nothing but a monster."

Igor's voice is as smooth as ever. "Oh, sweetheart, I hate to burst your bubble, but that's not exactly an original insult. People have used that word to describe me my entire life. My siblings, mostly. Monster. Freak. Wacko." His voice sharpens. "They didn't want me to lead with them. But my mother insisted. 'He's your brother,' she said. But they never called me brother."

His face twists with a different kind of madness than Arledge's face had worn. Madness born, not of hope, but of hatred.

"It was I who got them the power they so desperately craved," he goes on. "My elixirs that killed six Merpeople in a single night.

But instead of gratitude, I received contempt. 'Poison master,' they called me. 'Death dealer. Monster.'"

His words are coming quicker now, eyes widening, bulging slightly, red irises flicking furiously from side to side. "So I thought to myself, 'You say I'm the lord of death, my beloved siblings? I could be that. With the help of a monster.' So I began to travel, telling my siblings I was abducting Mermish captives to feed the monster caged in Loch Ness. But in reality I was searching the Mediterranean for a fabled locket that would allow me to control the menace in the North." His lips twist. "In the course of my travels, I ran across a mangy group of scavengers who told an outlandish story of a little, blue-haired Crura maiden with a miraculous voice. And I thought, 'If I have her, perhaps I'll have no need of the locket.' My pursuit of her led me to the foot of the Rayan Mountains, where I captured a member of her group, planning to use him as bait to lure the little witch to Atlantis." Igor's eyes seek Darin's. "But when I was captured, I thought any possibility that my revenge would succeed was gone. I would never be able to ensure my siblings' demise, making me sole ruler of Atlantis."

His smile is wide as a shark's, seeming to be comprised of as many sharp, glistening teeth. "But things have turned out better than I could have dreamed." He points. "The little witch is here. And she's brought me the locket."

31

LOCKLYN

MY FINGERS FIND THE LOCKET'S CATCH. Press down so hard that the metal digs a divot into the pad of my index finger. And the silver halves fall apart.

I am no enchantress. I have no way to control the voice flowing from the locket, but I hope—believe—that the most beautiful voice under the sea doesn't need me.

The song coming from the locket is not the same one I heard the first time it was opened in my presence. But, like the first time, images swirl through the water around us.

A red-haired Mermaid dancing in the city square of Aquaticus, twirling and laughing with her sisters.

A red-haired woman running through a field of some golden Surface plant chased by a laughing, dark-haired man and a mangy dog, skipping and laughing and joyous in the sunlight.

A red-haired Mermaid sifting through a pile of treasure that has just been brought to the palace with her sisters, gasping with delight as they hold up strange and wondrous objects.

A red-haired woman curled on a rug in front of a blazing fire with the dark-haired man and the dog, following her husband's finger as it glides down the parchment in front of her, her voice sounding out halting words, occasionally bursting into laughter at her own mistakes.

And as I listen, enchanted for the barest fraction of an instant, I hear the laughter in the music, the notes skipping and bubbling into a dancing melody.

Then I shake myself and nudge Orwell's shoulder. His face turns to me, slowly, as though his reflexes have been stupefied. Not daring to speak, I tilt my head toward the door. He gives a slow nod. His hand reaches to brush Ginevra's shoulder, and my stomach rolls again at the sight of the red and purple pustules encasing his hand like a gauntlet. At his touch, she also turns, her normally sharp eyes slightly glazed. My gaze flickers at Igor, and I see that he is frozen, his eyes bulging with greedy delight, staring at the images swirling through the water. From the looks on their faces, it is fear, rather than wonder, that holds the guards spellbound, but they too are paralyzed, jaws slack and eyes popping.

One by one, the members of our group rise through their paralyzing wonder and begin to drift toward the door. I wait, fingers trembling on the locket in my hands, fearful that the slightest movement on my part will shatter the precarious spell holding Igor and the guards at bay. Gold glints in the corner of my eye as I hear the scrape of a key in a lock.

Then I feel the prick at the base of my neck. My eyes find Igor, lowering the blowgun as he glides up to me. I try to swim away, but whatever was on that dart is racing through my veins, locking my muscles in a poison-induced paralysis. His arm hooks around my neck.

"Not so fast."

The guards shudder back to life as Igor reaches out and clicks the locket shut. He tugs it from my clenched fingers. In the open doorway, the members of my group turn, freezing at the sight of Igor's arm around my neck.

"I don't need her anymore," Igor says dismissively, but there is an edge in his voice as he yanks the dart free. I can feel blood leaving the wound, dissolving into the water, and I will my fingers to move, to reach up and staunch the bleeding. But my muscles remain unresponsive, beginning to cramp, sending licks of pain through my limbs. Something cool touches my neck, softly at first, then pressing into the wound left by the dart until a gasp slips from my lips. "A few drops of this in her bloodstream," says Igor into my ear, "and your little friend will be joining the snitch and his sister."

"What do you want?" Darin's voice is low and tense. My eyes drift sideways to find him, and I see him glance at me.

"Why, I want you all to accompany me on a little trip." The sweetness of Igor's tone makes my flesh crawl, and I clench my fingers into a fist.

I just moved my fingers. The poison is wearing off.

"I can't let you stay here." Igor's tone is calm and reasonable, like someone explaining basic facts to a child. "Not when you might go swimming off to my siblings, inviting them to send the full strength of Atlantis after me before I can free the real monster. No, no, no. I think you'd better accompany me to the North Sea. There you might be of some actual use. Or at least . . . provide some entertainment."

His twisted smile morphs into a grimace as I jerk around in his arms and strike him in the throat. From behind me, I hear the sound of blows and a strangled yell from one of the guards.

I knew I could count on you, Darin.

Squirming from Igor's slackened grip, I whip my tail into his side, hard enough to drive any remaining water from his lungs. Pandemonium has broken out behind me, but I don't look as I lunge for the blowgun still clutched in Igor's hands. But just as my fingers close on the cold metal, there is an explosive bang behind me, accompanied by a brilliant flash and a wave of water that knocks me head over tail.

Oh, no. Oh, no.

The moment I am able to right myself in the water, I spin, straining through the bubbles for a sight of my companions, begging the Wave Master for help. Hoping the spume will not clear to show me the bodies of my friends littering the tile floor of the Halls of Knowledge.

I think I catch sight of a flash of gold, right before a thin, metal tube connects with the back of my skull. Darin's voice echoes in my mind as black dots swarm my vision.

Distraction is fatal, Locklyn.

And, through the whirling blackness, I see the cool white tiles rush upward to meet me.

32

ONE HUNDRED YEARS EARLIER

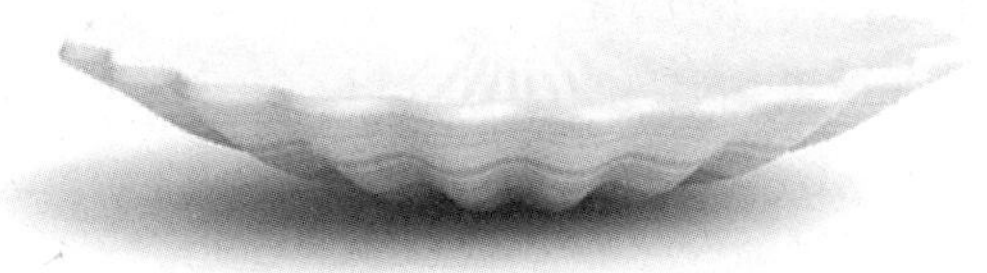

"MY LOVE, THE STORM IS GROWING worse. The captain thinks we should try to return to port."

Llyra gazes at Marcus with red-rimmed eyes. "I have to give the locket back, Marcus. Then she'll return Reef to us."

Marcus wraps his arms around his wife. "I can't believe that after today, I'll never hear you speak or sing again."

"It will be worth it, if we're reunited with our son."

The ship lurches and someone bangs on the cabin door. "Your Highness?"

Marcus makes his way to the door, bracing himself against the walls while the ship continues to heave as he exits the cabin.

Llyra knows it is time. Before the storm began, the captain had told Marcus they were about an hour from their destination.

She removes the locket from around her neck and opens the clasp. Holding the necklace in both hands, she repeats the words to the spell Circe taught her. The locket begins to glow. Llyra takes a deep breath and begins to sing. Images fill the air around her as she sings of her love for her husband and son. With each note, her voice grows fainter. The locket grows brighter. A tear runs down her cheeks.

When her voice is completely gone, she clasps the locket closed and tries to stand. There is a sudden grinding crash. The motion of the ship causes her to collapse back onto her seat. The door opens, and Marcus stumbles inside. “Llyra. We struck a rock. We’re sinking.”

She tries to speak, but no sound comes out.

Marcus makes his way beside her. He takes her hands. “I love you, my Mermaid.”

She leans into him and weeps.

Reef is lost to them forever.

This cursed locket is dragging them to the bottom of the sea.

33 LOCKLYN

I KNOW WHERE I AM.

After all, I've been listening to that metal, whirring sound for the better part of two months now.

I keep my eyes closed, sifting through my memories.

The escape from the dungeons of Atlantis.

The Halls of Knowledge.

Arledge's betrayal and death.

The fight.

And then . . . nothing.

The sensation of chains binding my hands behind my back slowly emerges into my consciousness.

Igor told us we would be accompanying him to the North Sea.

On the plus side, we didn't have to steal a submarine. On the minus side . . . the chains.

A voice I recognize speaks quietly. "Conway."

"I'm in shock. I can't remember the last time you voluntarily greeted me, Ginny."

"Clearly, shock has no effect on your swollen head."

"And being chained up has no effect on your sweet disposition."

"Keep talking like that, and I'll really show you sweet." But the usual edge in her voice is gone. "I can't believe I left Rihanna alone as regent. What was I thinking?"

"What was the warrior council thinking to vote Michal out? Fringeheads."

Her laugh is soft. "True."

"Was Michal upset when it happened?"

"You know Michal. All she wanted to do was help Ri. I was furious enough for both of us." There's a pause. "I think she got all the goodness for the family intended to be split among the three of us. But people still mock her. And underestimate her. And take advantage of her. And that makes me so angry, I can barely see straight."

"That's a kind of goodness too, you know." I open my eyes at that. Conway and Ginevra sit directly across the submarine from me, chained to the opposite wall, neither looking in my direction. Conway's face is turned towards Ginevra, whose head it bowed, her silvery braids falling between them. "That 'can-barely-see-straight-because-you-hurt-someone-I-love' feeling? It means you care, Ginny."

She looks at him through her hands. "But the caring doesn't help, does it? Because she still gets hurt. And all my caring can't stop that."

"But when she does get hurt, she has you to come back to." He continues to look down at her, his expression unreadable. "Who do you come back to, Ginny?"

A beat passes. "My mom is dead. My sisters need me. Who's left?"

"What about an old friend?" The words are hesitant.

"I've been a bit of a sea slug to him of late. And if you say you have a weakness for sea slugs, I will murder you. Don't think the fact that my hands are chained behind my back will stop me." The laugh that erupts from him is loud, and her shoulder knocks into him. "Do you want Igor to come back here?"

"I'd like to see you murder him. With your hands chained behind your back. And don't worry, I abhor sea slugs."

Listening, a thought swims into my mind.
Maybe we'll actually live to see Undula and Nebula united.
Despite the chains, I find myself smiling.

34

DARIN

"I HAVE A PLAN."

Darin watches Igor's pale form, reclining next to the submarine's controls.

"A plan to develop insomnia?" He hadn't noticed Locklyn was trying to sleep. The words are so bland he grins, blowing it out in a stream of tiny, noiseless bubbles.

"Ah, no. That would irritate Igor, and his punishment for disturbing his rest probably involves injecting the culprit with a concoction that causes excruciating pain."

"That's not funny, Darin." He blinks in confusion. Then she says, "Arledge."

A memory surges of Arledge spasming in his arms, clearly in agony, and shames him. "That was far too insensitive. It wasn't intentional. You're so right, it's not funny at all. I'm sorry, Locklyn."

She shakes her head. "I saw you try to save him, Dar," she says. "It's not that I thought you were mocking just now. It's that Igor is fully capable of torturing you for the most minor offense. Or no offense at all."

"Nothing's going to happen to me, Locklyn."

"That's what I thought once too."

The sentence stings more than she could possibly know.

He waits a moment before speaking again. "I have a plan," he repeats. She doesn't say anything, just waits, with her eyes moving every so often toward the achromos's prone form. "We're a day away from Svengd."

To his surprise, delight sparkles in her now emerald-green irises. "You can still do it!"

He stares at her. "What?"

"You can tell how much time has passed," she says to him. "Without an hourglass. When I was little and you took me out looking for wrecks, you were always able to get us back to the city just as they were closing the gates. At first I thought it was luck. But then you did it every single time."

Well, that was good to know about himself.

"We have to try to get control of the submarine before we reach the city," he goes on. "Right now, while Igor is alone, is our best chance. As soon as he has reinforcement in the form of dozens of Isja warriors, escape will become a lot harder."

Locklyn nods slowly. "Lucky that Igor freed your hands."

"It was lucky. I had no idea how to trick him into putting me in the neck shackle."

This submarine was designed specifically for transporting prisoners. Eight sets of wrist shackles are set into each wall, spaced between the portholes. Unfortunately for Darin, the wrist shackles had been designed for prisoners with average-sized wrists. But Igor did not seem to notice or care that Darin's manacles were cutting off the blood flow to his hands. On his third day in the craft, Darin noticed a single metal loop set into the back wall near the ceiling.

"Igor."

"Yes, Mr. Aalto?"

"My shackles are too tight. Could I be moved?"

He had been sure the request was pointless even before seeing Igor's derisive sneer. "Do I look like a fool to you, Mr. Aalto?"

Darin didn't answer.

Igor smacked Locklyn's elbow with his blowgun. An involuntary groan escaped her. "I will not be ignored."

"You are no fool." It took effort to keep his tone emotionless.

"You are right about that," Igor said. "I will not free your hands to save you a little bit of discomfort."

Darin hadn't even been thinking about the possibilities the neck shackle would offer. As the days had passed, he searched desperately for a way to convince Igor to move him.. Again and again, he was stumped by the fact that Igor would never jeopardize his control of the submarine by freeing Darin's hands.

Three daily events broke up the monotony of his endless brain wracking. Once a day, Igor would swim between the prisoners followed by an enormous, skeletal anglerfish he called Vir, placing black, pebble-like objects in each of their mouths. The first time this happened, the achromos explained that the objects were seeds from the alacritas plant, which had been specially bred by Atlantean scientists. Each seed, though smaller than a moonstone, contained energy equivalent to that found in a seven-course banquet.

Every so often, he would skip over someone for no apparent reason, feeding their seed to Vir. Several hours after this feeding, Igor would use a silver hook to lock the submarine's steering mechanism in place, and then he would swim slowly back and forth down the central aisle of the craft, twirling the ring of keys to their manacles around one long, white finger and hinting at the horrors waiting in the north. Finally, there would come the eventual moment when the achromos would drag a black shade across the glowing white stone set in the ceiling, pull the rod to halt the submarine's progress, and lie down to sleep in the small control alcove.

Two days ago, as Igor droned on about the barbarism and bloodlust of the Isja people, Vir suddenly darted at Darin's manacled wrists. Darin tried to twist away from the angler, wondering what had provoked the fish to attack.

"Darin, you're bleeding," Ginevra pointed out.

Igor stopped his speech and swam forward, pushing Vir aside. Darin knew he should feel the achromos's fingers, but his hands had been numb for days now because of the too-tight shackles. At first, he had felt painful tingling in his fingers. The sensation caused him to twist his hands, trying to induce circulation, but all that had resulted was a painful welt on his wrist where the shackle cut into his skin.

"Now, now, this won't do." Igor drew back, crossing his arms. "I can't have my best prisoner arriving in Svengd without functioning hands."

He glanced toward the locked chest at the front of the ship, which contained all his concoctions. Then, his gaze swiveled to the other end of the craft. Darin waited with bated breath, hardly daring to hope. Igor's lips curved as his gaze recentered on his prisoner.

"Very well, Mr. Aalto," he purred. "I think I can help you." And he smashed his blowgun into Darin's temple.

When he regained consciousness, a lump throbbed on the side of his head, and cool metal encased his throat. Igor hovered before him. "Let me warn you, Mr. Aalto. If you try anything, I will administer such rebukes as I see fit to your little, blue-haired friend. Perhaps the thought of her writhing in agony will induce you to choose a wise path."

"The problem is that Igor is expecting us to try something," Locklyn's somber voice pulls him back to the present.

"I don't want to risk him hurting you, Locklyn. But if we don't try now, we may not get another chance. Thanks to Arledge, we don't have a lot of options if we actually want to destroy the locket."

"It won't be your fault if he does hurt me." She gives him a reassuring smile. "So what is your plan?"

"I need your elastika."

Locklyn glances down at the rope twined through her belt. "Getting it to you is going to be a little difficult at this precise moment."

"I think you might be able to convince the anglerfish to help you."

Her eyes flicker to the fish, and she gives a brief smile. As the prowling fish swims by, she begins to sing under her breath.

"Come," the music says. "Take." And he watches, mesmerized anew by her magic, as the angler swims forward and pulls the rope into its huge maw. The meaning behind the melody changes and the fish swims forward until it is close enough for Darin to reach out and remove the rope from its mouth.

He grins at Locklyn. "Now, about tomorrow."

35

LOCKLYN

"IGOR?"

The achromos pauses in front of me, his fingers closing around the ring of keys he's been toying with during his usual promenade.

"Have you ever wished for a tail?"

Igor's eyes narrow in disgust. "Wished for a tail? Do you not understand what you have lost? Legs are an anomaly under the sea that confers true uniqueness, child. Possessing them is a sign of being destined for greatness, called to–"

My eyes flicker over his shoulder as Igor rambles on. Darin begins to unwind the elastika rope carefully wrapped around his chest under his shirt.

"Now you are common," Igor is saying. "You have lost that which set you apart." Out of the corner of my eye, I see a flash of motion. On cue, I begin a lullaby, just as Darin yanks the loop now wrapped around the achromos's ankle and pulls him backward through the water. Igor's eyes widen a moment before falling shut, then Darin takes the ring of keys from his slack grasp. As he sticks one of them into the lock of his shackle, pain suddenly lances through my arm, and I cry out.

Igor's head jerks up, just as Darin's neck manacle springs apart. Vir's teeth are clamped around my forearm. The ribbons of blood drifting up from innumerable puncture wounds make my stomach turn. A strangled shout from Darin jerks my attention back to him, just in time to see Igor's fist connect with his jaw.

I hurriedly begin to sing again, but the moment the first notes cross my lips, Vir's mandible tightens, and the music fades into a whimper as I thrash against my chains, fighting to throw the angler off.

"Darin, the keys!" Ginevra shouts, but in the split second Darin's eyes go to her, Igor's hand snakes out and the needle he holds in his long, white fingers pricks the inside of Darin's elbow.

It is like watching someone turning into stone. Darin's arm jerks weakly as he tries to throw the keys to Ginevra, and the silvery screws sink slowly through the water to the submarine floor. His neck spasms, and I know instinctively that he is trying to throw himself at Igor, but whatever paralyzing substance was in the needle prevents him from doing so.

Igor hangs back, watching with a smirk until Darin's body falls completely still. He swims forward and pats Darin softly on the cheek before shoving him into the neck manacle. "I could have used a concoction that would have rendered you senseless instantly," he remarks, stooping to retrieve the keys and securing the restraint. "But I wanted you to see this."

He turns toward me as I meet Darin's alarmed eyes.

Igor reaches into the pouch at his waist and withdraws a small pair of tongs. For a moment, I think he is going to use them to remove my eyelashes or something, and my heart pounds harder. But he only turns and swims languidly to the chest in the corner. After pressing his foot to the pin lock, he rummages inside.

I catch Ginevra's eye, and the tautness in her face increases the pounding of my heart. The achromos returns with what looks like a rectangle of purple jelly dangling from his tongs.

"I've been waiting for you to attempt some foolish escape plan. Ever since I changed your position, I've been carrying a needle imbued with paralyzing serum in my pocket. I've also been considering what would make the perfect punishment for your insubordination."

I press back against the submarine wall, realizing as I do so that Vir has released my forearm. Darin makes a strangled sound, and I know the paralyzation must be wearing off.

The achromos smiles sweetly at me as he raises the tongs. Then he lovingly lays the purple jelly along the exposed skin of my collarbone.

Agony explodes through my body, and I clench my teeth, fighting the screams wanting to escape. This pain is not an ebb and flow like Amaya described labor to be. It is a high note with no diminuendo, singing along my nerves in a cacophony of anguish.

The sight of Darin's face makes me bite down harder as tears come to my eyes. Because I know my screams will torture him like nothing else ever could. Ginevra and Conway are both yelling at Igor, but I can't make out the words through the haze of my pain. Through my slitted eyelids, I see Michal chained across from me, her lips moving as though in supplication.

Please, I can't do this anymore.

A shriek explodes from my lips, sending ribbons of red into the water in front of me. Darin doubles as though the sound was a physical blow. I can't help but scream again, eyes squeezed tight as the tears begin to pour down my face.

A never-ending circle of suffering.

Wave Master, please.

The sweet blackness of oblivion releases me.

36

DARIN

"WE'RE JUST IN TIME, MY LOVELIES." AT Igor's loathsome voice, Darin's hands tighten into fists. Branded across his eyes is the image of Locklyn writhing and shrieking as blood streamed from her mouth.

Wave Master as my witness, if that scum ever falls into my hands, he's going to know what pain is.

"Just in time for what?" Despite everything, Ginevra retains her sharp tone.

"For the Sterbfall Games, dearie. They start tomorrow. And look, we're just entering Svengd."

Darin looks through the viewing port and sees a line of tiny, domed houses, built out of some sort of white stone, whipping past. "There are no walls around Svengd?"

"Why would they need walls?" Igor's tone is patronizing. "After they were destroyed when the monster first ravaged the North Sea, the Isja people saw no point in rebuilding. Clearly, walls wouldn't stop the beast. And the Isja are the only Mermish hardy enough to call this icy marine home."

"And the Sterbfall Games are . . . ?"

Igor's bejeweled incisors flash. "The Sterbfall Games are a series of duels to the death. The winner gets an incredible prize."

The achromos pauses, and the implication of the words "duels to the death" hang in the water. Conway eyes him. "And what prize might that be?"

Igor's smile widens. "Why, to stay alive. All the losers"–his lips form a pout of fake distress–"are the monster's monthly meal."

Playing with the monster's food. That's what the Isja people have decided to do.

They have created a set of gladiatorial games for their own amusement. The monster won't care if its dinner is dead or alive. So why not create an entertaining spectacle beforehand? One desperate winner who will kill his fellow Mermish to save his own sorry life. And twenty-seven corpses to dump through the magical hatch into Loch Ness and keep the monster appeased.

The submarine shudders to a stop. "Here we are!" Igor chirps, darting forward to slide the submarine's door open.

A crowd waits outside. The Mermish people stare in, slanted gray eyes wide, black hair with streaks of red swirling above sealskin-clad torsos.

"Oh, I'll be betting on him!"

A middle-aged woman with a double chin and crooked teeth points at Darin. His brows lower into a scowl, which would have convinced the castle not to cheat him in his Schatzi days. But instead of shrinking in discomfort, the Merwoman's face lights up with a triumphant grin.

"See? See? He's a fighter, that one!"

"Out of the way! Coming through!" A pompous little Merman with red-streaked hair teased into position with walrus blubber pushes his way through the crowd, a squid-ink pen with an unusually sharp tip poised over a thick sheet of what looks like ice.

When his eyes light on Igor, his twitchy movements still. "Your Highness? We–I was unaware–is the chieftain expecting you?"

Igor's jewels glitter, and it is clear that the other's discomfort is balm to his crooked soul. "Oh, it's just a little Atlantean surprise, Sven. The Council wanted a firsthand report of how the Games are going. Not to mention how Nessie is faring."

The Merman called Sven stares at him, slack-jawed for a moment, before hitching his face into a painful simper. "Of course. I will escort you to the guest quarters myself. But first"–he points with the tip of his pen–"seven new contestants for the Games tomorrow?"

At Igor's nod, Sven clicks his tongue, gesturing behind him. Four soldiers come forward as Igor unlocks the chains from the side of the ship and shoves his prisoners toward the submarine entrance.

Reaching Darin, the achromos wraps chains around his wrists before unlocking the neck manacle. "I hope you get sent into the arena before Locklyn." His teeth gleam. "It would be dreadful for you to have to watch her suffer."

"Pray your life never falls into my hands, Igor." Before the other can respond, he uses his tail to propel himself through the doorway.

The guards hustle them through the crowd of onlookers, most of whom are speculating whether they should bet on Darin or Orwell. Darin catches a glimpse of Locklyn twisting to look back, and he follows her focus to where Llyra's locket glitters atop Igor's potion chest. Her face is a mask of despair.

The entrance to the largest white dome leads through a side door into a cramped hallway lined with cells. As the passage curves slowly, Darin is sure the "contestants' quarters" surround the central arena used for the death matches. Finally, just before the passageway ends, the guards jerk their prisoners to a stop.

"Let's just split them up between the last four," one of the guards grunts, and the others make sounds of acquiescence. Darin's guard works the lock of the nearest door. "Stand back," he barks as the lock clicks. The door swings slowly open, but the cell beyond is so dark that nothing is distinguishable.

"In!" the guard barks at him. He and Locklyn are shoved inside.

The lock clicks, and a voice says, "So, I have company."

They still as a faint red glow appears in the back corner of the cell, growing stronger until the dim outline of a Mermaid is visible, rubbing a small stone between her hands.

She continues to rub until the stone glows strongly, then raises it above her head and peers at them. She is young. For a moment, they study each other. Then the Mermaid launches herself at Darin, fingers scrabbling at his throat.

"Where did you get this? Answer me!"

37

LOCKLYN

THE MAD MERMAID IS SO FOCUSED ON Darin that I am able to swing my tail into her side, sending her reeling backward. I half expect her to dart at Darin again as soon as she gets her breath back, but she doesn't. She stares at the pearly inside of the clamshell half dangling around Darin's neck from a copper chain. Darin had startled, but says nothing.

My heart jolts as I see she is wearing a necklace that is identical, save for the fact that her clamshell faces the other way.

As I watch, the girl's eyes slowly widen. She seems to be trembling.

"He's dead, isn't he?"

You brought us to her, Wave Master.

Darin now speaks. "Is the 'he' you speak of the one who gave you the necklace you wear?"

Her eyelids flutter, and she squeezes them closed, her face one of misery. A pause follows. "He made them," she says eventually. "He wanted to give me a ring. But my father disapproved of him because he was poor and uneducated and not good enough for a prosperous merchant's only daughter. So he made the necklaces and gave mine to me on my eighteenth birthday. He told me it was a promise we would be married, as soon as he had built enough of a business to support me. The day after my birthday, the soldiers came for me."

When she doesn't go on, I ask, "To give you to the Atlanteans?" I look at her more closely. "Where are you from?"

"Proluvies."

My soft utterance of comprehension is met with Darin's confusion. "There are three kingdoms in the Mediterranean," I tell him. "Proluvies is the capital city of Lympha. But Lympha is so much smaller than Undula and Nebula, it is easily forgotten."

Darin's attention remains on the Mermaid. "Go on," he says.

"Usually Atlantis forgets about us too," she says. "But there were rumors about Undula and Nebula paying them off to save their youth, so they came to us. Our monarchy doesn't have enough treasure to keep the streets of Proluvies paved, let alone pay bribes of protection. So they drew lots to pick seven boys and seven girls to send to the North Sea. Everyone was told Atlantis was planting a colony–that it would be a better life for us. But when they said we would never be able to return, I knew it was a lie."

The Mermaid's voice falters before she continues. "He promised to come for me. He said he'd swim all the way to the North Sea if he had to. He said he'd get the money to buy my freedom. But I told him it would be foolish to do anything to anger the Atlanteans and that he was not to endanger himself for me. When he wouldn't listen, I grew desperate, so I told him my father was right. I said I'd decided I didn't care about him–that I was too good for him." Her voice cracks. "The look on his face still haunts me. He asked for the necklace back. I forced myself to take it off, but then he stopped me." Her voice breaks completely now. "He said, 'Why should I worry about half a clam shell when you'll always be the other half of me?'" Acidic, green tears slide down her cheeks, leaving inky trails.

Something about the finality in her voice makes me try something. I bend my body, curving my tail upward until I am able to ease my chained wrists beneath it, sliding until my shoulders feel as though they are about to leave their sockets. Right when I am sure I will never be able to get out of this contortion, my tail slips downward, and my chained hands move in front of me. I inch toward Darin, looking up at him with a question in my eyes. "Take it, eel-girl," he says, and I manage to lift the necklace over his head.

The chain pools in the center of the shell as I hold it out to the Mermaid. Then Darin says, "If I could tell you anything about your fiancé, I would. But my memory is gone. I can't even remember his name."

"Pike."

"Pike," Darin repeats.

"And what is your name?" I say.

"Marella. But Pike always called me Elle." She hesitates. "I can take your chains off if you'd like. I got out of mine so many times, the guards gave up putting them back on."

"That would be great," Darin says.

Elle flicks her braid over her shoulder and pulls out a small hook made of what looks like bone. "Luckily, the cook here doesn't much care what goes into the stew for the prisoners." She moves behind Darin, inserting the instrument into the lock on his cuffs. A moment later, a click resounds, and as they fall away, she moves toward me.

"Don't worry," she says to us as my chains land on the cell floor with a clatter. "I won't be a concern for you tomorrow. I don't have any reason to try to win this time."

I stare at her. "You've–you've won the Sterbfall Games before?"

Elle's eyes meet mine. They are dark brown, flecked with specks of silver, unique and beautiful as the pieces of wood Darin would sometimes bring back from the hulls of wrecks. "Twice," she says. "The first time I was put in the second-to-last round. I only had to kill twice to win." I try not to react to those words. "But the second time . . . well, the winner from the last Games goes in the first round. And they fight until they win. Or die."

Darin speaks. "I thought the winner of the Games gets to live."

Elle's laugh is dry. "Oh, you do. Until the next Games. You buy yourself another miserable month alone with your guilt."

"I wouldn't kill you," I say. "So you giving up won't change anything if we have to fight."

Elle looks at me oddly. "Do you know what they do if two contestants won't fight? They send in an orca. To kill them both. And believe me, getting torn to death by teeth is a much more unpleasant way to go than a thrust through the heart."

She turns away. I feel fingers close around my wrist. "Let her alone," Darin says in my ear as Elle sinks down in the corner of the cell furthest from us. "Nothing you can say will help her now."

I turn to look up at him. "But she doesn't even know for certain that he's dead," I argue, loud enough for Elle to hear me.

"Sometimes people just know," Darin's voice falls flat.

My heart sinks as I look again toward Elle's forlorn figure. "Love connects us," Chantara used to say. So perhaps Darin is right.

"What are we going to do?" I ask as we swim to the opposite corner from Elle.

"First, you need to tell me about the locket."

My heart thuds against my ribs. I had forgotten to tell Darin. While on the submarine, I had refused to talk about how I had come to possess Llyra's locket for fear of Igor overhearing. "You remember how I told you the favor Circe wanted was extremely strange?"

"Yes . . ."

"When she came to Atlantis, she gave me the locket and told me that, as the favor I owed her, she wanted me to travel to the North Sea, place the locket around the neck of one of the corpses from the Games, and make sure it was dumped into Loch Ness. She said the magma in the creature's stomach would melt the locket, destroying it for good."

"And why would she want that?" Darin's tone sounds skeptical.

"I have no idea." I bite my lip. "But, to be honest, I was afraid she'd ask me to do something much worse. Not to mention, I was headed to the North Sea anyway."

He turns to look at me. "Circe plus Llyra's locket, or Igor plus Llyra's locket? Which do you prefer?"

"The honest answer is that I prefer the locket melting in Nessie's belly."

"So how do we get it there?"

"First, we have to figure out how to get out of dying tomorrow," I say. My eyes flit to Elle, and my stomach turns. "Or killing anyone."

"I'm not sure both those things are possible," Darin observes.

"Killing someone or being killed? Which do you prefer?" I'm trying to make a joke, but the words come out cynical, sharp-edged.

"I prefer for you to stay alive."

"Even if I had to kill someone?" I turn to look him full in the face.

"If I were being selfish," he says quietly, "I'd say yes. Anything to keep you alive. But when I think of how that would break and scar your soul, I don't know."

"You mean I'm too soft."

"Too soft?" His expression is incredulous. "No. It's just that you're not a killer, Locklyn. There's no shame in that."

The wave of memory when he said those exact same words soothes me in their wake. He's still my Darin. Even without his memories, his core is the same. Blazing gold, as radiant as Earth's center.

I gaze at him, all my feelings renewing.

He utters something I don't hear, caught in the gold of his eyes. He leans forward, gaze searching mine. He finds something there and breathes my name before I kiss him. It is like the cool familiarity of waves rushing up in greeting when one leaps into the air above The Surface.

When we finally break apart, he keeps his face close to mine, our foreheads brushing. "If we survive tomorrow," he whispers, "I'll find you another anklet."

"But I don't have ankles anymore," I whisper back.

"This won't just be any anklet," he says, and his voice is serious, though I can hear a smile beneath the words. "It will be a message anklet."

"Really?"

"Yes. It will remind you every day that your husband loves you with or without legs."

My heart is pounding. "But I don't have a husband either," I say.

"Something tells me you will." He pauses for a fraction of a second. "Am I right, Locklyn?"

"Something tells me you are." The volcano Purkagia seems to have erupted inside my chest, spreading crashing waves of warmth and light, but with none of the destruction and pain. I smile. "You'll have to get me that anklet before I can tell you for sure."

38

LOCKLYN

THE CREAK OF THE CELL DOOR OPENING jerks me from sleep. For an instant, my heart is weightless, floating in a sea of golden happiness inside my chest.

And then my heart plummets into my gut, forming a hard, heavy lump.

To be married will only be a possibility if our escape plan works.

An escape plan that has innumerable holes.

And far too many unknowns.

Last night, we talked for hours, trying to formulate a strategy. Eventually, Elle uncurled herself and crept close to join our conversation, helping with descriptive details of what we could expect tomorrow.

The guards would come around dawn. They would shepherd all the prisoners out of their cells and chain us together. Then they would lead us into a metal cage on the edge of the arena, where we would be forced to watch all the other duels.

“Is the dueling area enclosed?” I asked, sure it must be. The Isja wouldn’t want to risk the prisoners teaming up to attack the spectators instead of each other.

Elle had nodded. “The glass dome to enclose the arena floor was a gift from Atlantis, I'm told. It arrived in two halves on a special express blue whale, a few months ago when the Games started."

She then told us that her first opponent would be selected by Axel, the chieftain of the Isja. And the selection would not be random. In her last fight, he had picked the weakest-looking of the other captives for the first match, wanting to save the more exciting duels for later in the event.

"There will be a whole wall of weapons for us to pick from." Elle's voice was resigned. "Then we fight. Whoever survives has to battle the next opponent Axel picks immediately. That's why it's unlikely to have the same champion time after time. By the time you reach your last few duels, you're so exhausted that you're much more likely to make sloppy mistakes. This gives your opponent an opportunity to strike."

"How many guards are in the arena during the Games?" Darin had wanted to know.

Elle shook her head. "All the Isja are fighters from the time they can swim straight. You might as well count hundreds of guards into your escape plan."

"How close are the exits to the enclosure where the prisoners are kept?"

"Not close," Elle replied. "The prisoners are kept right on the edge of the dueling pit, next to the royal family's seats. Axel wants his victims to get a close-up view of what happens to their friends before it happens to them."

My stomach twisted. "If you taught Darin and me to pick handcuff locks, could we free enough of the other prisoners for us to overpower the guards before we even get to the arena?"

"Maybe we wouldn't need to overpower them." Darin's voice suddenly sounded excited. "Locklyn, if you could sing them to sleep, that would buy us enough time to uncuff everyone and find a way out."

"Sing them to sleep?" Elle's voice was sharp with curiosity.

In answer, I began to hum, then sing, crooning the words of the lullaby I had used against Pike and his cronies. My heart ached as I offered the song as a tribute to the white-blond Merman I had assumed to be a villain, rather than a broken-hearted youth, willing to do anything to save the girl he loved. I stopped singing when I saw Elle's head begin to nod in the red light of her illuminator stone.

"That was amazing," she breathed, giving herself a shake as the induced drowsiness faded away. "We might actually have a chance."

She spent the next several hours teaching us to pick our handcuffs, snapping them onto our wrists again and again. Finally, when she deemed us proficient, she withdrew two more shards of bone from her hair and passed one to each of us. "Hide them in your hair. The guards don't normally look there." Then she had drifted back to her corner, curling up on the floor. "We should sleep. There's no way to make this plan any better. There are too many unknowns."

Now three guards crowd into the cell, one latching onto each of us immediately. An enormous Isja warrior with a red and black mohawk jerks Darin's hands behind his back, securing his wrists with . . . a piece of rope. I look toward Elle. Her eyes are wide, and she shakes her head ever so slightly. Ropes must be a new development. Perhaps a result of Elle's well-known proficiency for lock-picking.

I swallow. We'll just have to swim together after I sing the guards to sleep. Not ideal. But still possible.

Then the guard who has been knotting my hands behind my back suddenly appears directly in my line of vision and reaches forward, pinching my nose shut. My mouth opens reflexively, gulping in water, and the Merwoman shoves a wadded up piece of fabric inside. Face twisted in a leer, she pulls a second piece of fabric from a sealskin pouch on her belt and wraps it tightly around the lower half of my face, knotting it at the back of my head, effectively preventing me from making a sound. My eyes dart between Darin and Elle, and I see my own terror and distress mirrored in their eyes.

"We've heard so much about you, *kultaseni,*" my guard sneers. "How you've got a talent for making your guards feel like taking a little nap. But the Games are better sport for everyone if we all stay awake and alert."

The guards herd us into a clump, knotting the ends of our ropes together, Elle in front, Darin behind her, and me in the back. Then they usher us out of the cell into the brightly lit passageway outside, already congested with guards and prisoners. As our guards elbow their way toward the front of the line, pulling us along with them, I push desperately at the rag in my mouth with my tongue, trying to make a sound. But no sound emerges, and as the guards begin to chivvy us down the passageway, my terror mounts.

Wave Master, please.

There's no other way to escape.

If we can't stop this before we reach the arena, we're all going to die.

I redouble my efforts, contorting my tongue to push at the cloth. The lead guard opens a door halfway along the passage, and as Elle swims slowly inside, I stop fighting, knowing our chance to avoid the Games is gone.

The arena stands are packed.

And completely silent.

As we swim along an aisle, heading for the arena floor, a cry rises from the crowd, high and keening. The sound causes barnacle bumps to erupt on my arms. I know next to nothing about the customs of the Isja. But I recognize that sound for what it is. A death wail.

My eyes flicker forward, fixing onto the sparkling glass dome drawing steadily nearer, and my gaze moves along the seam of the two halves. So that's where I'm going to die.

Then something catches my eye and I squint. *Was I imagining it, or . . .?*

A vibration.

The faintest shiver of the glass along the dome's seam.

As the wailing of the crowd fades into silence, the glass stills. Looking over Darin's shoulder, I see the guards cutting Elle free from the rest of the line. Then they shove Darin toward the door of a cage covered in metal spikes on the very edge of the glass dome, looking down onto the sandy floor of the combat area. Right before he enters, another guard cuts the line binding us together, then the line binding me to the Mermaid at my back. I feel a tug at the base of my skull, and the cloth around my mouth loosens and falls away. Drawing water in through my nose, I shoot a jet through my mouth, expelling the wad of cloth as I follow Darin and take the seat second furthest from the entrance. As the rest of the prisoners follow us, I stare down, watching as Elle slowly enters the pit. Her face is drawn, and she makes no move to acknowledge the cheering that has erupted from the crowd at her entrance. A knife with a curved, pure white blade dangles limply at her side.

Walrus tusk?

The cheering dies abruptly, and a throbbing silence fills the arena again. Then a Merman appears outside the prisoners' cage, in the small space between the enclosure and the glass dome of the combat pit. His torso is swathed in a jerkin of white polar bear fur contrasting sharply with the black and silver scales of his tail. His waist-length hair is silver, rather than black, and the scarlet streaks hang in thick braids, like serpents sprouting from his scalp to mingle with his graying hair. His face is stoic with shrewd eyes that dart from prisoner to prisoner as his fingers stroke the pearl-encrusted shaft of the tall scepter in his hand. The three walrus tusks curling from the top look like an upside-down version of the anchors the Land Dwellers use to attach their vessels to the ocean floor.

Chieftain Axel pauses directly in front of Darin and me, and my heart gives a strange, hiccupping leap, its rhythm stuttered.

Not Darin.

I can't watch him die.

Pick me.

The moment stretches. I know Axel is allowing the tension to build on purpose. This is a spectator sport, after all.

Then he lifts his scepter.

And points.

Directly at me.

39

DARIN

AS LOCKLYN RISES SLOWLY FROM HER seat, her eyes on the Isja chief, Darin fights fruitlessly against the bonds.

I didn't think she'd be the first.

"If I were being selfish, I'd say yes. Anything to keep you alive. But when I think of how that would break and scar your soul, I don't know."

It is clear, without a shadow of a doubt, that she won't kill Elle. Which means that Locklyn is going to die. Before his eyes.

He bumps her hand with his shoulder, and she looks down at him. Her eyes are light blue, soft and gentle.

"I love you." The words must be said before the blue-haired girl with changing eyes who's always had his heart is gone.

Tears well in her eyes, their green sheen obscuring the blue of her irises for a moment. Her fingers brush his forearm. "When you enter the Wave Master's Realm, today or as a weathered Schatzi of a hundred, I'll be the second thing you see. His smile first. Then mine. Because I'll be waiting to go and see those Brushstrokes with you."

"Do you think there are Aurora Borealis in the Wave Master's Realm?"

"They're His brushstrokes, aren't they?" she says. "I think they'll be there. Or else something better."

There is a banging on the glass and she bends, brushing her lips, feather-soft, against his. "Till then, my Darin."

His eyes follow her as the cage door opens and she swims out, pausing so the guard outside can slash through her bindings. For a moment, she is out of sight, and then he sees her entering the combat arena, armed with a knife no longer than her hand. The blade looks to be made of a shark's tooth.

Elle darts at her so quickly that Darin inhales a gulp of water in a gasp. Locklyn's knife is too small to parry Elle's blade, but she manages to avoid the blow by dropping to her stomach on the arena's black, sandy floor.

He expects to see her slash at Elle's tail, but instead Locklyn merely rolls to avoid a downward jab from the walrus tusk and darts upright in the water, clearly waiting for her opponent's next move. When Elle flies at her again, jabbing viciously, Locklyn turns tail and zooms away from her, following the curve of the glass dome.

Boos rise from the spectators, and he leans forward, staring intently at the speeding blue blur below, knowing she must have a plan. Three times, Locklyn and Elle spin past, the distance between them closing with each lap around the arena.

Then, Elle's arms snake out, seizing Locklyn's blue hair and dragging her back against her chest. Locklyn lets out a shrill scream that catapults Darin out of his seat. And as the scream goes on and on, rising in pitch and volume, he scans the enclosure frantically for a way to escape–to reach her.

At a vibration, his roving eyes catch the seam of the dome surrounding the arena. Elle's arms fall from Locklyn's chest, and she backs away, wrapping her hands around her head as she sinks to the arena's floor. For a moment, Locklyn's voice fades as she visibly takes a breath, lungs expanding.

The note pours from her mouth with the force of a tidal wave. It seems to stab a nerve at the base of Darin's skull, and through a haze of pain, he watches the Isja in the audience contort themselves, clutching their ears in a vain attempt to muffle the sound.

The glass dome shatters. Screams erupt as the audience scatters, desperate to escape the raining glass. Darin flattens himself to the metal bars of the prisoners' enclosure, trying to see what is happening outside. Locklyn's blue hair flies past as she throws herself toward the royal box, the small knife still glinting in her hand. Her tail whips into Igor's face and he collapses, blood pouring from his nose. Locklyn fumbles with the locket on Igor's neck, brandishing her knife to dissuade any of the other occupants of the box from intervening.

"Aalto!" Orwell's voice jerks Darin's attention to the door of the pen, which is standing open. He catches a glimpse of Elle's flaming hair and realizes she must have picked the lock. His tail propels him through the opening after Orwell, pausing only to use one of the spikes protruding from the cage to saw through the rope around his wrists. He is just turning to find Locklyn when a scream rips through the water, and he spins back and freezes.

An Isja warrior with half her skull shaved has used a long pole with a cruel-looking hook at the end to stab through the thin, rubbery flesh of Elle's fin. Elle moans in agony, wriggling to free herself as the woman drags her backward. Ribbons of scarlet twine from the wound, drifting upward. "Help." The syllable is a plea as her eyes meet his.

Immobilization evaporating, he shoots forward, but the Isja warrior gives her staff a yank with one hand while reaching with the other to bury a shark-tooth knife in Elle's ribs.

"No!"

Darin's tail connects with the Isja's side, sending her cartwheeling away. He catches Elle as she slips down in the water, her blood soaking his shirt as she lets out another moan.

The hook.

Reaching down to catch the staff, its dragging handle almost certainly adding to her agony, Darin swims toward the exit into the catacombs, heart sinking as he catches glimpses of his companions, who are all locked in combat with Isja warriors. Hearing shouts behind him, he whips his tail harder, fear spurring him on as Elle's moans fade, and her body becomes heavier in his arms.

Two Isja dart suddenly into his path, blocking the way to the door. There is no way he can fight them without dropping Elle. He turns back, scanning wildly for another way out, but sees only five more Isja guards swimming directly toward him.

Orwell is locked in battle with the Isja chieftain a few spear-lengths away, his scarlet tail and flying fists matching the blows of the other's staff. Ginevra and Michal are fighting back-to-back, teeth gritted in matching expressions that make him see the familial resemblance between them for the first time. Conway leads a formation of prisoners, Kai among them, who have procured weapons from the table in the arena in an attempt to break through to the exit. None of them are in a position to come to his aid.

Then a single word, sung on a high, clear note, breaks through the tumult. His heart leaps.

"Stop."

Every face turns to the blue-haired girl hovering at the far edge of the arena, an orca whale on either side of her. Her song tune is calm.

"They will attack on my command." A perceptible shift seems to ripple through the crowd at her words. The Isja closest to him stiffen in the water, fear evident in their tense forms. "You will let us go." Locklyn is still calm, and it is clear the music is exercising control on the orcas as much as on the Merfolk around them.

There is a pause. Then, the chieftain drops his three-pronged staff to the sand. All around, the Isja back away, hands raised in surrender. Locklyn swims through the crowd, the orcas following docilely behind her. As she passes him, Darin hears her humming a brisk, inviting melody. He follows her and her strange, black-and-white entourage through the door which an Isja guard holds open. It is then he realizes Elle's body is now completely limp in his arms.

Behind him, he hears movement and knows the others must be following, but he does not look back. He follows Locklyn as she swims to the cell where they were imprisoned with Elle. She directs the orcas inside and closes the door. As she turns toward him, Darin looks down at the girl in his arms, taking in the pallor of her skin, the stillness at her throat. Locklyn moves forward, her fingers probing Elle's neck, and he waits, staring numbly at the blue head bent over the body in his arms.

"She's alive, Darin." Locklyn's eyes find his, sapphire-blue in this moment. "Barely."

Mixed emotions cascade over him, but Locklyn's gaze moves beyond his. "We can't stay here." Her voice is taut with something he can't identify. "We have minutes–at most–before they come after us." She swallows. "There's something I have to do. Orwell, I need you. The rest of you should try to commandeer a submarine."

Then Ginevra's cool voice says, "We came in that way," and the rest of the crew begin to squeeze past Darin, moving up the passage.

"Locklyn." Her name is mostly bubbles, but she turns. "Where are you going?"

Her hand rises, and he catches a glimpse of silver and moonstones. "To pay my family's debt."

40

LOCKLYN

"HOW FAR IS THE GATE?"

The muscles of Orwell's broad back are knotted with tension, and he doesn't turn as he answers, "Svengd was a mass of rubble the last time I saw it, and I'm not sure if they rebuilt on exactly the same site. But if they did, the gate is about a three-hour swim to the east."

The locket with its sapphire and moonstone designs is held tightly in my hand. I have no idea what exactly I am going to do when we reach the gate. There is no body to put the locket on. I wonder if Circe would count my end of the bargain as maintained if I just threw the locket through the hatch. I don't even know if I will be able to open the hatch, or if there is some specific spell that is necessary to unlatch it.

Bubbles from Orwell's wake tickle my arms, and as I struggle to keep up with him, I am reminded of the days when Darin would forget about my legs. It was a rare occurrence, but he would always realize what was happening before I had to say anything. Then he would turn with the smile that set my insides ablaze and say, "I'm getting a little tired. Lead the way, Stellvertreter."

It was what Schatzis called their seconds.

"I love you," he had said, before I entered the arena, and as

I sang to break the glass, I replayed those words over and over, turning them into strength and determination, into a will to break free so that I would be able to hear him say those words again, and say them to him in return.

Orwell is pulling ahead, and I increase my speed, trying to focus on something that will distract me from the discomfort beginning to prick at my hip bones. I think of the others and wonder how we will find them again after completing this task. My stomach aches as I think of Darin, and I wonder if he is still in the tunnels, trying to revive a girl whose life is slipping away as surely as the tide.

What if he's been recaptured?

This is the second time I'm leaving him. And look what happened the first time.

Flashes of red in the water draw me back to my surroundings. The landscape Orwell and I are swimming through is strewn with chunks and spurs of black rock, on which splashes of scarlet seem to shine through the darkness. I dip downward to take a closer look and feel a smile tug at my lips. The rocks are carpeted with anemones unlike any I have seen before–bright vermilion, with streaks of orange, purple, and cream on their tentacles. My finger strokes one, and the tentacles latch onto my finger for a moment before curling inward.

Beauty.

Even here.

Thank you, Wave Master.

Glancing around, fear replaces my delight. Orwell's scarlet tail has disappeared. Darting up, I begin to hare in the direction I last saw him going.

"Orwell?"

There is no answer, and the water seems to grow colder around me. I shiver and remember the furs the Isja Merfolk wore. Maybe they weren't purely decorative.

"Orwell?"

In the shadows ahead, something moves. I stop. If it is an orca,

I should be able to handle it. My connection to members of the dolphin family is stronger than to any other sea creature.

I begin to hum a soft, coaxing melody, reaching for the shark-tooth knife stuck in my knot of hair for safekeeping. The shadowy form does not move, and I infuse more urgency into my music.

Come, the notes say. *Come.*

"That won't work on me, dearie."

I know the voice, and my anxiety swirls into panic.

"Circe?"

The shadow moves, drawing nearer. A blue glow flickers and then grows stronger. A coiled rope of what I am certain must be oublier faire kelp gleams in the hands of the Mermaid hovering before me.

But it is not Circe.

Bile rises inside me at the sight of the pale, flaking scales of the tail from which a fin dangles limply on a thread of skin. The flesh of the hands twisting the blue rope of kelp is so puckered with purple and red scars, the scarce healthy skin looks like pink veins.

The face is skull-like, with wide, gaping sockets around the eyes and lips pulled back from gums with loose, barely-connected teeth. The thin layer of skin that has managed to grow back over the bones is almost transparent, and the short, frizzled hair through which the scalp peeks is charred, sooty black.

"Tsk, tsk." Circe's voice emanates from the creature's mouth, sweet and lilting as ever. "You don't look a bit pleased to see me, sweet. I must confess, I expected a little more enthusiasm since I was so kind as to free you from the dungeons of Atlantis last time we met."

My breathing has become shallow, water barely sliding over my tongue toward my throat before it is expelled again. My eyes drift down to the locket, its chain tangled in my fingers, and the tumbling pieces in my mind fall together into place.

"T-Talia?"

The face in front of me contorts, and I flinch. "Now, now," the Mermaid says, poison tinging her lovely voice. "There's no need to be offensive. It's your friend Orwell's fault that my looks aren't all they once were."

The sense of doom swells inside, but I attempt to regulate my tone. "Circe, I'm trying to do what you–"

"I am not finished." The fury in her voice is barely controlled, and I fall immediately silent, drifting backward in the water. "Where was I? Oh, Lief Orwell." Her gray teeth bare a snarl. "He told me he loved me. That he would protect me. That nothing would ever hurt me while there was breath in his body.

"He also said he needed my help. That if I really loved him, I would join his quest. He said it was selfish of me to allow my fear to stand in the way of his greatest chance at fame. He promised nothing would happen to me. 'This is the best crew that has been assembled in a thousand years. What could happen?'"

Talia's smile is so horrific that my eyes flicker away. "And then, he watched me burn. Locklyn, my sweet, I have spent the last hundred and fifty years in constant pain, biding my time, looking for a way to regain the magic I lost when the scar tissue wrapped around my vocal cords took away my ability to sing. And a hundred years ago, I found it, when a little red-haired Mermaid came to find me, promising me anything I asked, if I would allow her to join her one true love on land." Talia's face spasms. "You know what happened next, dearie. But I'd waited too long to give up. There was a reason my life had been spared. Lief Orwell will not pass peacefully from this life. He will burn. With the knife of betrayal buried deep in his back."

The blue kelp rope in her hands twirls once, flying through the air, and I am too caught in the hypnotic spell of her words to move. The noose of the oublier faire tightens around my throat, and the sweet, familiar smell rises into my nostrils, sending fog swirling through my brain.

I thrash, but Talia jerks on the noose, cutting off my water supply. The moment I relax, the noose loosens, and the aroma fills me again.

Lecker.

The scent of a merchild's head.
The open ocean.
Darkness.

41

DARIN

THE COLD BRUSH OF OPEN WATER ON her face causes Elle's eyelids to flutter. Carefully, he lowers her onto the black sand next to the door of the catacombs. She moans at the movement, and he takes a breath at the sight of the dark stain surrounding the knife still embedded in her ribs.

Pulling his shirt over his head, he wraps it tightly around the blade's handle, applying pressure and praying this small and seemingly pointless gesture will slow the bleeding enough for him to figure out what to do.

"Please." He startles, then leans over Elle, bringing his ear close to her lips. Bubbles brush the side of his face as she speaks again. "I don't want to die."

"But, last night . . ." he starts, unsure how to phrase the question.

There is a hissing gasp. "Last night I was sure I would rather be killed than do any more killing," she says. She takes random shuddering breaths as she tries to go on. "But as soon as I entered the arena, I couldn't seem to stop myself from fighting, from trying to survive. All I felt was blind panic at the thought of passing into the dim unknown beyond death." She shivers, and a tear drips from one closed eyelid. He takes her fingers and squeezes lightly, the pressure the only way he knows to express to her that she is not alone. "I've taken the lives of scores of the Wave Master's creatures. Taken them brutally. There must be some reckoning coming for what I've done. And I don't know how to face it."

"I don't remember anything about my past." The words float out in response. "Everything before the past month is a blank. I'm sure there is sound doctrine about death. And about the Wave Master's Realm and the reckoning. But I don't know it." He pauses, the remembered panic of being trapped inside his own mind rising in a sickening wave. It is only the sight of the red beginning to press into his shirt that allows him to force the feeling away. "What I do know is that since the day I woke up remembering nothing, I've had to fling myself on the Wave Master's mercy again and again. I may have done egregious things in my past, things I will never be able to make restitution for. I have to trust in His forgiveness. His unmerited kindness." He looks at her compassionately. "That's all any of us can do, Elle. Throw ourselves on His mercy. It must be at least as deep as these seas He created."

Her chest rises as she exhales a deep sigh. "It's not that I don't believe you." Her voice trembles. "But, Darin, I don't want to go like this." A tear slides down her cheek, chased by another and another. "Everything I've done in the past months–" Her voice breaks. "You're the first Merperson who has touched me without the intent to harm me in almost a year. Dying now would feel like drowning in a crimson sea, strangled by my victims' hands." She takes a deep breath, and he sees with relief that her tears have stopped. "I'm my parents' only child. It nearly killed them when I was taken. Before I left, I was teaching my little cousin to make sea snail chimes so she would have something to sell at the weekly market. My best friend was pregnant with her first baby. I want to see the little one. So much." Her voice breaks again.

She begins to sob softly, and he stays quietly beside her as time slips past, until gradually her sobs subside.

"That girl is on Death's doorstep." The unexpected voice causes him to throw himself forward so that his body shields Elle's prone form. When he looks up, he sees amused, crimson eyes staring at him. "I think I have something that could buy her a little time," Igor says, reaching into his pocket and withdrawing a small, corked vial of purple liquid.

"If you come near her with that, it will be the last thing you do," Darin growls, surreptitiously seeking anything in the vicinity that could be used as a weapon.

Igor laughs, the sound high and grating. "Suit yourself." He slides the bottle back into his pocket. "You're not harming anyone but your little friend."

"You work with poisons," Darin spits at him. "I don't want you to help her in the same way you helped Arledge."

Igor lifts a shoulder. "This is a poison," he remarks, gesturing to his pocket. "Anyone who imbibes it will fall into a coma-like state. For most individuals, that would be unfortunate." Darin snorts derisively, and Igor ignores him. "Your friend is at Death's door," the achromos repeats. "In her case, the coma would buy her enough time for you to find someone who could heal her."

Darin raises an eyebrow. "Any Isja doctor would send her straight back to the arena. And I very much doubt that a coma would buy her enough time for us to return to the Mediterranean."

"I'm not talking about a doctor." Igor's tone is supercilious. "The Sea Enchantress could heal her."

"Circe?" Darin barks a laugh. "Circe isn't here."

Igor cocks his head. "Of course she is. Do you really think she would have let her precious locket go to the North Sea without her? She's been following us since Atlantis."

Confusion sends Darin's thoughts spinning. "And you let her? You want that locket yourself. To release the monster in Loch Ness."

"Why would I stop her?" Igor's jeweled incisors flash as he smirks. "I was intrigued to see what she would do. And I wanted to leave myself the option of an ally, should our aims happen to align. But your time is running out." He gestures downward, and Darin sees with a jolt of panic that Elle's face is the color of skim dugong milk, and her breathing is so shallow, it's barely discernible. "Come,

come, Darin. What does she have to lose?" Igor twiddles the bottle, which seems to have magically reappeared between his fingers.

"What do you want?" The words taste like sand in Darin's mouth. Igor raises his eyebrows. "In return," Darin adds, scorn coating the edges of his syllables.

The purple bottle twirls in Igor's hand. "I want the locket back. And while I hope Circe and I can reach an understanding, I am prepared to use force if necessary. That is where you come in. You are not inept as a fighter, and should I need a diversion, you would prove useful."

"So you administer the elixir, and then I help you find Circe?"

"Oh, finding her shouldn't be too difficult," Igor says. "She wants the locket. Your little blue-haired friend has it. So we just need to locate her. I'm sure Circe won't be far behind. And I'm sure that you know exactly where the girlie went."

Darin looks down into Elle's face. *Please. I don't want to die.*

The two clamshell halves, now joined together on the chain around her neck, draw his gaze, and he knows, despite his blank memory, that he must have made a promise to this unknown Pike.

He asked me to save her.

"Give her the potion."

Igor's incisors flash, and he moves forward, stooping over Elle and forcing the open mouth of the little bottle between her lips. "Smart choice, Aalto."

I am not so sure.

42

LOCKLYN

MY HANDS FLY OUTWARD, STRIKING something that yields under my touch. For a moment, my eyes stay closed as I probe at whatever encases me. It is soft and supple, moving with every pressure.

Slowly, I open my eyes.

I am surrounded by water. Not the water that is air to Merfolk. A thin, undulating wall of water. My gaze flies down, up, side-to-side, and I realize I am encased in a bubble. Experimentally, I smack my tail sideways. The side of the bubble balloons outward for a moment before returning to its original position.

A glimpse of crimson out of the corner of my eye pulls my head around, and I see a second enormous bubble suspended next to mine, with Orwell hanging limply in the center. He appears unharmed. As I watch, he stirs, and then his head snaps up, eyes opening to scan his surroundings. Taking in the bubble enveloping him, he carefully pats the interior before swinging his tail violently into the side.

"Orwell," I call out, and he spins wildly, trying to locate my voice. "The walls must be magically reinforced," I say when he meets my eyes.

His eyes widen briefly, and then his face seems to spasm. "Where is Talia?"

"Here I am, dearest." Talia hovers before what, at first glance, appears to be a wall of rock. Then I catch glimpses of silver sparkling in the crevices where the stones join together. Spells.

I hear a short exclamation as Orwell's hands touch the surface of the bubble in front of him, straining toward the disfigured Mermaid floating there. I look away, suddenly unable to gaze at the expression on his face.

"You're alive." He clears his throat. "I was so sure–"

"You call this alive?"

Tingles shiver up and down my back at the menace in her voice.

"I'm sorry," Orwell says, almost helplessly.

"Oh, that changes everything. The fact that you're sorry. One hundred and fifty years of agony–erased by two words."

I want him to say something. To defend himself. To ask what else he can possibly do. But her venom seems to have penetrated deep into his soul, and he appears to be shrinking, folding in on himself.

"You're pathetic." The ice of the northern glaciers fills her tone, and every word is a knife's edge, deliberately carving deep into the Merman. "I thought, when I finally resurfaced, that you would have had the decency to slit your own wrists. Throw yourself into Oro's volcanic heart. Kiss a blue-ringed octopus. But, no. Like the piece of sea slime that you are, you skulked off to the mountains. Allowed your fame and mystique to grow. Lived a nice, quiet life, while allowing a monstrous crab to protect you from your enemies."

She drifts forward, her barely-attached fin fluttering limply beneath her. She is directly outside Orwell's bubble now. "Look at me."

I see Orwell flinch.

"Look at me!" This time it is a shout, and he looks at his former love, his face ashen. "A nice, quiet life. Isn't that all I ever wanted? Did I want fame, Lief?" Her teeth are bared as she lunges toward him, her scarred hands pressed on the outside of his prison. "Did I?"

"No." His lips barely move, but in that word, his admission of guilt seems to echo around us.

Talia drifts away from him, calm again, no hint of her near breakdown evident in her sweet voice. "You got exactly what you wanted, Lief. And you got what I wanted too. But, luckily for me, desires change. I've waited a long time. But I'm finally going to get my heart's desire."

She turns to the wall behind her and begins to chant, her hands tracing strange, intricate patterns through the water. Dread knots my stomach, and I glance at Orwell. His eyes meet mine for an instant before he says quietly, "Leave the girl here, Talia. She has no part in this."

The wall of rocks swings silently inward. Talia turns to look at us, and there is a faint smile playing about her misshapen mouth. "Oh, but you are wrong, dear Lief. Her part is to die a torturous death in front of you. I want her screams ringing in your ears as the magma turns your skin into ash."

Then, with a cascade of foul words, she flings up her hands, and our bubbles fly forward, sending us tumbling toward our doom.

43

DARIN

THERE IS A STRANGE, RESTLESS FEELING gnawing inside as he and Igor fly above black, wicked-looking outcroppings of rock, liberally overgrown with crimson and orange anemones. They must hurry to reach the gate of Loch Ness. Elle's comatose state can only keep Death at bay for so long.

And yet, the feeling is an itch in Darin's mind, urging him to turn off the path they are following and swim away into the unknown waters on either side, searching for . . . what? The past remains a black abyss, but the feeling is still familiar somehow, as though it is as much a part of him as his copper tail.

"What exactly are you planning to do with the monster, should you and Circe reach an understanding?" he says to Igor. "In Atlantis, I gathered that you wanted to show your siblings how much of a monster you are, but I'm still a little fuzzy on the specifics."

The achromos twirls his blowgun in a graceful arc before answering. "I have been debating the specifics myself. A reign of terror is somewhat pointless if it has no subjects. So I must find a way to wreak maximum destruction while still leaving enough Merfolk alive to experience it. And once that campaign is completed, I must also find a way to dispose of the monster, since it will be hard to exercise continuous control, even with the locket."

Darin stares at him in horror at the level of evil and lunacy necessary to allow someone to speak of wreaking maximum destruction in the same tone as someone planning a dinner party.

His fingers twitch subconsciously toward his empty hip, where his knife sheath used to reside. With no weapon, overcoming Igor will be difficult, but if he waits until Circe and a mythical monster are part of the mix, it will be virtually impossible.

"Are you married?" he asks abruptly, eyes scanning the surroundings. *I won't know where to go until we reach the mouth of the River, so I need to time this perfectly.*

"What did you say?" The sharpness of Igor's tone tells Darin he has struck a nerve.

"I was just wondering if there is an heir to take over your kingdom, or if one of your siblings' children . . ."

"My siblings' children will be the first to meet the monster's jaws!"

Darin raises his eyebrows. "Forgive me mentioning it, but that doesn't sound like the attitude of a loving uncle. I can see that your siblings may have wronged you, but your nieces and nephews would hardly be old enough to have done any–"

"It's not what they've done," Igor retorts. "It's that I–"

"Are you unable to have children?"

Igor turns, and the fury on his face is so blinding, that for a moment, Darin wonders if the other is about to attack him.

When the achromos speaks, however, his voice is icily calm. "I don't owe you any explanations regarding my life, Aalto. But I wouldn't want you to leave with the wrong idea. Were I able to find a wife, I am certain I would be as able to produce a child as any of my brothers. However, when I came of wooing age and began to seek a bride among the elite of Atlantis, it became clear that my siblings had spread their poisonous lies about me far and wide. Every Mermaid I approached had an excellent reason why she was unable to accept the honor of my proposals." Igor's mouth tips upward into a leer. "It is amazing how many of them contracted mysterious ailments that prevented them from ever donning their bridal purple at all."

Darin's insides pinch. "You poisoned the Mermaids who rejected you?"

His tone appears to incense Igor, and the achromos speeds away in a whirl of white, heading for the dark opening that has appeared ahead. Darin darts downward, scooping something from the crags beneath them.

"They had an opportunity and refused to take it," Igor shoots back. "It is time the people around me learned there are consequences for their actions!"

"You're right," Darin agrees. "There are consequences." And the dark hunk of rock in his hand flies through the water, connecting with the back of Igor's white-blond head. As the Atlantean jerks, Darin hurls himself forward, wrapping one arm in a crushing grip around the other's windpipe, while yanking the blowgun from his hand with the other.

Igor fights back, but the lack of water weakens his usually formidable strength, and gradually his thrashing turns into erratic spasms before he goes limp. Darin maintains his hold for a moment longer before lowering the achromos to the rocks below and fishing in his pockets for the vial of purple liquid he administered to Elle. There are still a few drops inside.

"This isn't enough to cause a true coma, but I can't have you waking up and following me," he says quietly before pinching the Atlantean's nose and dripping the leftover potion down his throat.

Then he leaps upward, the stolen blowgun in his hands, and heads for the mouth of the Moray Firth.

44

LOCKLYN

THIS FEAR IS WORSE THAN THE FEAR I felt when I saw the white shape of the Anakite hurtling toward me. A fear so potent, it is a drug–addictively mesmerizing, making it impossible to focus on anything but terror. The water around me begins to shift, with soft, caressing movements that normally wouldn't register against my skin.

My hands fly out, the gesture reflexive. My fingers encounter nothing. The bubble surrounding me is gone. And so is the veneer of protection it afforded. My body curls in on itself, eyes squeezing tightly closed. Somehow, the thought of seeing the monster coming for me is even more terrifying than the specter of Death itself.

You can't just give up, Locklyn.

The voice in my head sounds like Darin's, but it is as though the words are echoing to me down a long tunnel. The fear is a whirlpool, sucking me inexorably down toward its dark heart, and I am paralyzed, unable even to thrash against the panic holding me in its icy grip.

Save me!

It is not really a prayer, more an internal scream, and I expect no response.

"Locklyn!" For a mad moment, I wonder if the voice is the Wave

Master's, if with death so close, the barrier between His realm and ours has thinned, or even vanished completely. Then a powerful, calloused hand grips my arm. "Locklyn!"

The touch is my lifeline, pulling my mind back through the swirling eddies of panic. I open my eyes to see Orwell is beside me, deepened lines around his eyes and mouth his only sign of emotion. "We have to try to find a way out. She's gone for the monster."

I scan the lake that has imprisoned a fire-breathing fiend for over a century. It is barren. A wasteland. Grayish white particles float all around us. Instead of flora or fauna, the rocks of the lake floor are covered with dark scorch marks and disfigured with long gouges, whether from claws or teeth, it is impossible to tell.

I turn to speak, but he is peering intently at something through the murky water. Then I hear it. Drifting toward us, faint but audible. The sound of a voice singing.

For an instant, Orwell and I are frozen, his fingers still clutching my arm. Then we quickly begin to swim backward. "Talia told me there was a hatch in the gate," I say, trying to steady my voice. "Do you know if it is locked with spells?"

"It was only possible to open the original hatch from the outside," Orwell tells me. "But there must be a way out, or Talia would never have been able to escape all those years ago. Then she knew only the Wave Master-given power of music, not the black arts which have made her feared as the most powerful enchantress under the sea."

The gate, shimmering with its silvery strands of magic, looms out of the water before us. Orwell darts toward the hinges, hands probing the rocks along the articulation. Hanging suspended, I watch him, mind whirling.

We can't probe every inch of the rocky walls and floor of the lake. Already, I imagine I can hear the music drawing nearer.

We just need somewhere close by that we can go—a place where the monster can't follow.

I know what to do. "Orwell?"

He turns.

"Can the monster breathe on land?"

His head moves from side to side. "No. If it could, it would surely have left the lake by now. Loch Ness is not deep. And–"

Then understanding dawns on his face, and we both swim swiftly upward, parallel to the gate. I know now I am not imagining the faint music I hear, and I double my speed.

If we can only reach the shore, Orwell and I can crawl on land to a place in the River Ness beyond the gate. Then we can swim back and warn the others.

The melody is growing louder. I recognize Llyra's voice, but the images swirling in the water are no longer of a red-haired Mermaid and her dark-haired prince. The images are of a blue-haired Mermaid, and a Merman with a crimson tail, and the music is pulsing a single command, over and over again.

Hunt.

Hunt.

Hunt.

As my speed increases, I realize that even if we can reach The Surface, our plan will never work. Talia knows how to open the gate. If Orwell and I remain on land, we could possibly save ourselves. But Talia would simply direct the monster down the River to destroy Svengd. And in Svengd, waiting for us to return after destroying the locket, are Ginevra, Conway, Michal, Kai, and Darin.

I think of him as I saw him last, bending over the broken, red-haired girl in his arms, and my tail strokes falter. Orwell, who was already ahead of me, begins to pull away. But reaching land is our only chance of buying enough time to figure out what to do next and strike again. My heart lurches as I hear a voice echoing through the water behind me.

The words are unintelligible, but I feel their evil radiating through me, down my torso and then into my legs.

My legs?

I look down. My tail is gone. In its place wave two gray, cloth-covered limbs ending in webbed feet. For an instant, a strange mixture of regret and elation sweeps through me, and then it is gone, replaced by the terrifying realization of how slowly I am swimming.

My head jerks sideways as I kick madly, and I catch a glimpse of a gargantuan, black shape shooting through the water. It is still some distance away, but any chance I had of outswimming it vanished with my tail.

Churning my legs and my arms, I follow the red streak above me that I know is Orwell's tail. A shout rises to my lips, but I bite it down, knowing if he turns back now, he will lose his own slim chance of escape.

I feel, rather than see, the dark, clawed appendage swiping through the water to my right, as the music peals out a command of, "Capture."

Cold scales wrap around my body, pinning my arms and legs. As I thrash, they tighten, and as the water whooshes from my lungs and my ribs begin to creak, I stop struggling. For an instant, I close my eyes.

The unknown is always our greatest fear.

It is Darin's voice again, words he said to me once when I asked him why he wasn't afraid to go swimming off into unknown waters searching for wrecks. He'd told me he was afraid whenever he stayed safe inside Aquaticus's walls. As soon as he was outside, with the open ocean whipping around him and the taste of wild brine in his mouth, the fear always melted away.

I'm going to die anyway.

My eyes open. Slowly, I turn my head.

The orange eyes of the beast glow in the darkness. With my head at this angle, I can't see its entire body, but it is clearly massive, many times the size of the orcas I had controlled earlier in the day. Black scales flecked with white ash cover its massive frame. Needle-sharp teeth hang over its massive jaw, and I know if it didn't feel like incinerating me, it could rip my head from my body with a single bite.

"Orwell!" Circe's sweet, clear voice rings through the water, and, rotating my head as far as it will go, I see her, perched on the beast's neck in her Sea Enchantress form. "I have your little friend. Will you abandon her too?"

"Orwell, keep going!" My scream rips through the water before a musical command from Circe causes the monster's claw to constrict again. This time, the squeezing does not stop. Pain in my ribs grows from a sharp ache to a torturous stab. There is a snap, and I feel a bone break.

I cry out in agony. The claw loosens slightly, and in a moment of timelessness, Circe, the monster, and I wait. To see if Orwell will save himself a second time.

45

DARIN

THE GATE IS CLOSED. AND THERE IS NO sign of Locklyn or Orwell.

Or Circe.

Darin tenses as he swims toward the faintly glowing gate.

Once there, he examines the stones of the entrance, carefully avoiding any contact with the strands of silver pulsing between them. At first glance, there doesn't appear to be any way into the Loch without opening the entire gate, but he knows there must be a hatch somewhere. There is no way the Isja would risk the monster's escape every time it needed feeding.

He finally spots a stone unringed by silver spellwork. Placing both palms against it, he shoves hard. Nothing happens.

The gate is not only boulders thick, but magically reinforced. The absolute silence means nothing. Locklyn's corpse could be floating feet from him, her skin blackened, her blue hair turned ashy white.

Skimming the seam between the portal and the rocks around it, his fingers find a notched groove. A few inches further on, there is another. Then another, this one filled with a rounded metal peg. A swift count yields a total of twenty-one grooves and five metal pegs around the perimeter of the hatch.

It is some kind of puzzle. Right now, the odds of him figuring out the lock in time to help Locklyn are about as good as the Loch Ness monster spewing lecker from its jaws rather than magma.

He looks at the silver-laced stones towering above. To go over the gate would take time, but probably less than trying to figure out this lock. But still . . .

Wave Master.

He begins to move the pegs at random.

Help her.

Metal on stone.

Shut the monster's jaws.

Scrape, clink. Scrape, clink.

Don't let me be too late.

There is a grinding, clanking sound. Darin takes his hand away from the peg he just slid into one of the grooves, examining the portal. Nothing looks different, but when he pushes against the stone, it gives way, swinging inward.

The elation bubbling up inside turns to shards of ice as a heartrending shriek reverberates from within the lake. He throws himself through the barely open hatch, wriggling as his shoulders stick. The hatch must normally be held open by one person while the feeder dumps the bodies through.

He manages to pull himself through the opening, and the stone clatters back into place behind him.

Through the fine, white film of ash drifting in the water, he stares into the glowing eyes of the nightmare floating directly in front of the gate. Its fang-lined mouth opens at the sight of him, revealing a bubbling red spot at the back of its throat. But then, a strand of calming melody floats through the water, and the giant mouth slowly closes.

"Mr. Aalto."

It is the lovely, golden-haired woman, whose face above a cup of poisonously blue potion is his first memory. She is sitting sideways on the monster's neck, her light blue tail swaying gently.

The fingers of one hand encircle the silver locket clasped around her slim throat.

"How nice of you to join us."

46

LOCKLYN

I HEAR HIM THROUGH A HAZE OF PAIN.

"Let her go, Talia!"

I don't want him to come back.

She will just kill us both.

Even if he could somehow, miraculously, briefly incapacitate the monster, I can't swim. It is all I can do to keep from losing consciousness while dangling immobilized in the creature's claw. Every breath is agony, and I wonder dimly if my broken rib could have punctured my lung.

"Orwell." The word is barely a croak, but it is painful. I pull water into my lungs and know instantly that any chance of trying to control the creature with my voice is gone. The agony of singing in this condition would make controlling one of my own dugongs difficult.

I have to call out again and tell him to stay away. But at that moment, there is a flash of scarlet and green as Orwell hurtles in front of me to hover between me and the monster's jaws. He raises his arms, the movement somewhere between defense and pacification.

"Talia." His voice is throaty with emotion. "Talia, this is not who you are. You had the gentlest heart of anyone I have ever met.

You would never willingly harm another of the Wave Master's creatures. I beg you, do not do this. If you must exact retribution, take my life. Do not harm this girl, who has never wronged you and whose life is still before her. Do not destroy cities and kingdoms full of innocents. Doing so will not reverse the injury I did you."

"That was beautiful." Circe's voice is silky. She smiles at Orwell. "But you were always silver-tongued." Her words are growing hard and jagged. "I would never have come here with you otherwise, would I?"

"Talia, I–" Orwell begins, but she cuts him off.

"I should thank you. Once I was indeed soft. So soft that I allowed my heart to be carved into ribbons by a Merman who wasn't worth it."

Her eyes are darts. "My heart healed as it should have to survive, Lief. Hard. All those things I thought mattered when I knew you, love, family, and"–she scoffs–"sacrifice for others, were only myths. Fairy tales meant to keep people from pursuing the deeper, truer desires that drive them. The pain I endured and conquered was a gift." She smiles. "Because now I know the joy of inflicting pain on others."

Her white fingers flick open the clasp of the locket at her throat, and her lips move as she channels Llyra's voice. The monster's claw constricts around me again. I try to choke down my screams, but I hear another snap, and as a second rib breaks, a wail rips free.

"Locklyn!"

The voice is not Orwell's.

"Mr. Aalto." Circe's voice is silky once more. "How nice of you to join us."

I close my eyes, begging the Wave Master for the blackness of unconsciousness.

Because then I won't have to watch the man I love die.

47

DARIN

THE SOUND OF LOCKLYN'S SCREAM echoes through him.

He has no idea what kind of poison coats the darts in Igor's gun, but he pulls the tube to his lips, takes aim, and expels every ounce of water in his lungs. The dart embeds in Circe's neck, directly above the locket's chain. For an instant, she stares down at the finned head of the projectile, and then, as if in slow motion, her eyes close, and her body slips sideways, tumbling through the water next to the creature's face.

As her hold on the beast breaks, three things happen in quick succession. The creature releases Locklyn. She moans in pain. Orwell spins to catch her as she sinks, crying out again. And the monster of Loch Ness opens its mouth and brings its teeth together with a crunch on the body of the most famed enchantress under the sea.

"Aalto!"

He swiftly joins Orwell and reaches for Locklyn, who lets out a small cry as Orwell transfers her into his arms. "Follow me. Our only chance is if we can find somewhere to hide."

"Wait one moment!" Darin turns back toward the hatch. "There was no one to lock it behind me."

Orwell quickly propels himself over and slides his fingers under the edge of the bottom of the stone, pulling with all his strength. But above the grinding of stone on stone, there is another rumble. Whipping around, Darin sees the monster bearing down on them, its front teeth streaked with blood.

Locklyn whimpers as he shifts her weight to his left arm and pulls Igor's blowgun to his lips again. The dart lodges in the vertical black pupil of the creature's right eye. The monster bellows, and Darin expels water through the blowgun again, praying frantically that enough poison will be able to subdue a creature of this size.

But a stream of water is all the silver tube emits. The darts are gone.

"Orwell!"

The Schatzi's reply is drowned in a monstrous roar. One gargantuan limb claws at its eye as Darin spins toward the hatch. Orwell has managed to pry it open, but the crack is barely wide enough for a single Merperson. He will never be able to fit through carrying Locklyn.

"Orwell, go!"

"I can't leave you!"

"Then we'll all die." He forces himself to speak calmly. "Locklyn can't swim on her own, and I'm not leaving her. There's no way to save us, Orwell. But you can keep the others from waiting for us and risking recapture by the Isja. Please. Go quickly."

For an agonizing moment that feels like an eternity, the older Merman hesitates. Then he squirms into the crack he has created, wriggling to squeeze his body through. As the grating scrape of the hatch closing reverberates through the water, Darin realizes the monster has stopped bellowing. Turning, he sees a sight that causes him to back against the gate's stones, curling his body protectively around Locklyn's.

Blood dribbles down the center of the monster's injured eye, but its good eye is fixed on him and Locklyn. He braces himself for a pounce full of claws and teeth, but the creature remains still, observing them.

Then it opens its cavernous jaws so wide, Darin can see down its throat. A small spot of bubbling orange magma swirls, growing larger and larger.

Wave Master, let death be swift.

Don't let her suffer.

And a bubbling gush of liquid fire engulfs him.

48

LOCKLYN

WHEN DARIN PRESSED ME TO THE GATE'S stones, I was on the edge of consciousness. The light and heat explode, and I bite down, knowing that if I open my lips and inhale the blistering liquid rock, I will never be able to sing again.

I'm about to die. Why am I worried about singing?

Darin's body tightens against me as the wave of magma pours over him, and a moment later, agony sears over my skin as well. Fire is a torture artist, playing on the nerves with an excruciating pain like no other.

Soon I will not be able to keep my screams in.

Soon my vocal cords will rebel, responding to the agony rather than the signals my rational mind is trying to send.

I want to die.

When will blessed darkness come?

Darin spasms and lets out a guttural howl. I want to fight free of his arms, to cover him with my body, but I am too broken.

There is another flash, and I wait for another explosion of pain.

But it doesn't come.

Instead, arms wrap around the two of us as a shield, and everywhere the Stranger touches, cooling, soothing relief seeps into my skin. Through my eyelids, I can see light, no longer the orange glow of the magma, but a bright, steady, blue-white light. Slowly, I flicker my eyes open.

The Merman holding us is bigger than Orwell. Light emanates from every part of him–his tail, his arms, his torso, even his face, making his features difficult to discern. I look over his shoulder toward the monster and see, through the haze of blue-white light, that magma is still pouring from its jaws. There are walls of flame, over, under, and around us, but somehow we remain untouched.

The monster lets out a wrathful bellow, releasing another stream of magma. The Stranger releases us and turns.

"Enough."

With that one word, I know.

And I begin to tremble.

The Wave Master raises his arms, and as the stream of magma collides with the light emanating from his palms, it reverses course, flying back into the creature's open jaws. I watch as the creature's body convulses. It spasms harder and harder as the incoming magma fills its body. Then, at last, it disintegrates, turning into a billowing cloud of ash that surrounds us.

I can no longer see, but I hear the Voice, the one that makes my heart settle into peace and at the same time ache with longing. "Give her to me, Darin."

Arms take me, and I know that this Merman could crush my body with the tips of His fingers. With a single word. But there is nowhere else I would rather be.

"Come," the Wave Master says, and the ash suddenly clears away as the gate opens.

49

DARIN

I BELIEVED I WOULD ONE DAY SEE YOU IN Your Realm.

But You entered mine.

Darin follows the blue-white light away from the destruction of two of the most fearsome evils under the sea. The Wave Master leads him back along the river, setting a pace he can follow. His chest aches with a desire to hear that Voice again, a Voice which, despite his lack of memories, is as familiar as saltwater in his lungs.

They exit the Moray Firth, and the shining figure turns away from Svengd. Darin follows until they reach a strange tunnel of pure white rock. The Wave Master stops, Locklyn still cradled in His arms.

"Go through, Darin."

He is encouraging my heart's desire to seek the adventure of the unfamiliar, to pursue the lure of the unknown.

Darin plunges into the tunnel, swimming until it opens into a place so wonderful, he comes to an abrupt halt.

It is some sort of garden. White stones–similar to those with which the tunnel is made–stand at intervals, encrusted with sea urchins the color of Locklyn's hair. Swimming between them are pure white dolphins, the likes of which he has never seen before.

The sand below is as fine and sparkling as gold dust, and he is amazed to see sapphires, diamonds, and opals lying on the ground like pebbles. Silver kelp waves around the edges of the garden, and he is reminded of the oublier faire forest before he realizes something. This kelp is not emitting a scent. It is emitting a sound.

The kelp is singing.

At first, Darin can't understand the words, but as he listens, meaning begins to crystalize. The song is one of adoration, of wholeness, of knowing. True knowing that never grows dim or stale, but holds the lure of continued discovery with none of the fear.

He turns with widened eyes to the Wave Master, who smiles. Locklyn gazes up at Him, and Darin recognizes the expression of worship on her face, because he can feel it on his own.

"Well done."

There is no more pain. Locklyn utters a disbelieving cry of delight. It is gone, obliterated as though it had never been.

"Whatever you ask for is already accomplished," the Wave Master says. His eyes find Darin's. "What is it that you desire, Stellvertreter?"

The Schatzi word for your second. A deeper and stronger word than friend.

With a rush of joy, he realizes he can have all his memories back. The only One who is capable of such an impossible thing is before him, telling him that anything he asks for is as good as done.

I will remember every interaction with Locklyn.

Every quiet word from my brother's lips.

Every new wreck discovery.

Seeing The Surface.

Wrestling with my nephews.

I can have it all back.

But as his tongue moves to form the words, he sees the Mermaid he left behind in his mind's eye. A red-haired girl with blood soaking the sand beneath her body, her life ebbing away.

"I want to live," she had said to him.

His hand reaches unconsciously for his neck before falling

limply to his side. The clamshell necklace is gone, given back to Elle, but he knows, somewhere deep within, that it was the sign of a debt owed. A debt that must be repaid.

His mind fights to convince him there is another way for her. But he pushes such thoughts away, because his memories are not worth her life. And as surely as the One before him is his only chance at remembering, He is her only chance at living.

"Elle." He clears his throat. "She's near death, Wave Master. But I know you can still save her. I know you could even bring her back from the grave." He runs a hand through his hair, then drops it. "That is my request."

"It is done." The Wave Master's eyes do not leave his, and suddenly tears well.

I will never remember now.

Be comforted, my son.

It is the Wave Master's voice, but His lips are not moving, and it is clear these words are for Darin alone.

It is in the emptiness you will hear me in a way you never did when your mind was full.

He looks into the Wave Master's face.

Then it is worth it.

He doesn't know how long the Wave Master looks at him. Eternity and a split second.

Both and neither.

Then His gaze drops to the blue-haired Mermaid in His arms. "And you, dear one?"

50

LOCKLYN

I LOOK DOWN AT MY LEGS. ONCE UPON a time, my request would have been for a tail. For the acceptance and ease it would have brought with it.

My eyes lift to the face of the Merman hovering beside us. Once upon a time, my request would have been that my feelings for him would vanish if he didn't reciprocate them.

His golden eyes meet mine, and my heart aches with love and longing. He just gave his hope for memories away, willingly, so that Elle would have another chance at life. And I know what I want to ask for, but as I open my mouth, something holds the words back.

My mind goes to my home, embroiled in a senseless war of revenge. I remember the days in Imber–shark tooth-encrusted walls and a fire river and the stern, beautiful people there. I see Ginevra, huddled into a ball beside the submarine's wall in the middle of the night, her strong bravado broken as she weeps for the little sister she longs to fight beside. I glimpse Conway staring through the submarine's front window with glazed eyes, guilt over his family's aggression eating into his soul.

I want Darin's memory to come back. All the experiences we once shared now live only in my mind, and that hurts my heart. I know it will take decades for the sting of that loss to fade, if it ever does. Looking into the eternal eyes above me, I am sure He will not reproach me if I ask for Darin's memory to return.

Nevertheless.

"I want peace between Undula and Nebula," I find myself saying. "Not tenuous peace that could break at any moment. True peace. True unity. True striving for the other nation's good." I smile a little shyly at the Wave Master. "All my life, I would have said that such a thing was impossible. But not for You."

He does not speak, but He smiles and raises one hand. As if in response, the singing of the kelp swells to a crescendo, and images begin to swirl before us in the water.

A red-haired Mermaid lying on black sand stirs and opens her eyes. She pushes herself into a sitting position, hands patting at her torso, clearly looking for a wound. Then she shoots upward, laughing aloud as she spins in a circle, her body unbroken and gloriously alive.

The image fades, and another forms.

A small, pale Merman whom I recognize as Undula's steward, Wyre, is talking to a large Merman dressed in the uniform of a general. "The king is gravely ill. I considered this campaign ill-advised from the start, and now it must come to an end. Withdraw your troops, and pray that Prince Conway returns home swiftly."

The image fades.

"It is done," the Wave Master says again, and sudden, terrible realization floods me.

"You're going to leave," I say, around the hot lump swelling in my throat.

"You will see me again, beloved."

"I know." Tears come now, rolling in steaming trails down my cheeks.

His embrace grows stronger, and through the mist of my tears, I see him extend his other arm to Darin. As He holds us both, the kelp's singing swells again, the music speaking of joy and pain, having and losing, already and not yet.

When the music fades, I open my eyes, and the Wave Master

and His garden are gone. Darin and I are just outside Svengd, his arms holding me up. The burns are gone, but the pain in my sides has returned, and I realize that, for whatever reason, the Wave Master chose to leave the healing of my ribs to time.

I look up at Darin, and the sight of his face causes tears to well in my eyes again. "He's gone."

"I don't have any words." Darin gazes off into the distance. "But you know what it was like. What He was like." His arms tighten ever so slightly around me. "And, Locklyn, even though my other memories will never come back, you and I will always share this one. The best one of all."

The truth of his words sends warmth flooding through me. "You're right." The pain in my sides won't allow me to raise my arms, but I lay my head on Darin's chest, and he holds me, gently nuzzling his nose into my hair.

"Locklyn." Something in Darin's voice causes me to open my eyes.

"What?"

"Look down."

"You already know my legs are back, Darin."

"Something else is back too."

I look down. Silver and blue sparkles on my right ankle.

Even though it wasn't even a thought to ask, You knew how much it meant to me. To both of us. Thank you.

51

LOCKLYN

I DRIFT AWAKE AND HEAR GINEVRA AND Conway. They're sitting across from me, leaning against the submarine wall, their shoulders barely touching. Near them, a sleeping Orwell lies on his back, soft snores vibrating his enormous body. I lie still, fearful of the discomfort I know will break through the pain-relieving herbs Darin gives me every few hours, if I make the slightest movement.

"What now?" Conway says.

"Now you get a chance to put all your newfound maturity to use being Undula's new king. At least according to Darin and Locklyn."

"Crazy, eh?" Conway's voice is disbelieving. "That they actually met the Wave Master. And He gave them whatever they wanted."

"Not whatever they wanted." Ginevra muses. "Or Aalto would have his memories back. You know, if it were anyone else telling a story like that, I'd say they'd sniffed dried oublier faire."

"We saw the lake. The monster's gone."

"Not being the one with no memories, I am aware of that," Ginevra retorts. "I wasn't saying I don't believe them. I was saying if it was anyone other than Darin and Locklyn, I probably would think the narrative had been embellished."

There is a pause. Then Conway says, "You think I've matured?"

Ginevra's scoff causes me to smile. "Enough that I'll expect Undula's collapse in ten years rather than a month."

"Funnily enough, that means more to me than if anyone else told me I'd be the best king Undula has ever seen."

"Because you'd know that was a bold-faced lie."

"You're right, I would know that."

"Don't agree with me. It makes me nervous." She smiles at him, her usually hard face alight with something that makes my heart ache.

"I wish I could agree with you, Ginevra." His voice is suddenly sober.

"About what?" Her smile fades.

"You know about what." He turns to look her full in the face.

For a long, dreadful moment, there is silence.

He speaks again. "That's why I asked how you want it to be now. Do we go back to you hating me? Do we pretend the other doesn't exist until forced to meet at diplomatic events?"

"Is that how you want it to be?" There is no anger in her tone, only soul-crushing weariness.

"I want to stop hurting you." His voice is sincere. "I kept trying to force our friendship to continue all this time out of selfishness. Because there's no one else under the sea whom I can rile up as easily as you. No one else who will go on any adventure I ask them to. No one else who will stick sea urchin spines in my ego the second it gets the slightest bit inflated. Our friendship is one of a kind, because you are." He swallows deeply. "I didn't mean to say all that. What I meant to say was that I've kept trying to revive our friendship. And I shouldn't have. Because I think . . . you'll always hope that it will turn into more. And you'll keep being hurt when it doesn't."

She doesn't say anything. I half-expect tears, but her body remains still and silent as she continues to stare at her own pearly tail, twisting her braids between her fingers.

"Ginevra?" Conway says at last.

"I think it would hurt me more to lose you entirely." The words are business-like, but as she turns to look at him, I catch a glimpse of her face, and vulnerability rests there. "If you ever found someone else, I might feel differently, but for now . . ." She pauses, and the side of her mouth tips in a sad smile. "Be my friend, Conway. I won't ask for more." Her lips curve higher. "But I can't promise I won't be a sea slug to you again."

"I would have known that was a bold-faced lie."

She shoves his shoulder hard, and he bursts out laughing. "One more thing, Conway."

"Yes?"

"Stop calling me Ginevra."

52

DARIN

THE SUBMARINE SHUDDERS TO A STOP for the first time in two weeks. He glances at Locklyn, who leans gingerly against the side of the submarine, and then at the red-haired maiden close by.

"We're here," Conway says.

Stillness envelopes the craft. Then, as Elle turns to look out of the porthole beside her, Darin approaches Conway where he hovers next to the submarine controls. "Are you sure about swimming to Aquaticus from here?"

Conway's shoulders rise in a brief shrug. "It's only a three-day swim. I'll have Kai. Besides, Ginny's return to Imber shouldn't be delayed any more than it has to be."

Darin glances back at Ginevra, who sits in a corner with Michal and Kai. "I'm surprised she agreed to coming here first," he says, lowering his voice.

"As much as she wants to see Rihanna, I think she realized that forcing Elle's parents to wait any longer to discover their only daughter was alive would be a tad selfish." Conway hesitates, then drops his voice as well. "Speaking of selfishness, I'm wishing Orwell hadn't decided to stay up north and help the other contestants find a way home. I could have used his help with running a country for the first time. Especially since Igor might decide to return to the Mediterranean and muster an army to exact revenge."

"Do you think he's still alive?"

"I hope he got eaten by an orca. But that seems like too much to hope for."

"It doesn't seem possible he just vanished. I was sure the potion would keep him unconscious for a while."

"Maybe none of his concoctions have the same effect on him as on other Merpeople."

"Darin?" Elle's voice causes both to turn. The red-haired girl is hovering next to the submarine door, Locklyn beside her. "Will you come with me? To meet my parents? They'll want to thank you."

His eyes flicker to Ginevra, and her jaw tightens. "Go," she acquiesces after a moment. "But if you're not back in an hour, I'm leaving without you."

"Understood," he says, fighting to repress a smile as he claps Conway's shoulder. "We'll see you as soon as everything in Imber is resolved. Safe swimming, my friend."

Conway looks sideways at him. "If we're friends, then the emeralds must be forgiven and forgotten?"

A grin spreads across his face. "I've definitely forgotten them." Conway reddens and begins to apologize, but Darin forestalls him. "They'd be forgiven even if I could remember."

There is a pause, then the prince of Undula clasps Darin's hand and shakes it vigorously. Then Conway swims toward the submarine door, only looking back to say, "Coming, Kai?"

Kai rises from his position next to Michal. "I'm afraid not, Your Highness."

Conway gives a wry smile. "To think it only took numerous near-death experiences and a trip halfway around the world for you to grow a sense of humor."

Kai looks puzzled. "I'm not joking, Highness." He looks down at Michal, and something that is almost a smile flits across his face. "I will be making my new home in Imber with my wife. I am interested to learn their methods of mulciber husbandry."

"Your wife?" Conway's gaze flashes to Michal, whose eye is fixed on Kai. The prince throws back his head and laughs. "Kai, you sly cuttlefish!" Still chuckling, he swims over and takes Michal's hand. "For your lovely lady's sake, I suppose I'll have to forgive you for forcing me to endure three days of nothing but my own company."

"Darin?" Elle's voice is hesitant. He immediately leaves the bemusing scene and joins her and Locklyn.

"I'm sorry. Lead the way."

Locklyn's eyes flicker back toward Conway. "Safe swimming," she says kindly.

"Thank you." The prince's tone is curt, but pain masquerades as bravado in his eyes.

Elle pushes the door open, swimming out into the main street of Proluvies. Darin gestures for Locklyn to go ahead and pull the door closed behind them. As soon as the metal blocks Conway's line of sight, he loops his arm around her waist, supporting her.

"I guess they've never seen a submarine before." The smile in Locklyn's voice directs his gaze, and his mouth quirks at the sight of a crowd of some twenty merchildren, gawking at the silver monstrosity.

One of them, a girl with white-blonde braids looped around her head, suddenly lets out a gasp. "Elle?"

"Sereia?"

The other merchildren scatter as the little Mermaid darts through them, pushing those who are slow to move out of her way. "Elle! We thought you were dead! After the Atlanteans came . . . we were sure . . . no one ever returns . . ." She babbles as she flings her arms around Elle's waist, squeezing tightly. Sereia looks up into the red-haired Mermaid's face. "Do your parents know?"

"I'm going to see them now," Elle says.

"I'll go tell them! They'll be so ha–"

"No." The word is sharp, and Sereia flinches. Elle's tone softens. "Please. I haven't seen them in over a year. They don't even know I'm alive. I need to talk to them alone."

Sereia's expression is one of confusion, but she nods. "What about Pike? He went to look for you."

Elle looks in the girl's face, voice quiet. "He didn't make it, Ser."

Sereia's face goes slack, then taut. "How do you know?"

Elle touches the whole clamshell resting against her chest, and she gestures to Darin. "This is Darin. He brought me Pike's half of the necklace. He saw it happen."

"You weren't even with him? So he might still be–"

"He's dead." Elle's words are harsh in her grief.

Sereia gulps at the water around her as though it has suddenly become solid. She struggles to speak. "Who are they?"

"They're the reason I'm alive."

"But my brother's never coming back." Sereia's words catch in her throat. "My brother's never coming back, and you don't even care." She pivots and swims away, her shoulders heaving.

Elle's body is rigid as she turns abruptly and swims in the opposite direction, past the sea-snail-shaped buildings lining the street. Locklyn glances up at him, her eyes gray with concern before they follow.

As Elle's pace shows no sign of slowing, he feels Locklyn lean more heavily against him, her breathing becoming ragged. Pausing, he scoops her into his arms.

He nudges his nose against her temple. "If my ribs had been broken two weeks ago, I'd still be lying on the floor of that submarine."

She gives a weak smile, then sobers. "Pike's sister. That was awful, Darin."

"I wish I could remember. It might have eased some of the pain–just to know." Elle goes up an anemone-lined path to a domed house far larger than any they have passed. For a moment, the red-haired girl hesitates before bending down and blowing into the conch shell embedded into the wall next to the door.

The door opens.

The Mermaid hovering there is well-dressed, her purple jacket lined with threads of gold. Her face is not that of an old Merwoman, but her hair is as white as sea foam, bleached by intense suffering. As her eyes light on Elle, her face transforms, years falling from her like water at The Surface.

She flings her arms around her daughter as she shrieks, "Wade!" Within seconds, a Merman appears in the doorway behind her.

He stills, then tears come to his eyes. "The Wave Master has not forgotten us." He gathers his wife and child in an enveloping hug.

He looks over his reunited family's heads to Darin and Locklyn. "If you are responsible for bringing her back to us, thank you."

Elle's head comes up, and she quickly makes introductions.

"The pleasure is ours, sir," says Darin. "Elle will explain more in your time together, but meanwhile, the two of us must be off."

They bid their farewells, and as the door shuts, he says, "I think they have plenty to catch up on without you and me." He smiles. "And besides, I'm not risking Ginevra leaving without us. I need to drop you both off in Imber so I can go treasure hunting for an anklet."

53

LOCKLYN

I HAD NOT THOUGHT ABOUT THE FACT that peace cannot automatically undo the ravages of war.

But I think about it now as I hover with Ginevra, Michal, Kai, and Darin in front of Imber's gates. All along the banks of the Ustrina River, the helena algae that Merfolk plant on graves glows. There are so many that shimmering ribbons of gold line the red belly of the river on either side.

It is beautiful.

And yet tragic.

Tears stream down Michal's cheeks, but Ginevra's face could be carved of stone. She does not say anything, but turns away from what is now the River of Death and stares at the top of the wall. A moment later, the gates creak open.

Ginevra swims through so quickly that I have to climb onto Darin's back, looping my legs around his waist. "I'll never be able to keep up with her."

As we pass through Imber's streets in Ginevra's wake, I see Merfolk pointing at us and whispering. When they see me looking at them, they pull back, melting into doors or withdrawing down side streets.

I am about to say something to Darin when I hear a voice. "Well, well, well. Look who's returned to save her baby sister's hide."

We all turn to see the Mermaid I remember from the Council meeting, the one with yellow snake eyes. Two of the largest topazes I have ever seen sparkle in her earlobes. Clearly, the war has created no hardship for her.

"What are you talking about, Laguna?" Ginevra's question is frosted with dislike.

"Oh, haven't you heard?" Laguna moves closer to the Nebulae queen. What little deference she had possessed at the Council meeting is gone. "Rihanna Kaveri has been imprisoned as an accomplice to espionage. The fact that you, as the queen, left such an individual as regent calls your abilities as monarch into question. Prominent members of the Council are calling for the removal of the entire Kaveri family from power."

"Prominent members such as yourself?"

"You helped find a treasure which enabled Malik to hire the mercenaries who were nearly able to overcome our defenses. You have been absent during this entire conflict, leaving the defense of your people to others. And you left a child in power, who was not only too weak to lead our warrior maidens to victory, but was romantically involved with the spy who betrayed valuable secrets to the enemy."

Ginevra does not deign to respond. She spins away from Laguna, showering the latter with bubbles as she churns up the street. We reach the palace, and I slide off Darin's back as Ginevra speeds toward the massive iron gong–clearly mulciber-made–that sits beside the front doors. But before she touches the mallet, Michal catches hold of her arm.

"What are you doing?"

"Calling the warrior council. I intend to show them exactly how their queen deals with sedition and treason."

"Evrie, we have to see Rihanna first. We need to know what happened. If we come before the council without a basic knowledge of the facts, we will be playing directly into the hands of those who say we are unfit to rule."

Ginevra's fingers twitch, but her reply is calm as she says, "You're right."

The guard beside the door, who has been gawking at us as though unable to believe her eyes, falls into a bow as Ginevra faces her. "Lead me to the prisoner Rihanna Kaveri."

"Yes, lady."

We are led through the palace not, as I would have expected, to an underground cell, but to a room in the royal wing containing Ginevra's chambers. The guard stationed outside snaps to attention at the sight of the queen.

"I require an audience with your prisoner," Ginevra says regally.

The guards exchange glances. "Lady, the Council moved that, due to the severity of the charges against her, this prisoner was to be kept in solitar–"

Ginevra's knife flies from her hand. It misses the guard's ear by a breath and embeds itself, quivering, in the mortar between two stones.

"Open the door." Ginevra punctuates each word with a more intense glare, and the guard darts forward, fumbling with a key. The door swings wide, and Ginevra sweeps inside.

"I'd like to see them try to depose her," Darin remarks in a whisper as we follow.

The Mermaid huddled on a bed raises her head, and her tear-streaked face lights up. "Ginevra? Michal? Oh, oh!" She bursts into tears again as she throws herself at her two older sisters. Michal embraces her tightly, but Ginevra stands apart.

If I hadn't seen her the day Hugo arrived with Rihanna's message, I'd think she didn't care at all.

"Rihanna. Pull yourself together."

"Evrie–" Michal starts, but Ginevra yanks Rihanna from their sister's embrace. With a shove, she sends her reeling backward onto the bed.

"What is all this about you being romantically involved with a traitor?"

Rihanna chokes on a sob, but answering anger flickers to life in her eyes. "He isn't a traitor. He was told those notes he was placing on the wreck were love notes for an Undulae soldier."

"He?"

Rihanna hesitates, then says slowly, "Brosnan."

"The scullery boy?"

"Yes."

Ginevra's eyes narrow. When she speaks, something in her tone has changed. "How serious is it between the two of you?"

"I was going to marry him someday." Rihanna is defiant, but I can see anxiety sparkling behind the bravado in her eyes.

Ginevra opens the door. "Send for the prisoner Brosnan Shoal." The door clicks shut again as she turns back to Rihanna. "Tell me everything."

"I sent Hugo to find you the day after Undula attacked. I hoped you would come back, but I knew it would be at least a few weeks before I could expect you, so I gathered the most prominent warriors from the Council and began to plan a campaign. As soon as we had a plan, we tried to break the siege. But every move we made was countered so exactly by Malik's troops, and I began to suspect that whoever had been leaving messages on the wreck was still passing the Undulae information.

Rihanna draws in a deep breath before continuing. "Finally," she says, "after I was forced to instate food rationing, I planned a last attempt to break out of the city. I commissioned the mulcibers to construct seven heat-resistant suits from the skins of fire eels. Then I and six of our most skilled warriors swam out through the Ustrina River under the city gate. But when we surfaced, the River was lined with Undulae soldiers waiting for us."

A choked sob erupts from the youngest Nebulae princess's lips. Ginevra lowers herself onto the bed beside her sister, and motions for her to continue.

"I shouted at my team to go back," Rihanna explains, "but

Undulae archers were raining down arrows on us. I don't know how I made it back to the gate. None of the others did." Rihanna's breathing becomes ragged as she struggles to speak, fighting down the sobs threatening to break through. "The next day, Brosnan was arrested. The General told me she had received a tip from someone who had seen him depositing messages in the cleaned-out wreck on the Undula border. Brosnan admitted to leaving messages in the wreck, but he claimed a Mermaid had paid him to place the messages there for her lover who was an Undulae soldier."

"What Mermaid?" Ginevra asks.

"He didn't know. She wore a mask whenever they met because she didn't want the General to find out she was being courted by an Undulae. I tried to help him." Rihanna's eyes swim in a sheen of green. "I testified to his character before the Council. When they asked how I knew him, I told them the truth. But then they said our relationship was clearly the reason Brosnan had access to secret military plans. So they locked me up too, as an accomplice to treason."

There is silence, broken by a knock on the door. It opens to reveal Brosnan, looking much worse for wear than the time I saw him at the throwing range. His dark hair hangs nearly to his shoulders, framing a face disfigured by two spectacular black eyes and a split lip. But his swollen mouth still tips in a smile as Rihanna springs off the bed and rushes to him.

"Brosnan! What have they been doing to you?"

"Apparently, not meeting your quota of posidonia fiber ropes is frowned upon," Brosnan says lightly. He gazes at her. "I've missed you, Ri."

"Oh, Brosnan, I–"

"Enough." Ginevra's clear voice causes the young Merpeople to spring apart, but instead of looking piqued as I expected, Rihanna's face is alight.

"Everything will be alright now that Ginevra's back, Brosnan. She'll get us both out and make Malik catch the first blue whale out of the Mediterranean."

"We'll see about that." Ginevra's face and voice are expressionless. "Brosnan, is it? Tell me about the Mermaid who hired you to act as a messenger. When did she first approach you?"

"It was the day Michal was instated as regent, my lady. A masked Mermaid approached me as I was leaving the throwing range. She told me she was in love with an Undulae soldier, but due to the rising tension between our two countries, she didn't think it would be wise to let the General find out about their relationship. She gave me directions to a wreck on the Undula-Nebula border and asked me to leave a message next to the main mast, promising to pay me handsomely. No offense, my lady, but your kitchen staff is none too well paid. I took the job."

Ginevra's lips twitch, but all she says is, "Did you bring messages back from the wreck for this Mermaid?"

"Yes. A few days after I dropped off her message, she asked me to go and check if there was any reply. There was, so I brought it back to her. We began to fall into a rhythm–she would bring me a new message to deliver every few days, and after delivering her message, I would return later to collect the reply. She paid well, and even after the war with Undula started, I never suspected that the messages I had been delivering were anything but love notes."

"I know the Mermaid you worked for was masked, but was there anything distinctive about her?"

"Her clothes were too perfect," Brosnan says immediately. "I could tell she was trying to dress plainly, but there were no tears or stains, and her jerkins were made of sealskin, not posidonia fiber. She couldn't hide the fact she was rich."

"Laguna is one of the Council's most prominent members," Michal says thoughtfully, then looks at her sister. "But you said you were the only one who made it back to the city after the ambush in the River. Why wasn't she with you?"

"She was sick," Rihanna answers her.

"Sick?" Michal raises a brow. "Sick enough to miss a major battle?"

"That little sea snake." Ginevra's voice bites. "She must have begun plotting with Malik as soon as I left, thinking there was a high probability I would never return. I'm sure their bargain was that she would give Malik enough information for him to successfully conquer Nebula, and in return, he would instate her as his representative as soon as the war was over."

"We have to have proof, Evrie," Michal tells her. "After the war and your absence, Nebula needs stability. Starting another fight will only rip the country apart further."

Ginevra is still for a moment, then she nods to Michal. "You're right."

"Conway." Every head turns to Darin. "Send a mulciber to Aquaticus, asking him to confront his father," he says. "Malik is ill. His attempt to seize control of Nebula was a failure. He will have no reason to continue shielding Laguna, and he will probably be happy to have someone else on whom to cast blame."

"It's a start," Ginevra considers. "But Laguna will likely claim Malik is using her as a scapegoat. The Council will be more likely to trust the word of one of their own than the king of an enemy nation. Michal's right. It would be better if we had some sort of solid evidence."

"The earrings," I say suddenly. "The topaz earrings she was wearing when we just saw her. I've seen them before, on Llyra's ship. Conway brought them back as part of Undula's portion of the treasure. Malik must have given them to her as an advance payment for her services. Something to tide her over until she was able to assume the throne of Imber."

"That"–Ginevra points at me–"is the tangible proof we need. Michal and Kai, go and send a mulciber message to Conway. I will ask the General to set Rihanna and Brosnan's trial date for two days from now." Her smile is cynical. "We don't want Laguna to realize she is actually the one being tried."

54

DARIN

LOCKLYN TRIED TO DESCRIBE THE Council meeting she witnessed. But I don't think anything could have prepared me for this.

The pounding of the spears seems to reverberate in his chest as he and Locklyn hover near the doors to Imber's great hall.

"It's not the same without Rihanna's trident," Locklyn whispers, but he only has time to give her a confused glance before the thumping abruptly ceases.

"Warriors." Ginevra's clear voice rings to the furthest corners of the room.

"Lady." The bow of the Mermaids filling the room is as fluid and seamless as the breaking of an ocean wave.

"You all know we are gathered to expose and punish the treacherous in our midst." Ginevra stretches a hand toward the hall's doors, which swing slowly open. The crowd of Mermaids parts to the sides of the room, creating a pathway down which Rihanna and Brosnan swim, flanked by two guards. "In accordance with the laws of Nebula, I, as the monarch, will be joined in my judgment by the six judges currently presiding over the legal affairs of our nation."

Six Mermen swim out from the doorway behind Ginevra,

flanking her as she looks down at Rihanna and Brosnan. "Who accuses Rihanna Kaveri and Brosnan Shoal?" the queen asks.

"I do." Laguna emerges from the warriors on the room's left side. The onyxes in her incisors glint as she glances up at Ginevra. "As the one who first exposed Brosnan's treachery, I will plead our nation's cause against him."

"And who will defend the accused?"

"I will." Michal advances from the right side of the room. "As the heir to Nebula's throne, I have an interest in protecting both our nation and the ruling family."

"Wave Master as your witness, do you both swear on your spears to uphold truth, justice, and the interests of the Nebulae people?" This question is posed by a Merman with close-cropped black curls hovering to Ginevra's right.

"We do," Michal and Laguna answer in unison.

"Then let the accuser speak."

Laguna swims forward, her hands clasped loosely in front of her. "About three months ago, Brosnan Shoal approached me while I was on guard duty. He asked me to open the gates to allow him to hunt for mulciber cast-offs on the bank of the Ustrina. Thinking nothing of it, I allowed him to leave the city. However, as Brosnan's excursions started to become regular, I began to grow suspicious. Three days after Rihanna Kaveri was instated as regent, he approached me again. After letting him out, I asked a friend to take over my post and swam after him. He led me to a wreck on the border between Undula and Nebula. I watched him leave a bottle containing a message next to the mast. When he returned to the city, I retrieved the bottle and read the message inside. It was addressed to King Malik, informing him that Nebula's fate rested in the hands of a fifteen-year-old, and advising him that now would be an ideal moment to attack."

"Permission to speak?" Michal lifts a hand and, at Ginevra's nod, continues. "You say you discovered this incriminating message over two months ago. Why did you fail to bring it to the attention of the General until recently?"

"I wanted to see if Brosnan Shoal was acting alone," Laguna responds smoothly. "A scullery boy seemed an unlikely mastermind for treason, so I bided my time, knowing if I accused Brosnan, the true traitor would become so cautious, apprehending them would prove almost impossible. However, as it became clear that Malik was receiving inside intelligence, preventing us from breaking Imber's siege, I decided I must reveal my knowledge to the General. When Princess Rihanna disclosed her romantic entanglement with Brosnan Shoal, it was evident to me that she must be the true traitor to Nebula."

"What reasonable motive could Princess Rihanna have for betraying Nebula to Malik?" Michal asks.

"As third sister, her likelihood of ever inheriting the crown was negligible. Desiring to become queen, she made a deal with Malik that if she handed him the information necessary to conquer Nebula, he would make her queen under him once his campaign was successful."

"This is surmise," Michal states. "You have no proof of this other than Princess Rihanna's connection to Brosnan Shoal."

"Oh, but I do." Laguna's smile is that of a shark. "If you go to Princess Rihanna's room, you will discover a pair of topaz earrings, which Malik received as part of Undula's share of Llyra's Treasure. I have here a message from Wyre, King Malik's steward, stating he was asked to send these topaz earrings to Malik's contact in Imber about a month ago."

Darin's jaw tightens.

Laguna had beaten them at their own game. She had planted the earrings on Rihanna.

There is silence at the declaration. He can tell Michal is frantically thinking, despite her calm expression. Then a voice rings through the great hall.

"I challenge the accuser."

55
DARIN

NOT AGAIN.

Locklyn's face has gone ashen, and Ginevra's fingers are clenched tightly around the railing in front of her. Rihanna's head is buried in her hands, and her shoulders shake. Only Michal is serene, her single eye fixed unwaveringly on Laguna's astonished face.

"You say Rihanna Kaveri betrayed the kingdom of Nebula to King Malik with the knowledge and aid of Brosnan Shoal in hopes of securing a crown. But I say it was you who betrayed Nebula and tricked Brosnan Shoal into being your messenger in hopes of seizing power. I say that you would not know about the topaz earrings in Rihanna Kaveri's room if you had not placed them there yourself, in a final attempt to discredit the Kaveri family and gain the throne." Michal draws herself up. "In accordance with the laws of Nebula, I challenge you to mortal combat, staking my life on Rihanna Kaveri's innocence."

Laguna's expression morphs from one of surprise to one of intense satisfaction. "I accept your challenge. And when your body lies beneath a helena plant near the Ustrina River, all will know that truth is on my side, and the Kaveri family has lost their right to rule Nebula." She holds her head high. "Our battle will take place at once. And our weapons will be bows and arrows. I don't want to soil my hands."

"How can you fight a duel with bows and arrows?" Locklyn whispers frantically.

Darin shrugs, his heart heavy as Michal and Laguna swim through the double doors, the entire company behind them.

Their route leads to a training facility on the outskirts of the city. In the center of a courtyard is a long, rectangular glass enclosure. Two hunks of rock stand at opposite ends of it, chains embedded in their rough surfaces. Michal and Laguna enter the enclosure and each swims to a rock, waiting in silence for the warriors who have followed them inside to tighten the metal manacles around their waists. Each length of chain is long enough to allow for small sideways movements, but nothing more.

Ginevra comes beside him and Locklyn. The queen's jaw is locked, but he sees she is trembling. Locklyn reaches for her hand, and, to his surprise, the queen of the Nebulae does not pull away.

The attendants hand wooden bows with strings of jelly thread to each of the Merwomen, looping quivers of dart-like, metal arrows over their shoulders. His eyes scan Michal's quiver, tallying quickly.

Seven arrows.

The black-haired Merman from the Council chamber moves forward. He holds a large pink conch in his hands. "Are the contestants ready to begin?"

Wave Master, you know her vision is impaired. Guide her arrows.

The blast of the conch shatters the stillness. Michal draws and nocks an arrow, and in the fluid motion, he catches a glimpse of the archer she once was. But as the arrow leaves her bow, the trajectory is wildly off. It flies far to Laguna's left, pinging off the glass in the corner of the enclosure.

An instant later, Ginevra lets out a strangled moan as Laguna's arrow soars through Michal's blind spot, carving a jagged, red slash into the skin of her shoulder. Laguna's teeth glisten as she fires a second arrow. Michal lunges sideways, anticipating Laguna's strategy of targeting her left side, but the chain impedes her motion and the arrow nicks her ear.

Michal lets another arrow fly, but overcorrects her previous shot. The projectile shoots harmlessly past Laguna's other side. Another of Laguna's arrows grazes Michal's arm. The water around Nebula's second princess grows cloudy, tinged with red.

His mind fills with memories of Michal over the past month. Her perpetual kindness. Her dry wit. Her humble spirit. His eyes shut of their own accord, because he cannot bear to watch any more. He knows how this fight will end.

It is a heart-wrenching scream from Rihanna that finally pulls his eyes open again.

The water seems to dim, tunneling his vision onto the arrow embedded in Michal's stomach. The regent of Nebula's head dips, looking down at her waist. Then her arm bends back, pulling an arrow from her quiver. Time slows as she pulls the shaft to her ear.

And lets it fly.

Its path is straight.

Laguna is looking out into the crowd, smirking in celebration of her lethal hit, when Michal's arrow buries itself in her throat. For a heartbeat, a look of shock crosses the Mermaid's face before she collapses through a crimson cloud of her own blood to the sand below.

The crowd roars, but Michal makes no move to celebrate her victory. Instead, she slides back through the water to lean against the rock behind her, one hand clamping convulsively around the arrow in her abdomen, while the other opens, allowing her bow to fall to the ground.

The Merman arbitrating the competition enters the enclosure and bends over Laguna's prone form. When he straightens again, his voice rings over the now-silent crowd. "Laguna Reva is dead." He looks toward the rock where Michal slumps, eyes open but glazed with pain. "Truth awards victory. Rihanna Kaveri and Brosnan Shoal are hereby declared innocent through the triumph of Michal Kaveri. By the power bestowed on me as head of the Council, I declare this matter closed." He swims from the enclosure, making a motion to two of the warriors waiting outside as he does so. They enter, lifting Laguna's body, and swim slowly back out and toward Imber's gates.

"Fetch a physician." Ginevra's voice is uneven.

When no one moves to fulfill Ginevra's order, Darin opens his mouth to reiterate her words, only to be stopped by a voice of command slicing through the water. "The queen requires a physician." Rihanna's face is taut with strain, but her voice is loud and clear. As soon as several attendants dart away, she swims to her older sister. "Evrie."

The sound of Michal's pet name for her seems to do something to Ginevra. Catching hold of Rihanna's elbow, she swims toward the enclosure's door. The crowd melts away before her. As she reaches the door, she turns back. "Come," she says to them.

"Where's Kai?" Darin asks, suddenly struck by his absence.

"He stayed up all night, helping to nurse an injured mulciber." Locklyn swallows. "Michal told me she sent him to bed. She didn't think he needed to see the trial."

As they enter the enclosure, the metallic scent of blood fills the water. Ginevra and Rihanna hover beside Michal, who seems to be struggling to remain conscious.

"We've sent for the physician, Michal." Rihanna's voice is no longer commanding, but tremulous.

"Thanks, Ri."

"Michal, he'll be here any minute." Ginevra's tone is sharp in her suppressed anxiety. "Any minute. You have to stay awake."

"You know no doctor . . . can fix this." The words are slurred as Michal's eyelids flutter more and more rapidly.

"Don't say that, Michal." Tears begin to slip down Rihanna's face, and she clutches at her sister with her still-chained hands.

"Listen." Michal draws in a labored breath as she attempts to hitch herself higher on the rock. "No, Evrie, listen. Tell Kai I'm sorry." A single green tear leaks down her cheek. "I wanted to have a life with him."

A choked sob beside him turns his eyes to Locklyn. She is hunched over as if in physical pain, weeping into her hands. He wraps his arms around her, drawing her into his side.

"I'm . . . going to the Wave Master." Michal's eyes begin to drift closed. "Don't worry about me." Her trembling hands reach to weakly grasp her sisters' hands. "But I'm . . . worried. About you . . . two."

"You don't have to be." Ginevra is not crying, but the agony in her voice speaks of sorrow too deep for tears. Her free arm goes around Rihanna's waist as she pulls her sobbing younger sister close.

"Good." A sigh slips from Michal's lips. "Nebula . . . will be safe . . . in your hands, Evrie. Be . . . her friend . . . Ri. Locklyn . . . Darin . . . don't let your . . . children forget what . . . we fought for."

"We won't." The words barely make it past the lump in his throat.

"Evrie." The whisper is barely audible.

"Yes, Michal?"

"Will you . . . do something . . . for me?"

"Anything, sister."

"Take care . . . of Hugo." Michal's eyes close as she exhales one final time.

56

LOCKLYN

WHEN I FINALLY GET MY ARMS AROUND my sister, I don't let go. Over Amaya's shoulder, my gaze catches the stunned and slightly concerned faces of my nephews, but in my mind's eye, I see Michal's lifeless body with her sisters bent over it—Rihanna hysterical with grief and Ginevra still and silent, looking as though her soul had died with her sister.

After several moments have passed, Amaya tries to ease away, but I hold on even tighter. I feel the bubbles of her breath in my ear as she whispers, "I thought you'd be angry at me."

Now I do pull away, looking into her face. "Why would I be angry at you?"

"I tried to stop you from going." Tears well in her eyes. "I knew how selfish I was being at the time. How weak and cowardly. But I couldn't bring myself to stop because I was sure you would never come back to me."

My throat closes, prohibiting speech. Just two days ago, before Darin and I left for Aquaticus, Ginevra and I had gone swimming beside the Ustrina River. Below us, mulcibers cavorted and fought in its waters, illuminated by the golden lights of the helena plants on the banks.

"I thought the worst was over." Ginevra's voice is still high, but the defensiveness it once contained is gone. "We survived a Kraken. Being locked in Atlantis. Kidnapped by a maniac Crura. The Loch Ness monster." She swallows convulsively. "I was sure . . . the people I loved would be safe."

There is nothing to say, so I reach out mutely to touch her arm.

"Rihanna needs me. And I did promise Michal she didn't need to worry." Her voice sinks. "Otherwise, I'd tie on weights and throw myself into the Ustrina."

"Well, that would certainly break your dearest friend's heart." Ginevra and I both swirl around. Conway hovers behind us, his customary black attire replaced by the white of mourning. Behind him, I can see an entourage waiting beside Imber's gates.

Ginevra's frozen stillness is broken. "Why are you here? You're king now. You're needed in Aquaticus."

"I'm needed here." He and Ginevra look at each other for a long time. Then Conway raises his arms and holds them out to her. At that, Ginevra completely breaks down for the first time and swims to him, burying her head in his chest, choking on sobs. Conway's arms close around her, and he looks at me over her head. His eyes are no longer those of the boy who crept into my room that first night in Aquaticus. Streaks of his lighthearted irreverence remain, but they are overshadowed by strength that is no longer tainted by insecurity. Conway has become a Merman. "I'll take care of her," he says. "Go see your sister."

"I wouldn't be sorry if she grew up to be exactly like you," Amaya's voice pulls me back to the living room of her little house. Avonlea has wriggled free of Beck's grip and swum unsteadily up to her mother and me, worming under our arms into the middle of our hug.

"A dugong shepherdess?" I tease around the lump in my throat as I release Amaya to hug Avonlea.

"A brave Mermaid," Amaya says. At that moment, the front door bangs, and Chantara bursts into the room, followed by Darin and Beck, who had gone to fetch her. Darin is holding a seaweed rope tied around the horn of a tiny narwhal, who swims in circles, seemingly intent on wrapping Darin in seaweed.

"My Locklyn." Chantara's arms close around me and Avonlea, squeezing so tightly that I let out a little gasp as my barely-healed ribs protest. She draws back and holds me by my forearms as she looks me up and down. "I'm glad to see you got rid of that accursed tail."

I blink at her phraseology, and am about to say I think she has it backward, since the legs were actually part of a very real curse. Then I remember the Wave Master's touch, healing my body. But He didn't change my legs. Apparently, He didn't see them as a curse, either.

I smile at her. "That I did."

Hours later, Darin and I leave the house hand-in-hand. We are going to my place in the reef. Amaya told me she and the children had been caring for Darya and the dugong herd. "But I think they miss your singing," she said. "They seem lethargic lately."

As we swim through the streets, the people we pass cast us looks of unveiled disgust, muttering behind their hands. Darin's fingers tighten on mine as a tall, beautiful Mermaid with sea glass adhered to her purple tail gives my legs a disdainful look and murmurs something to her companion in which the word "spindle-shanks" is clearly audible.

"Don't mind them," I say, as Darin makes a move to stop and confront the girl. "Wasn't it always you who was telling me not to care what ignorant, prejudiced people thought?"

The corners of his mouth twitch as he allows me to pull him onward. "Was I always telling you that?"

"I wasn't terribly good at listening to you."

"Not sure that should be in the past tense," he says dryly, and I laugh, bumping his shoulder with my own.

The city gates are drawing near. A thin, pale Merman hovers beside them, and my heart gives an odd, stuttering bump as I recognize him.

Maybe he won't recognize me. Darin and I can just swim through to my house. If he doesn't say anything, I won't say any–

"Spindle-shanks!" We are already through the gates when the shout rings out behind us. I close my eyes, drawing in a mouthful of water before gently freeing my fingers from Darin's and turning back.

Alun, the guard who stood by as Blackwell trapped me in the city gates, glares at me belligerently, one hand resting on the hilt of his coral knife. "Heard you got Blackwell killed on that fool quest you dragged him on."

"That fringehead got himself killed," Darin says from behind me.

Alun sneers. "Has the little spindle-shanks found herself a protector? Someone to use his treasure to shut everyone's mouths so they can pretend they don't despise the great Schatzi's wife while they whisper behind your back?"

"I'm not going to try to shut anyone's mouth," I say calmly. "You and the rest of this city are welcome to say and think whatever you like about me."

Alun stares, clearly struggling for a comeback. Finally, he says cuttingly, "False bravado."

"It really isn't," I respond, smiling before turning to take Darin's hand again. As we swim away, I say over my shoulder, "Because the people whose opinions I care about have never minded my legs."

The reef is as familiar as an old friend. Darin and I swim in silence until we reach the door of my hut. Then he says, "I have something for you."

My heart begins to flutter. "A message anklet?"

His dimples flash. "Close your eyes."

I do, holding out empty palms. But he doesn't place anything in them. Instead, I feel his fingers fasten something cold around my right ankle. My eyes fly open without his permission, and I stare down at the new anklet, which is a perfect match to the old one.

"What–? Where did–? How did you find a pair?" I sputter.

"I'm not called the most skilled treasure hunter in Aquaticus for nothing."

"Darin!"

"All right." His large, rough hands close gently over mine. "I commissioned Hugo to make it for me while we were in Imber."

"It's beautiful," I murmur.

"You haven't heard the message yet." He looks down at our joined hands and then back up into my face. "I can't remember if I used to be good at making speeches. I can't remember why I was fool enough not to ask you this question years ago. But I remember you blasting a glass dome to pieces with your voice. I remember you holding your friend's hand through her deepest grief. I remember you asking the Wave Master for peace when you could have asked for anything else at all. I remember you promising a broken Merman that you would help him make new memories. And all Schatzi know that only fringeheads leave a priceless treasure."

I let out a choked laugh, and he pulls me into him.

"I want to remember you always. As my best friend. As the mother of my children. As my wife. Will you make those memories with me, Locklyn?"

I can't answer him. My throat is choked with emotion. With the knowledge of how short and precious each moment of life is. So I take his face in my hands, and kiss him.

When we finally pull apart, he leans his forehead against mine. "I have one more thing to say before we go find some long-suffering dugongs."

"Really?" I whisper. "What's that?"

He grins. "I'm so glad you got rid of that accursed tail."

EPILOGUE

TEN YEARS LATER
LOCKLYN

MY RIBS HURT.

So do my calf muscles.

And my hips.

But in a few more minutes, it will all be worth it.

Ahead of me, my Merman companion pauses and glances back. His looks have changed very little over the years. His golden hair has lightened, and the lines around his eyes and mouth are deeper than before, but Mermaids still try to buy him drinks in the Shark's Fin on the nights we meet Amaya and Beck there.

"Lead the way, Stellvertreter," he says, and I brush against his shoulder as I swim past.

"I don't think my ribs ever healed right," I say, one hand massaging my side as I continue to kick upward.

"It probably didn't help that you spent the weeks after breaking them lying on the floor of a submarine," Darin says.

"We had to get back," I say. "Undula needed Conway. Nebula needed Ginevra."

"The idea of Conway being a king is still unbelievable."

"Dar, he's been king for ten years."

"And he's been a good one," Darin admits. "His crown is going to be difficult to fill."

"Someone who has ruled a kingdom as wisely as he has a better shot than most at selecting a good regent. He will need to get on it, though. He and Ginevra are planning to swim the Seven Seas for their honeymoon."

"I can't believe they're really getting married. After all this time. I was certain neither of them would ever marry. They both seemed so fully focused on the welfare of their countries. Until last year," he adds.

"Conway says his heart was changing before that. But by then, he was sure she had given up on him. I can't believe he couldn't see how much she's always loved him. She just made her peace with his indifference. She never cared about anyone else."

"I still wish I knew why I left you hanging for four years," Darin remarks.

"Four years is significantly better than ten. I feel pretty lucky."

His hand loops around my ankle, and he tugs me downward, one arm wrapping around my waist, while his other hand tangles in my hair. "Someone's lucky in this relationship. But it's not you."

I tilt my head toward the faint silver glow I can see in the dark water above us.

"Come on," I urge. "We've waited long enough."

Moments later, our heads break through the waves of the North Sea. Stars sparkle above us as we strike out for a shining white mound of ice floating nearby. Clambering onto it is more difficult than I would have anticipated, and there are several failed attempts resulting in one or both of us splashing, laughing, back into the water.

But, finally, we are perched on the frozen water, our hands linked as we stare upward into the sky.

"Oh," I breathe.

They are there. Blue and purple and green ribbons of light pulsing over and around the stars. I relax back against the ice, drinking in the beauty above me. The sight makes my chest ache, in the same way the songs of the Vocalese always have. Joy so poignant it is almost pain.

"The Wave Master's Brushstrokes." My voice trembles a little when I can finally speak. "I miss Him."

Darin's hand squeezes mine. "It won't be so long now, dearest. We'll see Him again soon."

I'm looking forward to that day. But, for now, the seas are safe. Circe is dead. The monster is gone. My great-great-grandmother's voice no longer haunts the waters.

The bargain has finally been fulfilled.

And we survived the locket's revenge.

ACKNOWLEDGMENTS

This manuscript was the one I have (so far) struggled most to write. And yet, because of some very special people, it has turned into a book that I am delighted to send into the hands of readers.

Thank you first to Lisa Laube for helping to cull the extraneous material I had allowed to creep in. Thank you to Steve for knowing that Circe would be the best option for the cover. To Lindsay, Sara, Avily, Charmagne, Trissina, and Jamie, thank you for helping me through the process of launching a sequel (which is not for the faint of heart). And a massive debt of gratitude to Kirk DouPonce, for his patience in the process of designing another gorgeous cover.

To my parents, true paragons of grandparents, I hope that I'm half as good with my grandkids as you are with the Muggles. Thank you for giving me the time to pursue this dream.

To my wonderful endorsers, your support and kind words mean so much. I look up to each one of you, and getting to have your words on this book is an honor.

To Helena and Mum, thank you for being excited every time I place a new manuscript in your hands. I value your feedback, but I value your enthusiasm even more.

To Rachelle, I love having a friend who understands the craziness of the publishing world. Thanks for keeping a bed for me during author events.

To Leah, you've probably learned more about writing and the

publishing world than you ever wanted to know on our morning runs, but you still ask. Thank you.

Kyle, you've supported me through this wild ride of pursuing writing dreams, but more than that, you've made real life so good that I wouldn't choose to live in Atlantis even if I was offered the possibility. Thank you, sweetheart.

To Micah, Caleb, and Juliet–you three are the true fulfillment of my dreams. You love reading already, and I hope you never stop (at risk of being disinherited).

And to the One who stands with us in the flames, thank you for being a God who cares about both things as big as the Northern Lights and as small as the objects we cherish. Be glorified through this tale.

ABOUT THE AUTHOR

L.E. Richmond was practically born with a book in her hands (the result of being raised by an American writing teacher and a German bookseller). From a tender age, fairy tales have held a special place in her heart, leading to this spin-off of Hans Christian Andersen's classic as her debut novel. When not crafting stories rooted in lore and fairy tales, she can be found chasing three little readers-in-training, running crazy distances, and brewing homemade kombucha. She has never yet met a mermaid, but when she and her husband eventually complete an Iron Man, she plans to use the 2.4 mile swim to search for one.